They are Trying to Break Your Heart

They are Trying to Break Your Heart

DAVID SAVILL

B L O O M S B U R Y

LONDON · OXFORD · NEW YORK · NEW DELHI · SYDNEY

Bloomsbury Publishing
An imprint of Bloomsbury Publishing Plc

50 Bedford Square	1385 Broadway
London	New York
WC1B 3DP	NY 10018
UK	USA

www.bloomsbury.com

BLOOMSBURY and the Diana logo are trademarks of Bloomsbury Publishing Plc

First published in Great Britain 2016

This is a work of fiction. Names and characters are the product
of the author's imagination and any resemblance to actual
persons, living or dead, is entirely coincidental.

British Library Cataloguing-in-Publication Data
A catalogue record for this book is available from the British Library.

ISBN: HB: 978 1 4088 6575 0
TPB: 978 1 4088 6576 7
ePub: 978 1 4088 6577 4

To find o[...] [...]m.
Here y[...]

For Penny, Oren and Robin

'Losing too is still ours'

Rainer Maria Rilke, 'For Hans Carossa'

29 October 2004

London

Anya walked out of the lift to find the wrong picture on the corridor wall and a pot plant out of place. The lift had gone up, not down, and from here, the quickest way out of the building was onto the roof. At the top of the fire escape she barged through the smokers' exit and marched across the peeling bitumen, stopping only when she came to the rails. Over Exmouth Market, the pigeons were scrapping on the scaffolded tower of Our Most Holy Redeemer.

William had called the office. He had called her actual phone. Three years. And now he says, 'Hello you, what have you been up to?' Pleasantries. Questions about her work, and 'How have you been?' And 'Are you still living on Church Street?' And the way she played along – the way she tried to vaguely impress him by mentioning her new place in Walthamstow, her interest-only mortgage, her very slight promotion, whom she saw from the old days – the fact she even answered his questions annoyed her more than the questions themselves. They had been chatting about Bethany fucking Aldridge's bloody pregnancy. (No, the husband wasn't a guy William knew. Yes, Anya had been to the wedding.) Anya had always found it easy to talk to William. And perhaps that was the problem.

She smelt the smoke before she saw the man sitting by the air-conditioning unit and realised she had been muttering under her breath. Not a Dignity Monitor man (he was clearly over fifty for a start), more likely one of the chartered survey- ors from the fourth floor. She loosened her grip on the rail and not knowing what to do with her hands, tried to affect a casual posture by putting them into the pockets of her jeans. She was someone who came up here to take in the view, that was all.

'Smoke?' The man held out the packet as Anya headed for the roof door.

'There is nothing I would like more than to smoke a ciga- rette,' she told him.

'Oh, dear. I shouldn't tempt you, then.'

'Let's say it's been one of those days.'

'Always is,' the man said.

'Thank you anyway,' Anya said, then as she closed the door, 'you never know, tomorrow might be better!'

But today was not. She tried to pay attention to a young solicitor from one of the new agencies scooping up asylum cases. The woman had come to tell Anya the story of her Serbian client. What the solicitor really wanted was a human rights researcher to act as an expert witness. But Anya needed to see if the story added up first, and the solicitor clearly hadn't done this before. For a start, she had come without the client. The client was a man from Serbia, claiming a threat to life in the form of homophobic bullying. He came from the village of Gornja Slatnik, but when Anya pointed out there were at least two Gornja Slatniks in Serbia, it was news to the woman. In telling the story, the solicitor kept referring to 1998, but when Anya looked at the affidavit, the client had written 1996. They tried to call the client but he wasn't answering, and the difficulty of matching any information held by Dignity Monitor concerning the times and places in contention made Anya late for her regional-desk meeting with the programme director. Last through the door, she had to perch on a filing cabinet next to the old television, facing the backs at the table as Rhidian Keller talked about the effects of the Kosovan riots on regional funding and the need to redistribute further funds for election-monitoring activities in Moldova. She tried to follow, but the woman sitting in front of her was texting someone who wanted to know whether to pick up cereal at the supermarket, and for some reason this was a more compelling drama.

Yes, we are out.

The Shreddies, or the Cheerios?

Shreddies. NO MORE CHEERIOS.

Kids?

TOO MUCH SUGAR!

William had once tried to drown Anya's mobile phone in a river. In Brecon. A rare moment of anger. But he had chucked it over a stream so small it landed on the other bank and Anya had been able to cross over the stepping stones to retrieve it. The cracked screen was something she had come to regard with some affection.

'Can we work with that, Anya Teal?'

It was Rhidian.

'Sorry?'

Her seated colleagues had all turned their heads and were looking up at her with the eyes of people anxious for a meeting to end.

'The Kosovan riot report?' Rhidian said.

'Yes—'

Anya intended to start a question, but Rhidian took it as confirmation and carried on.

'Good. So, unfortunately,' he said, 'we haven't yet got the green light to pick up on the Kosovan returnees' project.'

Anya stopped smiling. She had come to the meeting to challenge this very point. The returnees' project was hers. But before she could gather her thoughts, someone was talking about the new liaison for the Council of Europe and she had to wait until the meeting was over before she could catch up with Rhidian in the empty room.

'Would it help if I wrote a paper?' she started.

'The report on returnees?'

'I think the time to finish this is now.'

'Can you complete it from here?'

'I can't get the same buy-in from here.'

He turned from his laptop screen. 'We've had Abu Ghraib, the report on the riots – financially, I just can't get them to prioritise the returnees. Maybe if you do it from your desk, but another field investigation – I don't think so.'

It was no use making the argument alone. She should have caught him during the meeting and co-opted the other members of the team. Now, her arguments had the tired sound of lines well rehearsed; it wasn't always right to divert funds for emergencies, the bigger picture was more important, once committed their reputation might be damaged if they then scaled back on the report, or did it half-arsed. But Rhidian could nod in sympathy all day, the programme director was just a messenger when it came to money. It was the divisional director she needed to talk to.

Anya stood up. 'Well, I might just have to take a holiday in Pristina.'

'Anya, the way you work, you should take a holiday in the Bahamas, on a beach.'

'And have my nails buffed by Haitian migrants who get beaten up in detention cells?'

Good old Anya, Rhidian's smile said, Anya will pick up the pieces.

'And the riot report,' he added as she left. 'You'll add something to it? About Svinjare?'

Dignity Monitor had told Anya to leave Kosovo when the March riots began. On the phone from London a man from the emergencies team asked if she could recommend a fixer. Not only were they taking over, they also wanted her staff. But now, as the report was prepared for Legal and due to be published, they needed her. When she saw the draft it was clear why.

The draft lacked testimony from the first day of the riots. Anya was essential precisely because she hadn't left the country like a good girl, but asked her fixer to drive straight to Svinjare. On the radio there had been news of Albanians burning down Serbian houses.

What was it they were saying in the report's introduction? Numbers: 2 days, 550 homes burned, along with 27 churches and monasteries; 4,100 people displaced. From the UN Secretary-General to the head of NATO, around the diplomatic table it had been decided: 'organised extremists' were to blame. When you had fucked up as badly as the United Nations Mission in Kosovo, it was better to paint the enemy as organised.

But it wasn't organised. This was the point the report needed to make. The Albanian rioters had been stoked for months. They were reacting to the lousy way in which the

UN were running things. The UN's Kosovo forces could do nothing about it because they lacked any coherent policy. Anya had seen it herself. She had stood at the roadblock in Svinjare, 500 metres from a French military camp where hundreds of vehicles were still lined up in perfect military order and going nowhere. She had watched as the rioters walked straight past a handful of KFOR troops and the single UN civilian-police car that had troubled to turn up.

She returned from the water fountain in the office. The water was always too cold and it numbed her teeth.

In the village of Svinjare, she typed at her desk, *Albanian boys were seen torturing the livestock of Serbian villagers.*

Then she deleted the sentence. There was no room in the report for what she had seen behind the burning barn, for the boys who stood with flaming torches, lighting a pig hung from scaffolding and doused in petrol. The suffering of an animal didn't add anything to the main argument here. The problem in Svinjare was that the French in KFOR saw their role as the protection of people, not property. And so all the UN troops had done was bus the Serbs of the village to the sports hall of Camp Belvedere, leaving the rioters to do as they liked. By early evening, the base had registered 206 of the villagers, and Anya's notes were filled with their voices.

Finding the one that needed to be heard, she added it to the report first:

'If I had a euro for every international who has come around here and observed what is happening. For every foreign soldier who has walked through my village and done nothing. All this "help" that doesn't help. All these cars, and these helicopters, and all this money, and still they can walk into our village and burn our homes, when the whole lot – the whole lot of you who are supposed to bring "peace" and "security" – you are sitting here doing nothing. Worse than nothing – you're getting rid of us, and helping them, helping them, take what they want . . . If I had a euro for that!'

It was a voice loud enough for one moment to drown Will's out. When the office intern appeared at her shoulder, and like a schoolboy asked permission to go home, Anya found herself saying:

'Do you feel like getting drunk?'

If she was going to have a bad day, she might as well have a bad night. She didn't really mean to get drunk, but somehow they hadn't eaten. At one point in the evening Jack had suggested a restaurant, but she couldn't imagine the slow business of ordering food. He introduced her to a craft beer called Bruised Moon, and she introduced him to gin. Anya felt aged by his references. She didn't know the films and books he was talking about. He didn't know who Winona Ryder was and had never even heard of *Heathers*.

The howling carriages of the Victoria line transported them from Highbury and Islington to Walthamstow in an instant – walk in, bright lights, walk off. She couldn't remember stumbling down the cut, or along the terrace. They had been laughing about something to do with hipster hair, then as soon as the door of her house opened, she felt as if she were falling into the dark silence of a stranger's. When she found the light switch, her living room appeared to her like something that had been washed too many times.

When the door closed behind them, she was standing in her home with a boy about whom she knew practically nothing.

'I like it when they knock the rooms through like this,' he said, 'kitchen to lounge.'

She struggled to keep things from getting away. Kettle, tap, running water.

'Yes.'

'You have this whole place to yourself?' His voice seemed closer now. 'How many bedrooms is this? Three?'

She turned off the tap and closed her eyes. She wanted his breath on her neck and his hand on her belly. She wanted his fingers extended around her waist to make her feel small. But when she turned around to meet his face, Jack wasn't close to her at all. Never had been. He was as far away as possible, standing on the other side of the sofa and picking up a picture from the mantelpiece.

'Where's this?'

Anya put down the kettle and tried to walk around the objects of her house with grace. He was looking at the picture of the Roma girls in Stovnik. She took off her glasses so things didn't seem too real.

'It's from a field trip to Bosnia.'

'And you're working on Kosovo now?'

She didn't hear what he said next. She pressed her nose into his arm, felt his hands make a gift of her head, his lips brushing down her face, rough over her mouth.

'Wait there.' Anya took the picture out of his hand and put it back on the mantel.

Alone in her bedroom, she pulled her tights from underneath her skirt and threw them into a pile of dirty laundry in the corner. The underwear drawer offered a large pile of black knickers. She used to own something spotty – pale, blue spots – but at the bottom of the drawer she found only the straps of a suspender belt. Where was it? It was William who had bought the spotty set. There had even been a chemise baby-doll thing at one point. In the sock drawer, she found a pair of canary-yellow knickers which would have to do, but when she hoicked them on, they felt a little small. There was no full-length mirror, so she had to angle the spot-squeezing mirror on her chest of drawers just to look at herself.

Her glasses. They were downstairs – in the mirror, only the vague shape of a woman.

The shape slumped back onto the bed. She wasn't going to fuck the intern. Who was she kidding? Three years. Will had not called in three years, and now he wanted to talk as if nothing had changed; as if all that silence was OK, as if it meant nothing at all. They should 'catch up', Will said. She should come over at Christmas. He would show her Thailand. *Thailand*. And what she had wanted to say, what she had wanted to scream from the roof, came out now in a sad dribble. 'Fuck you,' Anya mumbled into the cradle of her hands. Fuck Will. Not the intern. She couldn't fuck the intern because Will had ruined that too. He had called from halfway around the world, reached into her life and swept it all away. And she couldn't fuck the intern, because the intern would be there in the office on Monday morning.

Will had talked as if nothing had changed. And he was right. They had been together thirteen years, and for that reason alone they would always be together in some way, and even the 'other side of the world' wasn't really the other side of the world any more. It was nine hours away and—

'Hi.'

She looked up. An attractive man, still young enough to look good in jeans, was standing at the door of her room.

'Is this like – the third bedroom?'

'Two here. And there's a loft conversion.'

Jack crossed the threshold and surveyed the room like a bad actor lost on the stage. 'It's so big. You could rent out the rooms.'

She could. She could rent out the spare rooms of this house – this house built for the ideal nuclear family she had not yet managed to produce. 'I'm looking for lodgers,' Anya said. But the truth was, she hadn't even advertised.

He looked at her dirty laundry and unmade bed. 'I'm going to have to say that I think this is probably not a good idea, professionally and everything.'

What was he? All of twenty years old? 'Professionally?' Anya regained herself.

He looked confused. 'Well, you didn't come back down,' he said. 'And I thought—'

'No, you're right of course. Too much to drink. Not a good idea. There's a bed made up in the room next door.'

'Right.' Jack looked crestfallen. 'Well, I mean if you still want to—'

'That's romantic!'

He held up his hands in surrender. 'I mean, whatever you want—'

Anya patted the bed. He did as he was told. Placing her hand on a thigh that was mannequin hard, she touched the stiff cotton of his jeans and walked her fingers up to the zip.

'Is it true,' he said, 'that you chased off some rioters in Kosovo? I heard you threw stones at them and told them their mothers would be ashamed? Something about a pig?'

Anya pushed Jack back onto the bed, and climbing on top of him, placed her hand over his mouth. 'For fuck's sake,' she said, 'shut up.'

'It is estimated 40,000 persons went missing as a consequence of the armed conflicts in the former Yugoslavia, of which around 30,000 are from Bosnia and Herzegovina. Some 14,000 people remain unaccounted for. Of these, more than 10,500 are linked to the conflict in Bosnia, 2,400 to the conflict in Croatia, and some 1,800 to the conflict in Kosovo.'

Amnesty International, 'The Right to Know' (2012)

Tuesday 5 April 2005

Bangkok

It is common enough to see the dead. Common enough to believe someone you know to be dead has just stepped onto a bus, or out of a shop door. In William's Bangkok, the dead are everywhere; hanging in the steam of street canteens, walking through the sliding doors of air-conditioned malls, moving in the watery reflections of the Skytrain as carriages of commuters slide through the glass buildings of downtown. William Howell is not a man of faith. He does not believe in the supernatural. But this does not stop him from seeing the dead in the faces of students who pour down the corridors of the school where he teaches English to a pre-intermediate class on a Tuesday afternoon. It is the last class of the day, and as he wipes the conditional tense from the white board, as the last student leaves, and the classroom door flaps shut, William feels Anya's presence at his back. When he turns, someone is there. It is one of his mature students. He knows her name is Anchali, because it is written on the food-court employee badge which she wears over the bone-yellow blouse of her uniform. Anchali is digging into a fake Burberry bag, and her hand is spotted with pale yellow scalds. When she presents the letter, she nods and smiles her yellow-toothed 'please', like the people on the street who sell things you don't want.

RE: CULTURAL ACTION PROJECT FUNDING. The paper carries the familiar letterhead of the British Council. It is one of those applications for training programmes the Council is so keen on: community theatre, Shakespeare performed by the paraplegic, et cetera. To exactly what kind of project the letter refers, William can't quite tell, he is too distracted by the poor English of someone employed by the British Council. (No one alive seems to know the difference between 'subsequently' and 'consequently'.)

'This is a letter responding to your project application?'

More nodding and smiling. Anchali has only scraped her way into the pre-intermediate class, and William has been wondering whether she might not need another semester in Basic. It's a difficult decision with the poorer students, the ones who squirrel away every spare bhat for the fees because they have no formal qualifications and English might just provide them with a better life. The students whose Daddys hold some political position, or who claim some distant rela-tion to the royal family, the ones whose ancestors have already ripped off the state, *these* students William would resit in a second. But Anchali from the food court – Anchali from the food court appears to have strung some philanthropic community project together, and now he has to tell her about the British Council's rejection.

'I understand, Mr Howell.' (The vowels in his name are a particular torture.) 'But do you know the letter, if it says why I don't understand.'

'Why you don't understand?'

'Yes. Why.'

'Does the letter tell you why you don't understand?'

'Yes. Don't understand.'

'I'm sorry. I don't quite—'

'Why no funding.' Anchali smiles.

'Ah! Does the letter tell you *why* you didn't get *funding*!'

'Yes!'

'You don't understand all of the letter!'

'Yes, Mr Howell.'

'No.' William reads over the short letter again. 'It doesn't say why you were refused funding.' And because he feels guilty the school has not done a better job of helping the woman through her Basic English class, because he is frustrated that even the British Council can't accurately employ the English language, and because the ghost of Anya is still standing behind him, William makes his excuses and leaves Anchali in the classroom, telling her he will keep the letter, call the British Council and find out.

And then there is Anya's voice. If she has really gone, why can he still hear her voice? Anya who tells him he should go out of his way to help his pupil. Anya who sits Will down at his office desk and has him looking for the number of the British Council. Anya in the bar of the student union telling a sleepy assembly of activists what the agenda of their next meeting will be. Anya who, at the age of nineteen, owned a Filofax she carried everywhere, its pages bristling with pink and yellow Post-its because she had to write everything down. Will who, at the age of nineteen, had nothing in his life worth writing down. When they moved in together she had filled their flat with those notes, THINGS TO DO went up on the fridge, career plans on the cork-board above the desk in a space which had to do for bedroom and lounge. It looked like chaos to Will, but out of it, Anya made her own order.

'Where do we want to be in twelve months' time?' No one had ever asked him such a question. William thought the point of being twenty-one was not to know what you wanted to do with your life, let alone with the next twelve months.

He scribbles the number for the British Council on a Post-it in his office and tacks it up with the others on the cork-board above his desk.

That suitcase isn't going to move itself, Anya says as he puts the pen down.

Yes, yes – he is going to pick up the phone and ring the airport. He is going to arrange a courier for Anya's suitcase. But someone knocks on the door, and suddenly, he has to decide whether to hide, or, in the course of answering, reveal the door to his office has been locked so that he can be alone with Anya.

'Missy Ammanucci called.' It is Karin, the school secretary. 'Something about work permits. Said it was urgent.'

William takes a note from Karin's hand, and feels her examining him through the thick lenses of her glasses. She has always made him feel like he was the child, and she his mother.

The order in chaos. He is not as good at finding it as Anya is. His computer desktop is littered with documents. There are folders within folders. Eight different titles for the draft time-tabling. He has to resort to a search on the name. His folders on employees have somehow become mixed up with Upper Intermediate Scheduling, 2002. Who the hell was Missy Ammanucci? He finds a CV, and a letter of application. Missy Ammanucci is the new American teacher who, because William wasn't paying attention, had breezed through her interview. He opens the file on her employment. For each employee he keeps a Scanned Documents file, a record of the paper trail between the school, the Ministry of Education, the Bureau of Employment and the Immigration and Visa Office. Missy should have six documents. But there is only one: the receipt from the Department of Foreign Workers. He has not done his job. He has not made an application to the Bureau of Employment for a new work permit for Missy. He has not collected the receipt for the application. He has not, therefore, taken the receipt to the Immigration and Visa Office in order to generate a new work visa. As far as the authorities are concerned, Missy Ammanucci is an illegal immigrant.

Take responsibility, William.

He picks up the phone, but whatever Anya says, he is stopped when he thinks about the apologies he will have to make. He could blame administration at the school, but fears the wrath of Karin. Putting down Missy's number, he picks up Anchali's letter, and calls the British Council.

'We can only talk directly to the bidder.'

William looks at the name beneath the signature on Anchali Changkhaochai's letter. *Mark Heatherington.*

'The bidder is a student in my class,' William explains. 'She wanted me to call and get a clear picture as to why her application for funding was turned down.'

'Ms Changkhaochai is welcome to call us herself.'

'Well, that's the problem, isn't it? Anchali is a student in my *pre-intermediate* class, and she's not quite capable of—'

The man interrupts to explain the rules of privacy in the application process.

'Is there a fee,' William asks. 'To apply, for this kind of project?'

'As I said, sir, I can't really comment.'

'But this is a line of general enquiry about the *bidding* process. Forget Anchali's application for a moment, I'm just asking you about the fee.'

'The Cultural Projects Funding application round is over.'

'But if I want to apply next year, is there *a fee*?'

'Yes.'

'How much?'

'Eighty-five dollars.'

'And did you meet Anchali?'

'As I said—'

'OK – so if I apply for a Cultural Projects Fund, how does it work? Is there an interview? Do I come and get the form from you? Do I apply online?'

'If you were to apply for a fund, you would come in, and we would talk before issuing an application form.'

'So presumably, when Anchali came in to talk with you, she did so with an interpreter? Or do you speak Thai? I mean how many people *exactly* do you discourage from spending eighty-five dollars for the privilege of just filling in these forms? Wouldn't it be sensible to discourage someone who clearly doesn't have the basic language skills to make an application, or resources to execute a project? Mr Heatherington?'

The fan above William's head seems to hurry the beating of his heart.

'Thank you for your enquiry.'

Heatherington hangs up. William redials.

'Hello?' It is a woman's voice.

'I'm calling for Mark Heatherington.'

'You've come back through to the reception.'

'But I was just speaking to him.'

'You spoke to him? And you want to speak to him again?'

'No – the phone didn't – I mean, yes, I *was* speaking to him and we got cut off, then I rang you back – I mean *him*, through you, and now his phone isn't answering.'

'Mark has probably stepped away from his desk for a moment.'

He tries to imagine the receptionist at the British Council as a real human being. She has a young voice. Someone just starting out in life. Landed a good job with travel. Probably highly educated. She does not think that she will live her *life* as a receptionist, she does not for a moment think she will live her life teaching English as a foreign language, or directing the business of a language school.

Life has happened *despite* him. Not enough twelve-month plans.

'Hello? Sir?' The voice in the phone sounds suddenly distant.

'Hello.'

'Would you like to leave a message?'

William cuts her off.

How do people do it? How do people keep going?

What do you think other people do? Anya had asked him that morning. But he couldn't just *do* things any more. Brushing his teeth had been a *decision*. Showering, a decision. Food was the most difficult decision. The decision to eat was life or death. He had followed his feet as they took him out of the apartment into the lift and outside. It amazed him so many people had made the same decisions. To wake up, to care for themselves, to put fuel in their bodies and keep going. Did they see the ghosts too? Did they feel the absence of people who had decided to not wake up that morning, or who hadn't got as far as the shower before jumping out of a window or taking a lethal dose of prescription medicine?

It's not all about you, Anya said, and William had found himself standing in front of a class of students, talking about conditional tenses, and somewhere in there, somewhere around the distinction between the modals could/would/should in relation to the pluperfect tense, he had not been thinking about where Anya might be.

He is still holding his finger on the receiver switch and there is a ringing in his ear. Is the phone ringing at the other end? Or is it *his* phone ringing? He lifts his finger.

'Hello?'

'Is that you, Will?'

'Who's this?'

'Anthony. I'm calling to confirm Saturday. Will? Are you still there, dude?'

'Sorry.'

The phone has moved, revealing the edge of a card.

Don Muaeng Airport Baggage Handling.

'Will? Are you there?'

'Sorry?'

'Saturday, Will. The tennis match. You're coming out. And if you don't I'm going to come round there and drag you out.'

Flight: PA 342 Phuket – Bangkok
Items: 1

'Tennis.'

'Yes, the tennis. Are you all right, Will?'

Date of Arrival: 17 February
Collection: Please collect within 48 days of notification.

'Fine.'

'Not having a moment?'

He looks at the date on his computer. Anya's luggage has been ready for collection almost seven weeks now. It should be on its way to her parents in England.

'None of this is easy for you, dude. We do appreciate that.'

Dude. Something about the ridiculousness of the word in Anthony's English, public school mouth restores him.

'Are you sure you're OK, dude?'

'I'll see you Saturday,' he says.

'Sure?'

'Yes,' Will lies. 'Everything's good.'

11 November 2004

London

Until she read the obituary, Anya had never seen his full name: 'Mohammed Yasser Abdel Rahman Abdel Raouf Arafat al-Qudwa'. Yasser Arafat was dead. As a teenager, Anya had bought an 'Arafat' headscarf before she even knew what it symbolised. In her first year at university, a campaign to see Israeli forces withdraw from the West Bank and Gaza Strip became the occasion of her first march. It had been William who scrounged MDF offcuts from Homebase. They had constructed the placards in her college room above the Cash Convertors on Whitchurch Road. 'Israel Out', 'Liberation not Occupation', 'Terrorist or Freedom Fighter?' Anya supplied the words, and William, with his artistic gifts, had supplied the penmanship. In the cold February air of the Whitehall march, William's signs had drifted, bobbing away like ocean debris over the heads of the crowd, until they were lost. To see that bit of William, to see his voice lose itself among all the others, had somehow been the most moving part of the day.

According to the French doctors in the Paris hospital where Arafat died, the Palestinian leader had suffered an 'haemorrhagic cerebrovascular accident'. It wasn't just the stupidity of humanity against them now, it was the Gods. (If indeed this was a natural death.) Arafat had been in a coma for weeks, and his survival the only topic of discussion in the Middle East section. Now her colleagues were hunched over their phones to fixers and journalists in Ramallah, Beirut and Cairo, not to gather news, but to dig up the gossip. Arafat had been declared dead at 3.30 that morning, and according to the BBC, the interim president of the Palestinian Authority had already been declared: Rawhi Fattuh, a moderate from the legislative council.

'Fattuh will be gone in months,' Rhidian told Anya confidently. 'It's all about Abbas now.'

An image of Clinton embracing first Arafat, and then Rabin, slipped over the screen in the office. Placards above the heads of wailing Palestinians, not in William's hopeful hand, but strongly suggesting Ariel Sharon's violent death. Clinton seemed an historic figure now, a man whose smile only evoked the thought of what his lips had persuaded another young woman to do. Arafat was dead, and Anya was probably as old as the tutors she had hated for being part of a scarred and pessimistic generation.

In the soiled newspapers of her college bar, she had religiously followed events leading to the handshake between Rabin and Arafat. She was one of those students who celebrated that night, one of the few, in fact, who knew what there was to celebrate. Clinton's easy smile, and porch-front talk, had convinced the young Anya that the Oslo Accords were a 'new dawn'. She had read into the history of the conflict, and argued in tutorials how, like the problem of Northern Ireland, the Middle East might be resolved now a new generation were coming to power. But a new generation doesn't always make progress, her professor would counter.

Take the Balkans, he said, the Balkans were still a horror show. And the crimes there were committed by the generation *succeeding* Tito. Politics in the Balkans were over.

All anyone could do for the Balkans in 1993, was rattle tins in the Arcades. And so they had. Anya and William had joined the Socialist Workers, raising money to spend on baked beans (which, as it turned out, the Bosnians hated), toilet paper, sanitary towels and soap. Men and women who were older and braver than Anya and William had driven donated trucks to towns declared 'safe havens'; towns with names made familiar from the news reports: Stovnik, Tuzla, Banja Luka. For these towns, they had climbed into a van with a cab that had the tired smell of weed, and been driven around the suburban supermarkets of Cardiff collecting unwanted grocery boxes. Not an enormous sacrifice, but as much as two students could reasonably do.

Hiding from the Middle East desk, Anya called her mum, but couldn't think of a way to introduce Arafat into the conversation, let alone explain why his death somehow felt like that of a distant relative. Instead, she spent a few minutes listening to her mother talk about the temerity of the council's plans to institute new zoning for parking. And when Mum began to talk about her father, and how whenever she saw him he was wheezing and psoriatic, Anya felt too sad to carry on. She could hear the wine glass clink against her mother's bracelet, and it was only midday.

With a hurried excuse she put down the phone and found herself staring at her desktop monitor, nursing a vague sense of guilt. She was so much better at work than she was at her family.

Anya should take a holiday. At least that's what people kept telling her. From her desk at the Office for National Statistics, Beth had even sent a link for something called

Solitair, a company which organised walking holidays for solo-travellers.

'You think he was poisoned?' Jack took a chocolate from the communal bowl Anya kept on her desk.

'I would say it was a distinct possibility. How could the peace process go anywhere as long as Arafat was still alive?'

Jack looked nonplussed.

'I mean – if someone poisoned him, and it turned out to be for the greater good?'

'That's dark.'

'But Abbas is a moderate. America can talk to him. So it's win-win.'

'What a world.'

'The world we live in.'

Jack walked across the office with a defeated look. She watched as in the glass-box kitchen he hunted the cupboards for his fruit tea. It was hard to imagine him in her bed, lying next to her, let alone imagine him inside of her. Afterwards, Jack had slept as soundly as a child. Anya had stayed awake most of the night, going over her conversation with William. Why had he called? Why now? In the rehearsal of the call she didn't babble on about herself. She asked him directly why, after three years of total silence, he had decided to call her. By seven o'clock she was scrambling eggs, and when Jack didn't appear, she ate them alone. He finally emerged fully dressed, and hesitated at the bottom of the stairs. Should he leave? Anya told him he was perfectly welcome to eat. He had eaten the eggs quickly and quietly in front of her, like a boy late for school.

We understand the solo-traveller is a free spirit with an open and enquiring mind. We understand the solo-traveller is looking for an independent travel experience. We also understand solo doesn't have to mean lonely. On our small group tours the solo-traveller can share experiences with like-minded individuals, and travel with the peace of mind that comes from company.

It wasn't India they were trying to sell, it was 'self-discovery'. It wasn't solo travel, it was dating. She unwrapped a chocolate.

Jack had thought because she made him breakfast they might spend the day together, and the following Friday, he had made an embarrassing suggestion they might go out again. But what was she supposed to do with a twenty-year-old boy who still lived with his college friends? After Will, sex was really all she had *needed* from men. When the great couple had decided to split up, her friends had commented on how well she was doing, how remarkable Anya just managed to keep going, but her indifference was the exact opposite of what it suggested. Somehow, when it came to matters of her own heart, knowing what was right wasn't the same as *doing* what was right. And so people thought her cold. Anya knew that.

She scrolled through the playgrounds of the western self presented by the website: Indian mountains, Nairobi safari, Thai beaches. *Thai beaches.* Curving shores fringed with palm trees. The black, broken teeth of archipelagos in the Indian Ocean. Was she really looking at the pictures and hoping she would see William?

Then she stopped. Not William, but something else.

Solitair is proud to introduce Kao Lak 'Heaven Resort'. Anya took the key to the stationery room from the hook behind a filing cabinet. The room flickered into life, narrow and long with metal shelving to the ceiling on every wall. It was called the stationery room because the shelves were still full of unopened boxes of printer paper, highlighter pens and desk tidies. But really, the room was the office dump: old beta cameras from field trips, ailing tripods, mosquito nets, rucksacks full of moulding clothes, a pair of walking boots dusted with sand that might have come from some Central Asian desert. When the organisation had moved from single offices to open plan, there had only been room for one small set of drawers beneath each desk, and Anya had wheeled her old cabinet in here, complete with the notes she should have destroyed or put into secure storage. In those days, when she was not yet a senior researcher, when laptops were still unreliable and too heavy, she had kept parallel notes on paper. Thank God.

Anya could say this for herself. Her filing was impeccable. The books for the year 2000 were easy to find. And her notes were as brilliant as her filing.

Ljuba Crvenović, a thirty-two-year-old woman, who lived on the top floor of a shoddy Belgrade block. Bogdan Banović, the investigating policeman in Stovnik who had ordered Coca-Cola with his Turkish coffee. Vesna Knežević, the young redhead who lived at 32 Bjelave in the hills of Sarajevo among sheets of washing and the thunder of feet from a school playground. Vesna had been Kemal Lekić's girlfriend.

Back at the desk she unfolded the newspaper with Vesna's picture in it. The journalist at the *Stovnik Gazette* had pointed out the four people shouldering the painted green coffin which was supposed to contain Kemal Lekić's body. Vesna was at the front.

'Vesna was his girlfriend,' the journalist pointed out, then fingered the others. 'His best friend, the father of the family he lived with, and this is Marko Novak, Marko was like his brother.'

The coffin they carried had been empty. After the shelling, Kemal Lekić's body had never been found. This in itself was not an unusual consequence of the kind of Second World War mortar rounds the Serbs were using. But it was the journalist who had first mentioned the rumours.

Kemal Lekić had escaped the shelling and been recruited by the CIA to fight against Islamic militants. Kemal Lekić had never even been present at the shelling, but had already left the country and was fighting in Chechnya with the rebels. Both of these rumours made sense if you worshipped the man as a hero. No one wanted their heroes to die. But the third rumour was perhaps the most plausible. Kemal Lekić was now living in Thailand, working in a holiday resort.

Anya googled Kemal Lekić straight away. There was a Wikipedia page now, dedicated to the heroic exploits of Kemal's brigade. But the story of his death at the age of twenty-two was still the same. She only knew his face from the obituary photograph in the *Stovnik Gazette*, and at a distance of more than four years, was surprised to discover how good looking he was. Handsome enough she had to remind herself of what he had done.

She has remembered it right. *Kao Lak, Heaven Resort*. The words in pencil on the last page of the book. The name of the resort in a holiday photograph, on the hall table of Vesna's house.

Beneath the ocean's surface, a tsunami travels unseen.
Only as the tsunami approaches shore, does its
energy take shape.

Tuesday 5 April 2005

Cambridge

There is a philosophical idea which says if something cannot be perceived, it cannot exist. Marko is about to ask Emeka whether he has ever heard of Schrödinger, when Emeka says: 'There should be a test you have to pass before they let you have a dog.'

'Like a dog licence,' Marko says.

'They *used* to have a dog licence in this country. Before this country started going to shit.'

Marko's Nigerian employee is watching the balding greyhound across the street. She is tied to a street light beneath the Airman. The owner of the greyhound is an alcoholic who stays for Tuesday lock-ins. The dog will lie on the pavement until the not so early hours of the morning, opening and closing one lazy eye to anyone who passes by, her haunches shivering.

A stagger of girls climbs the steps to the club. They might be too young, but they're pretty enough. 'In Bosnia,' Marko remembers, 'we used to say, if you want to be a host to a guest, you should also be a host to his dog.'

Emeka clicks his teeth. 'Fur all matted up and bones show-ing. It's disgusting.'

Marko's phone buzzes in his pocket. It could be the Roxy, or the boys at the Fountain. But there is no message, and the missed call only tells him it was an 'international number'. The second 'international number' of the evening.

Most likely a call centre.

'Boys.' The boom of the club opens up behind them. It is the head barman, craning around the porthole door, white towel over the black shirt of his arm. 'Those girls.'

'No?' Marko says.

'Kid in the kitchen goes to their school.'

Marko shakes his head, half apology, half self-disgust.

On a night like tonight, when clouds are low enough to mist the green, people leaving the street and crossing Parker's Piece momentarily drop out of sight before reappearing in the light of the lamp post which ties the paths of the park together. There is a moment of uncertainty, when it seems entirely possible one of the students, dog-walkers, professors or home-less drifters might disappear. They are in Schrödinger's box.

The door closes. Emeka hasn't moved. 'Someone should put that dog out of its misery.'

'Do something about it then.'

'It isn't my dog.'

Marko steps down to the pavement and crosses between the cars. The drunk's knot is so bad, the dog could have untied it herself. He leaves the rope at her neck and uses it as a lead. Her legs scuttle back as he pulls her over the road. 'You want to save the dog? Save the dog!'

Yellowing, soupy eyes, silvery bald patches over her back – the old thing stinks. Emeka gets down on one knee and strokes her neck. 'Greyhounds are made for running, you poor bastard.' He takes the lead from Marko, but when he reaches the edge of the piece and unknots the rope she doesn't move.

'Go on!' Emeka shouts. 'Run – run!' He taps the dog's backside with the toe of his boot, finds a stick and throws it into the darkness. When he tries to lift her haunches, the dog stands up, turns her back legs and sits down again.

Marko shouts from the steps of the club, 'She only plays for her master!'

Emeka puts his hands in the pockets of his jacket and shakes his head. 'Stupid dog.'

'Only for her master!' Marko smiles. 'That's why dogs are dogs!'

Marko's office is the table next to the jukebox in the Millennium Kebab. It is a short walk on Tuesdays, right next door to the Airman. Husni serves him pickled jalapeños at the end of a shift and he sucks them off the stem. He drinks yoghurt and a coffee but never touches the meat. There didn't used to be any Bosnian-run kebab houses. No real ćevapi, no burek. Only the Turkish places like Husni's. There were hardly any Bosnians in '96. Now there's a 'Balkan' restaurant out towards Grantchester, and cul-de-sacs in Cherry Hinton where Serbians face Albanians in capitalist harmony. Marko prefers to hide with the Turks and read his book for the night class. *Philosophy for Beginners.* He finds it easier to read in public, with the television of the kebab house and noise of customers. He can't concentrate when it is quiet.

'Your friend.' Husni slaps the dough for tomorrow's flat-bread on the counter. 'What's he do with dog?'

'He loves animals.'

'I love animal.'

'I love animals, but I know when something isn't my business.'

The last two college boys fall out of the kebab house, arms around one another, pavement a tightrope. In the end, Emeka had given up on the dog. She had kept walking back to the road, and it seemed safer to just tie her up again. Marko puts down the book, and scrolls through his missed calls. Before the international numbers, only Millie. Yesterday she had sent him on a diversion from the market to pick up some books reserved in the college library. Husni sits down, and Marko feels the plastic bucket of his seat tighten. The tables are modular, the seats connected like a see-saw without the action. Husni pushes a piece of thin blue carbon paper across the table. Some sort of form.

'DVLA,' he says. 'Speeding.'

The ongoing saga of the Turkish man's driving licence. Marko pushes his laptop to one side. Husni gives him a pencil, and Marko tells him he'll need a pen, a black one.

'I thought they cancel points already.'

Marko looks down the form and ticks the boxes. 'Did you have any valid reason for doing 53 in a 30 mph zone?'

'My wife was pregnant and I'm taking to hospital?'

Marko shakes his head. Husni doesn't have a wife. 'Something they can't check.'

'What do I know?'

'It was January.' Marko looks at the incident date on the form. 'I'm going to say there was a local fog, and it was impossible to read the signs.'

'I shouldn't be driving so fast in the fog.'

'Yes, but there's no law against driving fast in the fog.'

'But driving fast in the fog is dangerous!'

Marko studies his Turkish friend; this man who has been in the country longer than him, but still not learned enough of the language to understand a basic form. No wonder the British complain about people who don't integrate.

'Don't worry,' he says. 'Trust me. This is your best chance.'

Above the kebab house, Marko walks into the warm fug of Millie's sleep. When the shop provides so much heat, he can forgive the cold blue glow of its sign. In the bedroom Millie has bunched the duvet into her chest, bare leg shining in the light of the bedside lamp. Even after three years, there is an exotic quality to her dark skin.

She has fallen asleep on her book and he gently lifts up her head to remove it.

Jonathan Woolf, *Political Sciences in Post-War Europe*.

The theory baffles him, but he loves the history which contextualises each chapter. He has read 'The Eastern Front' several times.

Thirty-nine million civilians died in the Second World War. One in ten of the Russian population . . .

Marko sits up in bed.

. . . One in five of the Yugoslav population.

Before his family moved to Bosnia, his mother's grand-parents had been Croatian. His great uncles, their parents too. The one in five. The book describes columns of Croatians, Serbs and Bosnians, marching across the continent; 100,000 Croatians in post-war Austria alone. A map shows how in 1942, only Spain, Britain and Russia stood outside the borders of Nazi occupation.

We are still living with the social and political consequences of the mass migration of peoples.

He is a consequence. We are all consequences. Millie a consequence of Haiti, a consequence of slavery.

The sentences of the book range far above the events they describe, and Marko recedes, unimportant in the great scheme of things.

A consequence.

He closes his eyes. When the phone in his pocket rings, he does not know how long he has been asleep.

International number.

He closes the bedroom door and stands in the fluorescent light of the kitchen. 'Yes?'

There is a moment of silence, in which his voice is nowhere and anywhere.

When the man replying makes a question of his name, Marko lands in Bosnia, no longer the young man he is, but a boy.

'Marko?'

He is standing on the sidelines of the five-a-side pitch on their housing estate in Stovnik. His cousin is walking across the pitch in a Chelsea football shirt.

'Marko? Is that you?'

'Samir?'

'Marko, it's Samir. Can you hear me?'

He knows how long it has been since he last heard his cousin's voice.

He knows he has lived almost a decade in England. But now he is in Stovnik on the day he left.

'Perfectly,' he says. 'I can hear you perfectly.'

Christmas Eve, 2004

Kao Lak

On jet-lagged legs, Anya wobbled from the bathroom, into the lounge of the beach hut. Will handed her something champagne-y in a plastic cup, and poured himself a mineral water.

'Citronella!'

'Sorry?'

'The smell in the room, I was trying to think what it was. Citronella – for the mosquitoes.'

'Oh yes,' Will said. 'Cheers!'

'*Naz Drowie!*' When she looked up from the fizz, Will seemed to be inspecting the wooden slats of the bungalow walls.

'What a great place you've found!'

'Trip Advisor told me good things.' She wandered over to a raffia-work bookcase and its dog-eared collection of novels left by previous guests.

'I'm glad you wanted to do it,' Will started. 'I haven't really given myself a holiday these past three years.'

'I was coming here anyway.'

Since landing in Phuket, she had struggled with this petulant teenage girl sulking inside her and trying to get out; a girl looking for attention every time her mouth opened.

William had met Anya in Bangkok before the transferring flight, head poking above the others in arrivals. Anya had forgotten what a beanpole Will was; forgotten too that delicious feeling of her toes stretching as she reached up and threw her arms around his neck. But the embrace had been calculated on her part, a demonstration of the confidence she wanted to exude. From there on, it had all been improvisation; oddly easy, the conversation about the fatuous in-flight magazine, and predictably strained, talk of their lives in Bangkok or London. The charabanc ride from Phuket airport to the resort had proved awkward too. As the other tourists climbed onto the back of a converted pickup, Anya shuffled up, knee to knee, Will's hand resting between them like a lost glove she felt the need to pick up. She had to remind herself it didn't belong to her any more.

The busyness and noise of the journey passed, and entering the candlelit bungalow over the marshes, Anya suddenly wanted only to sleep. From the shelf, she picked up a Black Lace novel with yellowed pages. The bustiered heroine on the cover had blood-red hair and a severe fringe, and had trapped the neck of a man beneath the heel of her vermilion boot.

'Do you like Bangkok?' She tried again. 'I thought you were trying to get away from cities?'

'Away from cities – was I? No, I love cities.'

'You always said about London that you hated all the *people.*'

'Wow,' William laughed, 'sounds incredibly misanthropic. I don't know. Maybe I was just bored with London.'

'You always used to talk about moving to a small village and finding real "community".'

He was sitting in a wicker bucket seat with an ease she found oddly frustrating, and however much she tried, she couldn't stop digging at him. She wanted to say something about his clothes, about the saffron-yellow harem trousers and Birkenstocks. What had happened to Will? It just wasn't *him*. Will dressed almost religiously in black Converse and tan cords. The trousers with the linen shirt made him leaner and younger than she remembered. In fact, there were actually a number of perfectly nice things to be said about Will's appearance, but somehow she couldn't bring herself to say them.

'Is this a *new*, teetotal William?'

'Not teetotal exactly.' Will looked at the water. 'Just taking a break from booze,' he sighed. 'I thought getting out of the city I might try and get fit. You know, while you're off doing whatever you have to do, meeting and whatever. I thought I could get some swimming in.'

'Not a bad idea,' she said, and then realised it sounded like a criticism of his physique when all she really meant to say was – oh, *she might just as well shoot herself now*.

She didn't have to come to Thailand. She could have ignored his emails. And having decided to come, it didn't have to be this. She could have told him about her work plans, and left things at a meet-up, a coffee in Bangkok. Instead, she had used the notes on Kemal Lekić as an excuse to come to Kao Lak and then let William know this was where she would be. It had seemed clever at the time. Now it just seemed devious. And her eyes were burning. She rarely wore contacts and they had been in for twelve hours.

'You know I am just shattered,' she said. 'I may have to go to bed.'

* * *

It was a disaster. She shouldn't have come. It had been in Anya's power to refuse Will's suggestion. She knew when she was lying to herself but somehow thought that *if* she knew, it wasn't really self-deception. It was like that thing about madness, the truly mad not knowing they are mad.

In the mirror of the dressing table, she saw through the open door of her own bedroom, across the dim hall of the bungalow, where Will stood over his bed presenting his back to her as he unzipped his suitcase. Quickly, she pulled off her vest and pushed down her yoga pants. If he turned, he would see her. The knickers were duck-egg blue now, no more black. Although the nightshirt she needed lay right on top of her things, she lingered for a moment. She heard the sound of the door, then the mirror turned black, and there was a second in which she anticipated him stepping out of the darkness to appear behind her. But when she opened her eyes, the mirror reflected the gloom of the passage between their rooms, the shadows of his legs moving in the light between the door and the floor.

Lying beneath the single sheet of the bed, her mind raced to catch up with the body that had taken the journey. The oriental faces, the looping characters on signs, the airport advertising products she didn't recognise, the buzzing shoals of mopeds breaking around the charabanc, the people wearing shorts and vests and flip-flops at night, the palms springing out of pavements, the fairy-light fences and trees drooping with ribbons of torn clothing – *offerings*, William had said.

What did William Howell *want* from her? She thought about waking him up and asking. Cards on the table. She had no problem walking up to corporals at roadblocks and asking them what the rules of engagement were. She had no problem confronting men who killed for a living, but when it came to the man she knew better than any other, Anya couldn't quite summon the courage.

Not even the courage to hold his hand. All those years together, and she could still remember the first time she had done it. It had come a week after the sex in her mother's bedroom (which was no more than any other teenage experiment), and it was far more electrifying, more frightening than that. They had been standing at the window of a delicatessen on the high street of Stratton, Anya explaining how halloumi tasted, when suddenly she felt his palm slip into hers. Her first instinct was to pull away, as if he were kissing her in a public place. She had a feeling that it wouldn't do to be seen, she felt as though she were suddenly surrounded by her friends and family, a congregation in her mind. But then she checked herself. What did it matter? And so she had slipped her hand back into his, gripping his fingers tightly to mitigate any offence she might have caused. When they turned from the window, they had to negotiate the pavement together, discover what distance to keep so the link between them held. They had to find a whole new pace at which to carry themselves through the world. It was showing the world they *were* together. But to hold hands would never feel like that again. It became something they took for granted, then something reserved for crises, for the encouragement before exams or for the consolation of a failed job interview. And now what? To start all over again?

What did she *want* from him? That was the real question, and the reason she couldn't cross the dark corridor to ask him another.

Anya turned in the bed and fell through the floorboards. She dreamed of touching an elephant on the beach. A Bosnian woman stood next to it, not any particular woman (although Anya *knew* in her dream she was Bosnian), and behind her a man brushed an elephant with a broom. A sound like gravel being brushed from concrete. Scrape. Scrape.

Scrape. Her eyes opened on the bone light of mosquito curtains. She might have been asleep for hours, or only minutes. The room had filled with the sound of crickets. Wide awake and ready to work, she pulled herself up against the bedstead, and reached for her laptop.

Thursday 7 April 2005

Bangkok

William sits on the floor of his bedroom, back to the glass wall seventeen storeys over Bangkok. Something about the sound of the Windows signature tune stills him, like the tyres on the gravel of his childhood home or the hushing pipes behind the walls of a bathroom. Anya's computer hums with life on his lap. The blue screen blinks once, twice, then shows its bright, blank face. Ctrl. Alt. Del., and she appears: her surname, initial and a number. TEALA01.

Their first holiday: Lake George
Their first gig: Sebadoh
Anya's favourite Polish biscuits: Ciasteczka na święta
Anya's teenage crush: Luke Perry
Anya's school: Stratton Girls
Her research subject: Bosnia

After six attempts at the password, the computer locks him out.

Shutdown. Restart.

The traffic lights of Bangkok below. The red tail-lights of cars smeared in the rain, and a Skytrain's winking yellow windows threading a needle of carriages through glass buildings. During the day, William manages the commute to work. But at night he does not go out. He orders in food. He orders in films. Orders in eleven complete seasons of *Frasier*. He is not interested in the operation of the city below. All that movement. He can't understand what it is for, or where people find the courage for it. He prefers it up here, where red altitude lights on skyscrapers blink across the roof of the city.

Cairo
Juchinar
Four Winds
Underground
Hula Hoops
Stoke Newington

The name of Anya's first dog.

Her best friend at school.

The restaurant where they first met as waiters.

Her favourite film.

Her guilty pleasure.

The neighbourhood of London where they had their first flat.

All these things they shared. All these things had become a part of him. Now he has the laptop. A cold metal box which will not talk to him. When after the wave he visited the bungalow on the beach, William somehow felt he should take the laptop because it was one of those things people might steal. And one of those things he knew Anya would ask about straight away. Her laptop. Her work. She wouldn't want to be without it. The rest had been sent on. And he had every intention of collecting the suitcase from the airport. He had even got as far as stepping to the opposite side of the Skytrain platform, the side which would take him to the airport. But then he had discovered something he already knew but hadn't admitted. William could not deviate from the route between the school and his apartment. These were the co-ordinates pinning him to Earth. Without them, his feet would simply leave the ground, and he would drift into space.

He lies down on the bed and darkens the windows of the room with a switch in the headboard. Inside the sea is silent, and this silence is where he wants to return. Above the water, only noise; people shouting, car alarms, snapping buildings, cracking trees. It all happens in the roaring throat of the ocean. The unmooring of the world. The wave picks up a car and pushes it slowly through the window of a shop. The buildings drift like unanchored ships. The street slips, water grabbing William by the ankles and pushing him down where a cold silence pours in and he is free. Here in the wave, where he holds Anya's hand.

When William surfaces, it always takes him a moment to believe. To believe he can breathe. To believe in the dark walls of the bedroom, blinking red and then black, red and then black, a giant eye, opening and then closing.

On the first night in Kao Lak, Anya had stood in the dark of her room and he had watched across the hallway of the bungalow as she dropped her clothes, stepped out of her knickers and stood in her blue socks. She had a system for socks. White popsocks for trainers, and midnight blue ankle-length socks for everything else. William bought the same ones – still did – because then there would never be a problem with sorting pairs. It wasn't OCD, Anya had never been anally retentive about things. Quite the opposite, she was capable of being far more impulsive than William. It was just one of the extremely practical ideas she had brought to their life, along with the Post-it notes and the cork-board, and the twelve-month plans. Her actions in the bedroom that night felt as though they were planned too. A striptease, a performance, as if she knew he was there. And hadn't she known? She stood in front of her suitcase, but didn't turn. She waited for him, but he did not go. How many steps between them? It wasn't the physical distance that mattered. You could lie next to someone and, without touch, be on the other side of the world. It was Anya standing with her back to him but at the same time, an entirely new woman standing in the cottony light of the mosquito curtains; soft, flickering like a moth in the unstable glow of a weak electric supply. So luminous that, like the schoolboy he was when they first met, William had lost all belief in himself. No faith to take the steps which might have led to a different future, which might have led away from the path of the wave. No faith in the touch which might have sealed the canyon opening in the bed of the Indian Ocean. If he had gone to her then, where might they have been when the wave came?

In Bangkok, William has to believe in the touch of the cold carpet beneath his feet, the dull sounds of the traffic seventeen stories below; he needs to have faith the phone is ringing, or that any of his life now is real. As he treads the dark he lets go of Anya's words, the count before the dive – *Bosnia. Juchinar. Stoke Newington*, and—

'Hello?'

'Oh. Hey. William Howell?'

It is not Anya. It is an American voice. The American voice tells William its name is Missy. This Missy woman has been arrested. She needs him to come and verify her employment status. She needs him at the police station to sign the forms. William waits for Anya to tell him he should take responsibility. But Anya doesn't speak. He puts down the phone and gathers his clothes, creeping around in the dark until he realises he is not in his London flat, nor on the beaches of Kao Lak, and Anya is not there to be disturbed.

Sarajevo

Marko pushes his overnight bag through the headrests. It lands on the back seat in front of the cracked shell of a TAXI light.

'I'm not a taxi driver.' Samir lowers himself into the driver's seat. He sits half in, half out, detaches the left leg and pulls the right into the car. He gives the false leg to Marko. The cuff of his trouser is stitched around the remaining stump, and the stump pushes into some sort of metal lever connected to the pedals.

'I don't taxi.' Samir engages the engine. 'You can't make any money on it. What I do is I just drive our guests to and from the airport.' They pull out of the short-stay bay, and scrape over the speed bumps of the airport car park. The Renault's suspension is shot. 'With the taxi sign I can park right out in front of arrivals,' Samir explains.

His cousin's car smells like a basket of dirty laundry. In the passenger door, where the window handle should be, Marko finds only an exposed bolt.

Samir hands him a bent fork, and Marko cranks the window down.

'From last week,' Samir says.

A newspaper lands in Marko's lap.

For a brief moment the marks on the page are not a language but gibberish. Shapes without meaning. Then he learns to read again. It is not the lead story about negotiations between police chiefs in Sarajevo and Republika Srpska, or

the second story about the opening of a new festival of literature. It is at the foot of the front page.

Stovnik's Hero Comes Home
– and ten years after his funeral.

The body of a soldier presumed dead in Stovnik's Youth Day
massacre has been returned to the town almost a decade after
his funeral.

Kemal Lekić, commander of Stovnik's 2nd brigade, was
given a ceremonial burial in 1995, after searches failed to
recover his body from the shelling of Stovnik's Kapija.

Yesterday morticians in Stovnik confirmed they had received
the body of Mr Lekić, who died in a Thai hospital this January.

Doctors in Thailand say his death had been caused by head
injuries sustained in the Indian Ocean tsunami.

Problems of identification had delayed repatriation, but locals
who knew Mr Lekić were able to identify Stovnik as his hometown.

Mr Lekić was well known in Stovnik. His command was
considered instrumental in the operations which broke two
years of siege. The 2nd brigade created safe-corridors for
thousands of displaced persons from Biljelina and Srebenik.

Oslobodenje contacted friends of the deceased, but they did
not wish to comment on the news. Former colleagues in the
battalion expressed their shock.

A number of the shelling's 58 victims were also given
ceremonial burials after bodies were lost or went unidentified.

Mr Lekić had no surviving family.

'You look pale,' Samir says. 'You want to stay and get a tan.
You look like you've been living in a foxhole . . . in a forest . . .
under a fucking . . . mountain.'

'Just England.'

When Samir laughs, Marko might be seventeen again. Almost ten years. The man sitting next to Marko is definitely his cousin, but the brown cords and denim shirt are a costume, silvery stubble sponged on like stage-make-up.

They pass the housing estates near the airport, the patchwork tower blocks with their sticking plasters of pink alabaster and balconies boxed up to make spare rooms. Vesna's father had lived somewhere around here.

'Are you angry?' Marko asks.

'What do you think? Aren't you?'

Marko is looking at the picture of Kemal in the paper. It is the official brigade photograph, the one cut into Kemal's headstone. But anger isn't the right word for what he feels. It is too weak. That night there had been too many things in the flat Marko could break, so he found himself outside without any idea of where his feet were leading. The dark circling the lamp post of Parker's Piece was dark only when observed from the street. In the place of disappearing, everything became apparent. Marko could see across the green, as far as the chain of street lights, the old greyhound following the trail of kebab meat which he had left behind him like Hansel in the woods.

Marko brings one of Samir's cigarettes to his mouth. It had been a day, but he can still smell the dog on his fingers.

'Did you know?' Marko lights the cigarette.

Samir only has to look at him to register his offence. They swing around a hairpin turn. Beneath them, the city begins to fill the mouth of the valley. An illusion of completeness; in his memory still, the broken teeth of white towers so familiar from the news bulletins of the war. He knows it is supposed to mean something to him. He knows the word 'home' should contain some magic. They slow in the early evening traffic and light the colour of weak tea floods the hills.

'The little shit only had to call us,' Samir says. 'You were like a brother to him – and to think of your poor parents!'

'I don't know what the fuck *they* think,' Marko says.

He could have been telling his father Kemal had returned from the moon to lead an alien invasion of earth. When Marko called his parents that morning, he could hear the stately Austro-Hungarian calm of his grandparents' Zagreb apartment at the other end of the line. Clocks ticking. Newspaper pages turning. (All in his imagination of course.)

'I never expect the craziness of that war to end,' his father had said. He told Marko it would only upset his mother to come to the funeral. What did it matter Kemal had been alive? They had buried him once – wasn't that enough? Then before Marko could hang up, a final punch: 'You know it has been over a year since you called, Marko?'

They stop before a pedestrian crossing. An old woman in a headscarf wheels a shopping trolley behind her, and two dun-coloured street dogs follow silently. Marko thinks of the greyhound on Parker's Piece. When he killed the dog, he hadn't expected her to fight so hard.

'Do you realise that when we turn into the next street, we will be in Republika Srpska?' Samir says.

'What are people saying?'

Samir taps on the driver's window with his wedding-ring knuckle, 'Look. Half these graves are ours.' They are passing one of those prickly thickets of white crosses and obelisks which grow in the hills: 'Bosnian buses, Bosnian ćevapi, Bosnian dead. And now they call this Serbia.' Samir sighs. 'Republika Srpska. Kemal didn't do anything. He had nothing to run away from. I think he just wanted out. Can you blame him?'

Until now, Marko hadn't realised how much he needed to hear his cousin say it.

'There are stories about this and that.' Samir wipes his nose with the back of his hand. 'They say he might have crossed someone in the villages; someone's family.'

'*Crossed* them?'

They stop in the tail-lights of a bus. Red light fills the car. Samir says how it was all bullshit; not Kemal, he always played it straight, and Marko nods and agrees because this is how they always talked of Kemal. Because Kemal was the hero who died, and the friend they had grieved for, the only one whose life made any sense of the war, and if they didn't believe that, if they didn't believe in Kemal, then what the fuck had it all been about anyway?

The bus moves and Samir puts the car into gear. 'There were two women who went missing.'

'Missing?'

But Samir is already wagging his finger. 'No, no, no. It's just they were last seen at this place where the brigade was, but it has nothing to do with Kemal. I fought every battle with the man! The guy was a fucking saint!' Samir slaps the steering wheel. 'The bastard.'

They laugh. How has Marko lived ten years without this kind of laughter?

'Have you ever performed the ghusl?' Marko asks.

Samir shakes his head and tells him it's nothing, tells him you don't really wash the body, tells him it's just ceremonial.

'I'm not even a Muslim,' Marko says.

'The imam said it would be shameful to bury Kemal without the ceremony. If there are no Muslims it should be family. So I tell him there is no family and he asks after your parents, and I ask your parents and they suggest you. What can I do? A crazy Bosnian imam. Already the hospital autopsied and prepared the body to be sent back. What difference does it make?'

'Kemal never gave a fuck about imams or mosques.'

'I know.'

The car turns off the high road onto an old street, heading down between the lean-to houses built out of old shepherds' huts. Samir slips it into neutral, and the sound of the engine is replaced by the familiar popping of tyres over cobbles. They drop down to the centre of the old town, the low red roofs of the buildings in the Turkish quarter, where his cousin now runs a bed and breakfast. This was a place too dangerous to visit during the war. Although Marko had come here with Vesna.

Vesna was the last person Marko had seen before he left the country; Vesna standing on the banks of the Sava as the ferry, low with cars and cattle and people, drifted into the current. He knew he would not be coming back. This place had taken away his childhood and given him the opportunity to start again. He wonders now whether Kemal had known it too. Whether Kemal had stood on the ferry over the Sava. Whether Kemal had been drifting with the river current on the day Marko, Samir, Vesna and his father buried an empty coffin.

'Kemal would laugh,' he tells Samir, 'at the idea of me and an imam washing his body. He'd prefer a woman.'

It is an anger he is not supposed to feel. The anger he had used to kill the dog on Parker's Piece. Be angry with something else, not with the animal. Kemal had taught him to do this. To kill without feeling as the plastic bag tied around the greyhound's head became a thrashing balloon of spit. Without feeling, and with mercy. That was the trick. He was doing the dog a favour. He was doing the best he could.

'Is Vesna coming?' Marko asks.

'The invitations went out,' Samir says. 'But we never heard from her.'

The tip of Marko's finger has turned purple. He lets the lace of Samir's trainer loose. It is oddly light, this false leg, the shin a hollow rod of plastic. Not the shape of a real limb, but something approximating a Caucasian skin colour. Samir pulls the car up against a kerb, switches the engine off and takes the leg from him.

'It's just around here,' he says.

A tourist shop, postcard spinners and buckets of those giant sponge hands people wave at football matches, with 'Sarajevo' printed along the pointing finger.

'Baščaršija Bed and Breakfast'. The name of Samir's place is etched in English on the glass. So they are the ones running things now.

Bangkok

William closes the driver's door and seals them from the nightclub din.

'Pad Kee Mao – they didn't have Rad Na.' He offers Missy the tray of steaming noodles but she has fallen asleep, head against the passenger window and hands closed between thighs of denim shorts. Her hair is loose from its pins, a backcombed mess of curls over the glass. William thinks it may be dyed – no, *sprayed*! This strange American woman has sprayed her hair silver with the kind of stuff kids use on Halloween.

'I charge for looking.' Missy opens one eye.

'Pad Kee Mao,' he holds the tray out again. 'You asked for something to eat.'

She shifts with the over-meticulous care of a drunk and looks around the car as though she expects someone else to be there.

'Oh, Jesus Christ – so I *did* call you.'

'You called me from the police station,' William says. 'Remember?'

'They are going to deport me.'

'They are not going to deport you.' William rests the tray of noodles in the well of the handbrake, checks the rear-view mirror, tells her not to panic and knows he is really telling himself.

He hears the passenger door close. Missy is already out on the road, trapped by a tide of cars. She looks left, looks right and, with one hand on the car to steady herself, stumbles around the bonnet, extending her arm for a taxi, stupid hair wobbling like a head of candyfloss.

Well, fuck her then.

He is startled as water slaps across the window of the car. A man trips onto the pavement with something bright pink that turns out to be a plastic gun. The New Year's nonsense is starting already. The girl he is chasing runs clean out of her flip-flops, black soles of her feet flapping a few steps until she is cut off by a second jet of water. As the girl bends down to pick up her flip-flops, another man appears and drops a balloon of water over her head.

William turns on the windscreen wiper. Missy has reached the corner of the block. She stands by a road crossing, yanking her ridiculous silver hair into a small ponytail and dangling one foot over the road.

Technically, this was all his fault. Missy's visa had expired. The visa William was supposed to arrange. She had been taken to a police station with backpackers who didn't have the correct paperwork.

His hands open the car door. His feet walk him over the pavement. His shoulder leads him through the crowds. It is two a.m., a hot April storm has passed and the street smells rise from asphalt slick with neon colours. Missy is bending over a tuk-tuk driver.

'Missy, I think it's best—'

'I just need to get to the border.'

'If you wouldn't mind getting in the car first, we can talk—'

She shakes him off and heads back down the pavement. William wants to call her name but can't bring himself to shout in public. Instead, he half runs, half walks, until he catches her at the crossing which holds the night-market crowds beneath the Skytrain tracks.

She is looking at her feet. When she lifts her head it is with a deep breath, as if surfacing from the sea. 'I've had a little bit to drink – what with New Year.'

'That's fine. You're absolutely fine.'

'I was expecting the school to sort out my work visa. I don't know if that was personally *your* fault, but it *was* a screw-up.'

When he gets her to the car, she climbs into the back seat.

'I'm going to take a nap,' she says. 'And when I wake up, I'm going to hope it isn't in the backseat of my boss's car where I crashed out drunk after being arrested.'

She has closed her eyes. Beneath the vest her chest rises and falls. He clears his throat. Perhaps she had just decided the best way out of what she has just done is to hide.

What is he supposed to do with this tray of noodles?

'What am I supposed to do with this?' he asks.

But she appears to be completely out.

As William pulls away from the kerb, he realises, he doesn't even know where she lives. At the junction of Pitsanulok and Luang the lights stop them. On the wide corner of Bamrung Muang, a woman places an incense stick into a Buddhist shrine next to a stall selling bongs, hula hoops and water guns. Golden Buddhas, posters of South Korean pop stars in their underwear, dildos lined up in order of size and giant cactuses laid out on a Turkish carpet by the pavement chairs of an all-night Starbucks.

Where is Anya? Why isn't she talking to him? Only the failed passwords.

Hula Hoops, Four Winds, Underground.

Rama Road falls behind them; the Paragon Mall, the Bank of Thailand, the Metropole. He could take her home but he had cancelled his cleaner months ago – the sink in his kitchen is full of unwashed dishes, the fridge is empty, the bins are full of takeout boxes. The road rises on to the flyover where advertising hoardings loom and fall. The New Kia Cee'd, Louis Vuitton, and a sign that simply says: 'Thailand thanks the Rotary Club for helping eradicate cholera'. Beneath the tyres, the concrete sections of the flyover thump: *Stratton, Stratton, Stratton.*

He has done the border run before. Three years ago now; six hours to Aranyaphratet in Thailand, two in Poipet. He has heard the bureaucracy is worse these days. It takes twenty-four hours, maybe more, to turn a new entry-visa around. But what choice do they have? When the flyover dips down into a single lane between the shacks of the suburbs, William pulls over, rests his head on the steering wheel and breathes in and out to a rhythm dictated by the ticking of the car's indicator.

'What?' Anya would grin at William when she was driving, 'What are you looking at?'

He was looking at Anya. Anya who had passed her driving test first time. Anya who would give him lifts to their shifts at a restaurant. He had already failed the driving test twice. To sit next to Anya as she drove her mother's car was everything. The car changed the world they were in. They let the windows down, William lit her cigarette from his own, and they filled themselves like sails with the air rushing in. The dual carriageway that stretched out into the green belt wasn't just leaving the town, it was leaving everything they had been. It was all over. Not just the houses, and their parents, shrinking in the rear-view mirror, but the school with its teachers, the parks with its bullies, the girls who had broken his heart. All those battles were over and William had *won*. He had won! His arm trailed out of the window, palm batting the thick summer air.

William had won Anya.

'What are you looking at?'

Looking at Anya. At her eyes behind oversized sunglasses, her smile wide beneath them, arms stretched to the steering wheel and a tie-dye skirt falling between her legs. She was the kind of girl who knew who she was going to vote for in her first general election, and actually knew why. She worked to pay her half of the insurance on the car, she knew what settings to use on a washing machine, she could cook curries and moussaka, and ate olives when she drank red wine.

'What are you looking at?'

Looking at Anya, who treated the car like she did the cutlery and plates at the restaurant. She threw it around without fear of breaking it, jamming it into small spaces on the high street, heavy on the clutch, ruthless with the gears (in Anya's view, bumpers were for bumping). But William never for a moment felt anything less than safe. As with the rest of her life – the three dogs she walked, the two jobs she did, the political parties she had already joined – Anya seemed to be in control, to know what needed to be done.

'What are you looking at?'

Looking at Anya. Anya as she sits on the veranda beneath the palms. She smiles. She is wearing sunglasses again, but not over-sized. She is trying the Durian fruit he bought for their breakfast and the silence which follows contains their earliest memories. Sixteen years later, and William still feels like he has won.

'I love that we can hear the sea,' she says. And they can. They can hear the ocean sigh as it gives itself up on the shore.

Christmas Day, 2004

Kao Lak

Anya sat up in the bed. The book fell from her chest. She had fallen asleep with the dominatrix, a nineteenth-century Austrian princess cast out from her family to live a life of exile in North Africa, where she commanded a harem.

She opened the blinds. Through the heavy fingers of a palm there was a view of the walkway suspended over the mangroves. Three more bungalows in the trees. It could have been too early or too late for people to be up. She had passed the night in a jet-lag dream, waking to read again her notes on Kemal Lekić, and struck by a sudden doubt over whether she should be here at all. Not just because of William, but because of this business she had already fucked up once. Wasn't it a vanity? The real question was, what would Ljuba Crvenović want? The woman whose apartment in Belgrade had been spotless, baklava freshly made for her English guest. Ljuba had heard the English didn't drink coffee, and had been out to buy tea. Her children were at school. Her husband was at work. No mother of three could have always kept a place this tidy. When Anya used the bathroom, she found the end of the blue toilet paper folded into a neat arrowhead.

Finally, after years of petitioning, after years of campaigning for the eviction of the tenants occupying their old house, the Crvenović family had won their right to return to their village. It was one of those front-line places, awkwardly split between post-Dayton Bosnia and the newly created Republika Srpska. Ljuba and her husband were Bosnian Serbs, but they had not participated in fighting on the Serbian side, and in theory, their return should not have caused any difficulties in the community.

During the conversation, Anya had detected some stalling between Ljuba and the translator. But when it came, Ljuba's breakdown was sudden. Her village was only a twenty-minute drive from Stovnik. How could she go back? How could she go back, when men from the brigade were living in the town? The man she accused of her rape was dead. But the other soldiers knew. The other soldiers had witnessed what happened. And what of her friends? Her friends were still missing, and no one was investigating that.

Anya had told Ljuba she would be visiting Stovnik to report on the efforts of the local police to evict wartime tenants. What if she checked in to see whether there had been any developments in the missing person's case? Would that help?

In the bungalow, Anya's mobile wouldn't come to life. The heat drained her as she rifled through the suitcase for the charger and plug adaptors. What would happen if she just left the mobile turned off? The idea was startling. Her colleagues wouldn't believe it. But with the care of someone laying flowers on a grave, she put the dead phone back in the drawer, and then in the shower, let the cold water beat against her face, a light battering for all of yesterday's foolishness. There was no reason why it might not get better. They had twelve days together.

God. *Twelve days.*

She stood in a towel and cut off the price tags from a red one-piece bought on impulse at Heathrow. What if she knocked on William's door and woke him with a blow job?

But Will's bedroom door was closed. She put her ear to the warm wood, her hand on the cool porcelain doorknob, when something stopped her.

What the fuck was she *doing*?

'It was in the pool,' a man with a heavy German accent told the receptionist.

By its laces, the receptionist held up a dripping pair of trainers, looking uncertain of what to do with them. A second boy darted beneath the desk and surfaced with a bin-liner.

Anya waited and studied the leaflets in a carousel. Boat trips to islands, dawn parties on special beaches, tattoo artists, massage treatments and restaurants. Elephant rides.

Elephant rides. She picked the leaflet out. An elephant on a beach. The red tabard with golden brocades over its back and the name of the place. *Heaven Resort, Kao Lak.* There were no more pictures inside the brochure, only this paragraph in a number of different languages.

> Thailand famous for its wild Elephant.
> Beach rides at dawn and dusk.
> Ride this wild and magnificent animal.
> Hire only from boathouse.

Over four years ago she had written the name of this resort in her notes. But the picture of the elephant was something she had not seen since then.

Anya showed the receptionist the leaflet. 'Do you know where I can book an elephant ride?'

The receptionist said something and Anya had to ask him to repeat it. The elephants could be hired at the boathouse, down at the south end of the beach, not far, he said. She found herself walking through a restaurant, white tablecloths reflecting the sunlight, the percussion of cutlery, and staff threading through the room like ghosts in their grey pyjama suits. Outside, a pool area, hot flagstones and the resort falling away in tiers to the sea. It was Anya's first glimpse of the Indian Ocean and it blinded her. The sun on this side of the world seemed heavier, closer to the earth somehow.

William sank a penknife into a giant watermelon. 'Happy Christmas!'

He had been to the local market, and from parcels of brown paper, dished out Thai specialities as if they were Christmas presents. Sticky rice in baking paper; a heavy orange fruit about the size and shape of a large aubergine. As he cut the fruit open with a penknife, he tried to teach her the name. The fruit split into two pieces of yellowish flesh folded over with a startling resemblance to labia.

'And this rice,' he said, splitting it with a fork, 'funnily enough, sort of tastes spermy. But I think it's fish.'

She preferred the juice (his favourite apparently), a mixture of guava, lime and banana. He arranged everything in a line for her to try and although it didn't feel like breakfast time, she found herself hungry for it all. Somehow, she had forgotten Will could be fun.

'He lives in a room next to the school entrance,' Will was talking about the school caretaker, 'with a kettle and a cupboard of Pot Noodles – or the equivalent of – and a blow-up doll.'

Through the trees, on the veranda of another bungalow, a large, pale European man busily erected a picnic table for a family of what seemed like an impossible amount of children. Anya closed her eyes and let her head fall back. The light through the palms. She was a child trailing a stick along the iron bars of a fence.

'Doesn't attempt to hide it. Doesn't even see anything wrong with it. I caught him washing the doll down in the school shower.'

The noises cut through Will's chatter; cutlery against a plate; the sound of children's voices. Anya was falling and had to force herself to sit up and open her eyes. She hadn't been down to the boat-hire place, not yet. Even if Kemal Lekić was alive and had at some point been here, visited by his girlfriend, it didn't mean he was still here. And if he was – well, what was she going to do? In the pocket of her shorts she felt for the reassuring shape of her mobile phone. Returning from the reception she had plugged it in, and it was now fully charged.

'Christmas presents!' Will said. He produced another brown paper parcel from the bag.

'Oh, I forgot!' she said.

'Typical.'

'No – I mean, it's in my bag. I'll have to fetch it.'

'Never mind that now, look – you might not want to give me anything after this. I only just remembered myself and it's all they had at the shop.'

Anya opened the parcel. 'Wow.' She examined the box. 'This is – a *Franklin Roosevelt* action figure!'

'Also available – Copernicus, Mozart, Schopenhauer and Einstein – all from the same stall that brings you vaginal fruit.'

'And this,' Anya picked up a second thing in the bag, 'is – a *Chairman Mao* wristwatch!' She broke into the plastic packaging. 'I didn't think Thailand ever adopted communism?'

'And I don't think Roosevelt ever set foot here.'

'So what better gift from Kao Lak?'

'Exactly.'

It was the first real silence between them. Will began to clear the half-eaten food. On her wrist, Anya fiddled with the strap of the watch. She knew the silence was too long to be comfortable. He hadn't yet asked where she had been that morning. She thought about telling him but worried that if she started out on the story of Kemal, its pieces would somehow fall apart. He would think work was getting in their way again. But getting in the way of what?

'What are you looking at?' she said.

'Nothing,' he said, then 'you.'

She turned her head, looked into the twisted mangroves, and tried to hide her smile. 'I love that we can hear the sea.'

'Bosniaks and Croats consider the first casualties of the war to be Suada Dilberović (a Bosniak) and Olga Sučić (a Croat), who were shot after the declaration of independence, on April the 5th 1992, by unidentified Serb gunmen. Serbs consider Nikola Gardović, a groom's father killed on the 1st of March in Sarajevo's old town . . . to be the first victim of the war.'

Robert J. Donia, *Sarajevo: A Biography*

July 1991

Kletovo

Marko, Kemal, Samir and Vesna, lay on the steep garden of Kemal's family home, upside down in the tall grass, feet higher than their heads and the distant cornfields hanging over a purple dusk. Who would be the first to chicken out with a head full of blood? Vesna? Kemal? Samir? Marko? Somewhere in the house Jim Morrison was singing about enterprise and destiny and how stoned everyone was.

'I feel dizzy,' Vesna said.

'You are dizzy,' Kemal replied.

'It's your Croatian blood. If the world was always upside down,' Samir tried to control his laughter, 'our blood would have to pump up to our feet and we wouldn't walk on our heads but—'

'But we would constantly be shitting ourselves.'

'But gravity would be working the other way,' Vesna said. 'If we hung from the earth, you know, like spiders, we'd be sticking to it because that's what gravity does.'

'We *are* like spiders,' Kemal said. 'The earth is round. We *are* sticking to it – just upside down.'

Vesna moaned dramatically, 'Oh fuck – but now I really am upside down – so does that mean, I'm the right way up?'

A willow tree dangled in the sky; a willow tree holding a tyre that floated on the end of a rope, like a helium balloon on a string. Marko dug his fingers into the cold roots of the grass, closed his eyes and listened to the sounds of the party and the brook rippling impossibly over the rocks. Perhaps there was no such thing as upside down. Or the concept of being upside down was actually relative. But relative to what? Everything was upside down now. There would be no holiday in Bečići for the friends this year, where the beach days were long and the promenade nights longer. Family holidays together were the first thing the war had taken from them. Unless you counted Kemal's father. How could a boy live when his father had died? How could a boy talk and make jokes and kiss a girl – kiss Vesna? How could a boy whose father had died throw parties? Kemal's mother was away for work and they had all been drinking plum brandy since the middle of the day. Earlier that afternoon, someone had given Marko something to smoke. Kemal had taken it out of his mouth, smoked some of it himself, put it back in Marko's mouth and clapped him on the shoulder. Marko had never felt more like a man. The revolving rooms of the house. Bodies on the floor. Bijelo Dugme on the stereo singing '…all of that, my dear, will be covered in rosemary, snow and reeds', a conversation about Slovenian women that never seemed to end. In the garden someone picked out notes on a guitar, and the war was still in Croatia.

'I'm done,' Vesna said. Abruptly she rose from the grass next to Kemal. 'I think I'm going to be sick.'

Marko watched as upside down, hanging from the earth, or whatever it actually was, Vesna held her head in her hands. If she didn't hold her head it would fall off and drop into the sky. Kemal sprang up next to her and placed an arm around her shoulder and Marko felt something in his gut as sharp as the stubble in the meadow grass. He closed his eyes again. What Marko had heard was this: Kemal's father had been watching the television; the famous game between Zagreb Dinamo and Belgrade Red Star. The fans in the stadium had begun to fight, the policemen in the stadium had begun to fight the fans, the Croatian policemen in the stadium had begun to fight the Serbian policemen and Kemal's father had stood up, punched the air, told the world it could go to hell, then dropped down dead on the carpet. Just like that.

It was being a policeman that killed Kemal's father. This is what the mothers had said in the kitchen. As if being a police-man were like cancer. But *all* their fathers were policemen. That is how they had met, after all. And now Yugoslavia's policemen were being killed at barricades all over Croatia. Men like their fathers; twelve last week in that town not so far from the Sava. Not so far from the actual border. On the news they said the men had been found with their ears cut off. And what was left when you cut off an ear? Could you see the skull? Or could you see into the brain? Did the dark tunnels of the ear worm right into the brain?

Marko feels the pressure of a warm hand on his forehead.

'He's still alive.' Kemal's voice. Kemal upside down when Marko opens his eyes. 'You win.' Kemal offers his hand.

'I think I passed out.'

When he gets up, Marko isn't ready for his legs. He scrab-bles around to face the brook and the bottom of the garden where the willow tree is a stain in the inky evening. Girls are yelping and giggling and there are candles in the grass. Somewhere Van Gogh are singing the ballad about a sinking precious stone and the girls have waded through the shallow brook to sit up against a tree where they hold their knees and watch a boy standing in a tyre as he swings across the stream, whooping like a baboon.

Samir the baboon.

'I'm going to jump it,' Kemal says.

Marko takes Kemal's hand again. Finding his legs, he stands up in the righted world. 'Jump what?'

Kemal nods in the direction of the brook and before Marko can say anything, his friend is running, or *trying* to run; the steep slope tripping up his legs until he falls over himself. Marko follows, but by the time he sees Kemal fall it is too late.

When he lands, the water isn't deep enough to completely cover him. Standing up, he is soaked through. Marko drags his heavy legs to the other side where Kemal kneels on the bank. He pulls off his wet T-shirt and throws it into the grass. And for some reason he doesn't think about but only feels, Marko wrestles Kemal to the ground.

Kemal is the taller boy. At seventeen he has three years on Marko. In a fight with fists there is never any doubt Kemal will win. But Marko has won every category of the region's judo competitions since the age of eleven and now he manages to knock Kemal's feet away. They roll on the hard edges of the bank until Marko finds an arm, locks it and pins Kemal, face down, to the ground. Pure skill. Kemal goes limp. He is not fighting any more. And Marko doesn't even know why he has started it. Except that the girls are watching. Except that he wants to say something.

I met Vesna first. (This is what he wants to say.) Last summer, on the beach in Bečići, she spoke to me first. Vesna is my age. Not your age. Don't you have other girls – other girls your *own* age?

But Marko says nothing. Instead, he takes his knee out of Kemal's back and stands up to offer a hand which Kemal shakes. He embraces the younger boy and Marko can say nothing because in truth, even though he had met Vesna first, even though they are both fourteen, he had not noticed her until she stood in Kemal's arms. In Kemal's arms Vesna's body seemed to take on a different shape. The stupid thing was Marko had never thought about Vesna as a girl to kiss until he saw Kemal kissing her.

Friday 8 April 2005

Sarajevo

He lay awake on the springs of what was little more than a camp bed, and listened to the market waking up with him. It was a small, low-ceilinged room, dim orange light of curtains over a porthole window. Samir's bed and breakfast occupied four of these rooms, carved out of the two which had been above his uncle's shop. It was Friday. Marko should have been in the swimming pool at Cherry Hinton. Three times a week he needed to beat the water. Millie said she could always tell when he hadn't been for a swim.

You've got your bad head on.

At the reception desk he searched the Internet while Samir boiled coffee. In a full ghusl ceremony, they would have to begin by washing the 'excretory' organs of the dead body. Three washings with juniper water, camphor and then fresh water. Incense sticks, incantations. All that shit. It was a ceremony associated with the 'cleansing of sins'. But what were Kemal's sins? Kemal used to leave his dirty clothes on the floor of the bedroom and never remembered to open the window after using the bathroom.

But he had never crossed anyone in his life.

'Where does Vesna live these days?' Marko asked.

'And good morning to you too,' Samir said.

In Dobrinja, the sun rises behind the blocks of the estate. Marko crosses the playground of child-safe matting. The matting is new; the Day-Glo climbing frames too. During the winter of 1993, the people of the estate had broken up the old wooden climbing frames for fuel. With Vesna, Marko had come to Sarajevo during one of the war's last ceasefires, entering the city by bending double in the tunnel underneath the airport.

Samir said that after the war, Vesna had left Stovnik and come back to Sarajevo, but he'd never seen her again and he didn't know where she lived.

Vesna's father might still have the place in Dobrinja.

On the walls of the stairwell, Marko can smell the new paint, a bifurcation of pink and aquamarine, the colours of his child-hood school, his father's police station and all the institutional buildings of his youth. Black telephone lines, yellow Internet cables, potted cactuses guarding the front doors to apartments; Marko has climbed to the twelfth floor by the time he even thinks of the lift. He is not quite sure if this is it. There had been a windowless frame in the stairwell, where with Vesna's cousins he had shot at the 'PTT' hoarding on the roof of the building opposite. Now the window is double-glazed and the billboard advertising the postal system of Yugoslavia has been replaced by the neon pink tubes of the legend, 'T-Mobile'.

He knocks on the door. A light appears in the peephole, quickly darkened by an eye.

'The Knežević girl?' The man who opens the door wears a handlebar moustache. Silver hair touches the emerald-green tracksuit over his shoulders. It is not Vesna's father.

'You're after the Knežević girl?'

'Her father used to live here.'

'Who are you?'

This question proves more difficult than he thinks. He starts with his childhood friendship, his years away, but the man dismisses him with a wave.

'I have something here,' he says. 'Come in.'

From the apartment a loud cheer explodes. It is football on a television.

'I'll find it.' Barefooted the old man pads over the creaking parquet with a slight limp. Cigarette smoke curls into the corridor.

'My son,' he gestures through the glass doors to the living room where a man younger than Marko sits on an old sofa in his boxer shorts, legs spread in front of the screen.

The communal areas of the building might be clean, but this apartment isn't. It smells of damp and machine oil and a motorbike engine sits on the floor like something that has fallen off a spaceship and landed on earth. Apart from the sofa, the television and old dresser, there is no furniture.

'Two—one at forty minutes,' the boy tells him.

'What did you bet?'

'Three—one full time.'

Vesna's grandmother had been sleeping in here, on a threadbare divan next to the wall. There had been a dining table and chairs, and net curtains. The parquet floor Marko slept on the weekend of the tournament had been polished within an inch of its life.

They watch Stankovic pass long to Haag, and Haag thread the ball skilfully through the defenders.

'Only problem now is they play too fucking well.' The boy throws Marko a pack of Drina.

When the older man limps into the room, he is holding a bunch of envelopes. The door of Vesna's father's bedroom is open. There is a single camp bed on the floor. In Vesna's day, five people slept in there. The bedroom on the side of the apartment not facing the snipers.

'Right.' The man sits down on the sofa and shuffles through the papers. 'You said you were a friend of the family?'

Marko picks up a lighter from the table.

'Not a debt collector then?' The man is half-joking, but suddenly Marko feels the need to justify himself.

He tries to tell them about the trip, the judo competition, the airport, remembering as he does, how little he likes to talk about things that happened during the war, how little he has *had* to talk about them. He can't stop looking at the old man's right eye. Its black pupil swims like a glassy fish in a dirty pond.

'After her father died, the girl couldn't afford the loans on her own.' The man finds what he is looking for. 'This arrived not long ago.'

It is the handwriting of Marko's father, and seeing it here, is like meeting him in an unexpected place. Although they had no intention of returning to Bosnia, his parents had paid for Kemal's funeral and made all the arrangements. This is her invitation.

'You don't know her new address?'

'That's how it came.' The man reaches over and raps his knuckles on his son's knee. 'We couldn't find the address. Could we?'

'Couldn't find what address?'

'The new address – of the Knežević girl.'

The boy doesn't take his eyes off the television. 'We don't know where she lives.'

'You want a coffee?' the father asks.

'Did you meet her? Vesna?'

'Good-looking girl,' the father says.

'Is she still in Sarajevo?'

The man shrugs, showing Marko the cracked pads of his palms. 'I met her when we bought the flat – not since then.'

'Tourism,' the boy says. 'I think she was working for some tourism company.'

'She travelled?'

The boy shrugs.

'I told you – we only met her once,' the father says.

Marko knows it is a dead end. But he doesn't want to leave. Not yet. He asks if he can use the toilet.

Word of the funerals had gone out the evening after the shelling. People had left their homes just after midnight: fifty-eight coffins for the dead and the missing, most of them lighter than they should have been, and not just because they were constructed from recycled crates. The shell had left the kids in pieces, and some bodies seemed to have disappeared altogether. A number of coffins carried that night had been filled not with bodies but stuffed toys, favourite football shirts, or the guitars and violins the children played at school. Marko placed Kemal's medal and fatigues in the coffin. Before they closed the lid, he remembered a German porn mag beneath the bunks in their bedroom, and searching for it, found the *Tao of Jeet Kune Do*. The *Tao*. Their martial arts manual, the only book they both read, read again, and then read again until they had a store of its wisdom to carry around in their heads. They had annotated the margins and practised the book's moves together. Kemal drew pictures of Chuck Norris on the right-hand corner of each page, so that when you flicked through the book, the figure performed a flying roundhouse. They would always fight over who played Bruce Lee. *Chuck Norris vs Bruce Lee*; it was what they called their training sessions. Only as he sealed the coffin did Marko realise he would never fight Bruce Lee again. In the plywood crate, Kemal's last things slid about like loose change as Marko, his father, Samir and Vesna carried it through the town, a shoulder at each corner. The absence of the body should have given them hope. But they had all seen the town square after the shell.

As they carried the coffin, Vesna had sobbed for the man she was supposed to marry. Like all of them, Vesna had believed Kemal was dead. Hadn't she?

When Marko opens the toilet door, the teenage son is waiting in the hall.

'You were here in the war?'

Marko nods.

'Will you tell me something?' The kid leads him into the room on the right. Vesna's old room. 'Know why they did this? We were going to paint over it. But I sort of got used to it.'

The posters of Annie Lennox are gone, and the walls are bare except for Vesna's mural, tied together by the red line. The line loops up and down, painted in places to make the peaks of mountains and dotted with childish drawings of trees and villages. Marko explains to the boy that the wobbling red line had joined the bullet holes in the plaster. He points to the lowest ebb of the line, where a blue river runs through a forest. The bullet holes here have joined together to form a tear in the wall. Where the sniper had trained his aim, once, twice, three, four times. Whatever angle he was working, he couldn't aim any lower.

'She knew it was safe to sleep below this line,' Marko tells the kid. 'If they put the mattress on the floor.'

At the bottom of the stairwell, Marko doesn't stop at the ground floor, but finds himself down at the entrance of the basement service area, looking for something. The first thing to present itself is a recycling skip on wheels. He grabs it, pulls it out and pushes it into the opposite wall. Where the skip had been there's a broom, which Marko picks up and throws. When it doesn't break he retrieves it and snaps it over his knee. It is only when he punches the skip that he stops.

Outside, Samir is waiting in the car.

'Find her?'

Marko picks up Samir's leg and sits down in the passenger seat. His chest is still tight. 'Moved on.'

They drive off the estate, and straight onto the dual carriageway which carries the cars of the valley, north-east, past the first signs for Stovnik. Samir turns the radio on to some happy euro-pop. They glide over the railway station and its rusted lines, the grey basin of the Olympic Stadium, the apartment blocks of the Athletes' Village steepling the hills behind it.

'Apparently she works in tourism now.' Marko holds his right fist.

Samir turns the music down. 'Vesna? What? You think she was going out to Thailand?'

'Maybe.' Marko opens his bruised fingers. 'Maybe she was *in* Thailand.' The road crests a hill and Sarajevo drops behind them, the high valley and its hamlets, blinking in the morning.

He tests the splinter in his palm. Samir had told Marko not to visit Vesna. Not to dig around in case there was anything he didn't want to find. It wasn't just the missing women. There had been a woman in Serbia. A woman who accused Kemal of rape and asked for an investigation.

'None of it stood up,' Samir said. 'The rape. No evidence at all. The police – they asked everyone, and everyone told them the same story. The women were at the camp. And then they were gone. I know it myself.' Samir had been there. Nothing happened. Kemal wasn't capable of those things.

But still, Marko had wanted Vesna to tell him it wasn't true.

He listens to the gears changing as the car climbs the hills. Maybe he had just wanted to see Vesna.

'You know, Marko,' Samir says. 'What I would do if I were you? I would attend this funeral. Have a drink with your old friends. Get back on the plane, back to your woman, back to your life in England. Really. Move on. You're good at it.'

Aranyaphratet

The queue to drive through seems to move more slowly than the queue on foot. They park in a roped field, pay a boy in a Manchester United T-shirt fifteen baht for the spot and walk. In the morning heat, they wait before the border gate; one of those carved stone arches of miniature gopurams, replicating the temple at Angkor Wat. Inside a mobile hut which smells of antiseptic, the queue snakes until they reach a passport booth where a uniformed young woman with nail art and a smile waves them through. The Thai Visa Office on the Cambodian side of the border straddles a traffic roundabout bristling with parked mopeds. After three hours of waiting in a room where posters explain the equation between drug smuggling and Cambodian justice (Smuggle Drug + Cambodia = Death Penalty), a middle-aged woman with no nail art, and no smile, takes their paperwork, and tells them to come back the next day. Nothing William says or promises to the woman will make things happen today.

It is hotter back on the street than in the Visa Office, and William is blinded by the sun shining on the shoal of parked mopeds. The drive has finally caught up with him.

'William?'

He might throw up. The traffic queuing to get into Thailand has abandoned all discipline. The road honks and shunts. Their car is in a field on the other side of the border. They are stuck.

'I said what do you want to do? Find somewhere to rest up?'

William nods. The air smells of something he doesn't want to breathe. A giant truck has stopped in the traffic on the roundabout, the engine idling. Meat waste. Packed and stacked in translucent green bags behind the slatted panels of the truck-bed. The broken boomerangs of rotting legs, and the squashed faces of oxen.

It was the day after the wave, in a marquee at the roadside, at the gates to one of the temples where the bodies were kept. The woman pushed a pen and a piece of paper over the trestle table and asked William to fill in Anya's details. The sun was hot on his neck, the road at his back full of shunting traffic.

Name: Anya Teal.

Date of birth.

Here William faltered. He tried to work backwards. They did not go to the same school. They had met in the year *after* school. That was right. She had always been six months ahead of him. He thought of summer when he thought of her birthday, sometime early, perhaps June. Thirteen years together and he couldn't remember her birthday. The form asked William what the missing subject was 'last seen wearing'. But he couldn't remember. It asked him if Anya had any 'distinguishing physical characteristics'. He asked the woman what sort of thing was meant.

'Maybe any tattoos? Any birthmarks? Hair colour?'

William made a note of the tattoo on Anya's lower back. The hammer and sickle. They had been twenty-one. She had held his hand in the tattoo parlour.

'She has slightly red hair,' he told the woman. 'Not naturally, but dyed slightly red. Would you say that was distinguishing?'

'I would put it down.'

'It was called burnt amber!' William suddenly remembered.

'I'm sorry?'

'The hair colour she used – burnt amber.' It would bleed into the bath.

The woman's smile was thin. 'Did your girlfriend have a mobile with her, a telephone number?'

Why hadn't William thought of it before?

The woman gave him a mobile phone. He punched the wrong number in at first. And a second time. On the third attempt he finally got the number right and Anya's voice leapt out at him. '*Hello! This is Anya Teal's phone – I'm really sorry I can't speak right now, but if you would like to leave a message, please leave your name after the tone!*'

Anya's voice is still speaking when William puts down the phone. He opens his eyes to the dark and reaches for the remote control which adjusts the blinds over the window of his apartment bedroom. But the remote is not there, and somehow the bedside table has been knocked farther away from the bed. He sits up. He must be ill. Everything feels too sensitive. The sheets too stiff. The carpet beneath his feet too hard. When he reaches under the bed for Anya's laptop, the mattress is too thick, and then the board of the bed – he can't get underneath it. It is sealed to the carpet. Someone is knocking on his bedroom door. The wall is not where it should be. The door handle isn't the right shape.

'Hey.' It is Missy. She is standing in the hotel corridor.

'Sorry?'

'I said, I've been trying to wake you for, like, hours.'

'What time is it?'

'Ten o'clock.'

William doesn't know if she means morning or evening. There are no windows in the room. No windows in the corridor at Missy's back. Just a terrible watercolour of the temples at Angkor.

'You must have been pooped,' she says. 'I tried to get you on the phone and came knocking.'

'Yes.'

The stains on her red vest could be food stains. There are dark shadows of make-up around her eyes.

'Well,' Missy tries, 'I was hanging around to see if you wanted to go get something to eat?'

He tells her to wait, fumbles for the light switch in the bedroom, can't find it on the walls, then knocks into the bedside table and a lamp which casts a dim glow over the mess of a bed. He is clutching a bed sheet around his waist. His clothes are spilled over the floor. He picks up the phone and dials the number again.

This number has been . . .

'Look – I didn't want to disturb you.' Missy is still holding the door open. 'But I'm so embarrassed about last night, you have no idea. Fuck – I am *not* the kind of person you need to rescue—'

'When you lose a mobile phone,' William starts. 'Say you lost a mobile phone that had an answer message on it. If the phone was still operating somewhere, how long would it take for the message to be erased?'

Missy looks at him in a way that makes him realise what he is doing – half-dressed, clutching a phone in his hand.

'Um – I think the battery would die,' she says. 'Or the phone would go out of service and there would be no message.'

William sits down on the bed.

'So what I wanted to say,' Missy continues. 'You picked me up last night – and honestly, I was so drunk. I never would have called – I don't even know how the fuck the idea got into my head but now – well, are you hungry?'

'I'll order room service.'

Missy salutes and clicks her heels together. 'Alrighty then. Well, I'll go get something myself.'

He needs Anya to say something. He needs to hear her voice. In Bangkok she would speak to him. But when was the last time he heard her voice?

William manoeuvres himself back onto the bed like a sick man. There are empty minibar bottles scattered over the mattress. When he has stared at the ceiling long enough for it to start drifting away from him, he extends a hand from the safety of the bed, picks up the phone and dials Anya's number.

Tsunamis are usually formed along subduction zones, areas of the seabed where a lighter tectonic plate has been forced above a heavier plate. A tsunami is unlikely to form if the tectonic plates have split apart, or slide past each other.

October 1992

Stovnik

Marko tried on the uniform when Kemal was in the bath. The material seemed thin. No armour at all. The buttons were loose on their threads. It was a cheap trick. No magic in it. The battalion uniform was a shirt with a camouflage pattern, no more real than the Spiderman costume he wore as a child. The only thing real about the uniform was the smell. Cigarette smoke and earth, and the oily odour of guns.

Kemal appeared behind him in the bedroom mirror. 'It suits you.'

He had wrapped a towel around his waist. There had been no electricity all week and they were showering with cold buckets of water.

Marko sat down on the bed and started to pull off the uniform trousers. The fatigues drowned him. He was not a soldier but a fifteen-year-old boy three years shy of the draft.

They changed into their tracksuits and as Marko was leaving, Kemal grabbed an empty tennis bag. He had something to show him.

The lift hadn't worked for months, so Marko followed Kemal down the stairwell and out across the five-a-side pitch, through the first clean pinch of October's cold.

Like all the shops on the estate, Željo's windows had always been full: sets of hammers and chainsaws hanging from racks, toolkits presenting their gleaming drawers, the latest vacuum cleaners, the latest power drills. The bakery next door to the hardware store had always smelled of fresh bread; the launderette next door to the bakery always hummed. Marko had spent his childhood hanging outside these stores, and when he was really young, the things in Željo's were something to covet – the sculpted metal shapes of the hardware inseparable in his childhood imagination from those of spaceships and weapons. But the bakery did not bake any more, and the launderette did not launder clothes. The hooks in the window display at Željo's hung nothing, sheets flung over boxes gathering dust. Željo's stock had sold months ago and couldn't be replaced. What Željo did have left, no ordinary man could afford. These were siege prices. The aisles of the shop were dark and uninviting.

When Željo saw them enter he disappeared behind the bead curtains at the back of the store.

'What do you think?'

The gun Željo gave Kemal wasn't new. Marko could see that. It was a Second World War rifle, Partisan issue, like the one his grandfather used to have. But although the body was old, the barrel looked clean. Kemal handed it to him. The gun had been completely refitted and had a freshly oiled smell, everything wire-brushed.

Kemal carried the gun in the tennis bag. Marko followed him past the kids sitting on the wall outside a café that had been closed for weeks. They walked off the estate and up the old road, through people's emptied hillside allotments, past the bootlegging sheds, steep along the backs of the tower blocks, behind the stone hats of the ancient shepherds' huts, where the air smelled of manure.

Marko hadn't been here for a while, perhaps not since the summer. He kicked a bag along the road until it exploded, spilling nappies and sanitary towels into the long grass at the side of the track. There were scorched rings in the fields where rubbish had been burned. People used to have small plots for chickens and other fowl up here, but the fences had fallen in and the huts were empty. This was where the kids of the estate played on long summer days. Games of soldiers around the sinkholes of the old salt mines. Now, every night, the older boys dragged themselves in their fatigues over the peaks of the hills. And some of them never came back.

Kemal sat down on the broken bricks of an old shaft and unzipped the tennis bag. There was no need to show Marko how to load or aim. The gun didn't feel loose when Marko put the stock to his shoulder, the body didn't rattle like his grandfather's gun. It felt solid and cold and indestructible.

'I know your dad has guns.' Kemal picked up a piece of broken brick lying between his feet and stood up. 'But you can *work* with this one.'

'Work?' Marko looked down the rifle's sight and picked out a satellite dish on the roofs of their block. He swung around. A metallic crash followed by a boom. For a second he thought he might have pulled the trigger. But Kemal's brick had bounced off the corrugated roof that had been used to patch up one of the ancient stone huts. A dun dog sprang out of the dark.

* * *

The dogs were refugees too. Refugees of families who could no longer afford to feed them and had been too soft-hearted to kill them. Some of the dogs even came from the villages around Stovnik, following the trails of human refugees and looking for people who could barely house themselves, let alone the family dog. One dog had attacked a girl playing in the alley at the back of a primary school. A whole pack had caused an accident on the ring road. Swerving to avoid the pack, the driver had ditched into the river's concrete over-flow channel.

Some people suggested the battalion or the police start culling the dogs, but as many protested against it.

'We need two armies,' Kemal told Marko. 'One out there, and one back here. That's your job; to make sure the place doesn't go to shit.'

Marko missed with his first shot and the dun dog ran back into the shepherd's hut, barking murder. The kick of the gun vibrated through his shoulder, down his arm, finishing with a tingle in his groin, as if he had just been kissed. He stepped around one of the sinkholes and through the damp autumn grass, gun raised, nervous as a kid sneaking out of his room at night. Stopping a metre from the black mouth of the stone hut, he felt the cold soaking through his trainers and into his toes, the smell of ignition on his hands. Something moved in the dark. He brought the barrel to sight. No barking now, just panting. The dog was a silent flash of colour when it leapt out. It came right at him, teeth bared.

Marko's gun didn't jam. Marko did.

The dog jagged sideways, passing him, and sprinting along the path between huts. Marko took a moment to level the gun again, the diminishing target of the dog's rear much harder to find than its side. He took the shot. The dog tripped on its hind legs, picked itself up and tripped again. With the third shot, it stayed down.

'It's not dead,' Kemal said. 'You should put it out of its misery.'

The dog was on its side, front legs paddling without water. Marko stood over it and brought the barrel of the rifle as close to the animal's head as he possibly could. The dog's eyes were so clear and so round; the black pool of ink that spotted his mother's white tablecloth on the morning of his first day at school.

Marko pulled the trigger but hadn't thought it through. The stock kicked into his armpit and he stumbled backwards, off the path and into the grass, landing hard on his arse.

Kemal was clapping. When Marko got back on to his feet, he was glad to see the dog wasn't moving. The bullet had opened a small red cave in the animal's head. Blood, like red paint in the dun fur, black, as it made a river through the small stones of the path.

'What do we do with it?' Marko didn't know if he was asking Kemal or himself. Up until now, the fact that there would be a body to be disposed of hadn't crossed his mind. But now he knew. When you kill something, it becomes your property. They stood over the dog, looking down on their creation as if they expected it to do something.

Kemal told him to check the hut first.

Marko smelled dog even before he reached the mouth of the hut. He levelled the rifle again, taking careful steps. But nothing leapt out. He stepped inside. Nothing beneath the low ceiling, except the dogs' crap and some rubbish they must have been dragging in from the tips.

When he turned to leave he saw it. One more dog, cowering against the wall and moving strangely in small, rippling motions, until all of a sudden, it fell apart. Not one dog but a cluster of puppies. New enough not to be capable of finding their legs.

'Anything?' Kemal asked when Marko stepped back outside. The low light of the autumn sun formed a halo around him.

'No,' Marko said. 'Nothing.'

Saturday 9 April 2005

Poipet, the Cambodian Border

Either William has escaped a hangover, or he is still drunk, he
is not sure which. In the Visa Office, he can hear himself
performing the role of a school manager. Nervous of silence,
he fills it by telling Missy things she probably already knows:
how they should have taken her teaching licence to the
Department of Labour, and secured a receipt while the application for a new visa was being processed; how the visa was
always going to take more than seven days.

The point of the *receipt* was to stop Missy from being
arrested.

'But the application *isn't* in? We didn't have a receipt?'

'No, so I showed the police the contract, and persuaded
them we would leave the country to get a visa. The school –
we – had the responsibility of starting the visa application
process. So this was our fault. My fault, really.'

They are sitting opposite each other on plastic bucket seats
in a narrow, windowless room. Missy lifts up her foot and
rests it on her knee. He wants to tell her there is a flattened
cigarette on the sole of her trainer.

'I'm not a big drinker,' she says. 'I was out for the New Year. And let me tell you, you only realise how drunk you are when a Bangkok policeman starts asking for your ID.'

Behind Missy, the teller's window is empty. It is not yet eight o'clock in the morning. They are the first people in the waiting room. William's shirt is clinging to him. He is uncomfortable in yesterday's underwear. In Thailand, he is accustomed to starting the day with a fresh shirt, and wonders if there is anywhere he can get a new one. He has got to this point without once thinking about the decisions he is making. The decision to get up, to brush his teeth, to shower, to eat. He just knew he had to get here. Now he only knows he wants to get back to the car.

'So once I get the tourist visa here we can start fresh?' she asks.

'Correct.'

Missy is staring at something across the room, pressing her mobile phone to her nose. The wild silver hair is gone, replaced by the slight kink of a bob still damp from a morning shower. The panda eyes of nightclubbing have gone too. Stripped of the make-up, there is something childlike about Missy Ammanucci, sitting in a visa office smelling her phone like a child does a stuffed toy. The denim shorts and the vest add to this impression. There are bruises like thumbprints all up her shins and pink burns on her knees.

'Skateboarding.' Missy straightens her legs, feet together as if she is measuring one against the other. 'I'm heavy into skating – these bruises are my epic bails. It's so screwy that you can't get a tourist visa *in* country.' She sees the cigarette butt and flicks it away. 'I was meant to meet a friend today.' Missy thumbs around her phone.

Checking into the hotel had probably been the worst moment. Oceans of red carpet, everything gilded like a temple shrine, air filled with strings playing 'Dear Prudence'. Missy had been chatting away about the pool and the sauna. William felt as if he had a balled sock in his throat. He knew he was on the edge, and didn't want to go over it in front of Missy. Missy had come to his room. He had stood with a sheet wrapped around his waist. The mess of the bed, the minibar bottles. The dream about Anya's call.

'I hope you're not missing anything in Bangkok,' Missy says without looking up from her phone. 'You been in Thailand long?'

William clears his throat. 'Three years.'

'Me? Two years.'

He looks hopefully at the woman who has appeared behind the glass of the counter. She is holding a folder, looking through papers, approaching the glass. They will get Missy's visa and drive home. He will be with his television, and Anya's laptop, and the view from the window, and she will speak to him again. He will slip back into his routine, into safety. After all, he took responsibility, didn't he? It was what Anya was always telling him to do. He had answered Missy's call, met her on the street. He drove through the night. He made it through the heat, and the passport control, and was still here. Still breathing. No harm had come to him or to anyone else. There was no reason to be afraid.

So why did he feel so afraid?

The woman behind the glass jags to the right and out of the room without a glance.

'First time in Cambodia?' Missy puts the phone back into the pocket of her shorts.

William nods.

'I kept meaning to come,' Missy says, 'I really want to see Angkor. But then I never seem to get the vacation time. Or when I do, it's monsoon season or whatever. It's, like, always monsoon season. Right?'

He tries to remember what he should know about her. For some reason he thinks *New Jersey*. She is from the town with the name of an early Bruce Springsteen album. The tape he used to have. The one he would play in Anya's car. *Greetings From Asbury Park.*

'William?'

He looks at Missy. Her face is a question and he doesn't know what she has asked.

'I've just remembered I have something too,' he says, 'to cancel today. I don't have a mobile – can I borrow your phone?'

Kletovo

It was the last house of the Lekić family. A one-storey farmhouse at the end of a gravel track in Kletovo. Marko sits in the old van. Engine ticking as it cools. He can't believe his father garaged the thing. As if he knew his son would return. They all thought England was just an adventure in Marko's life, not the future. His responsibilities lay in the Balkans. The only child. He would join his parents in Croatia, or better, come back to Bosnia and invest in the security company his father had set up at the end of the war. *People need security like shit needs flies*, his father always said. *As long as people keep shitting it's good business.* Besides, why did Marko want to work doors in England when he could sit back and *manage* the men working doors in Bosnia?

Marko hadn't intended to get into the van but he had got into it. He hadn't intended to drive the van but he had driven it. He hadn't intended to do anything other than drive around the block, but he had left the block and found the road leading him out of Stovnik, over the hill, down into the next valley. He thought he might be heading for England, but then he noticed signs for Kletovo.

A breeze tickles the ears of wheat. In front of the farmhouse, the sail of a giant model windmill turns behind the painted blue fence of the garden and abruptly stops before starting in the other direction. The glove compartment of the van is locked with a twisted piece of old wire. Marko unwinds it, and the door falls open. His cigarettes. An ancient packet of Drina.

If Marko was ever tempted by his father, it had been last night. Barking in the hills. A football crashing a goal. The cries of children occupying the darkness of the playground. He had climbed out of Samir's car into the memory of the cool night air, the yellow and orange lights of the apartment blocks printed against a black sky. One of the town's dogs had stopped at his feet, sat down and looked at Marko as if his master had returned. On the sixth floor he had opened the door of number 67 as if he had closed it only that morning. The apartment was as clean as his mother had always kept it. Preserved like a museum of his childhood. The only change his bedroom. Every trace of the old room had been replaced. A single bed where the bunks had been. New cream carpet and magnolia walls. No trace of him. No trace of Kemal.

Next to the packet of Drina are some old tapes. Dino Merlin, Van Gogh, *Bijelo Dugme in Concert*. He is back where he was the moment he left. Kemal was dead, Vesna didn't love him and the next twelve months held only the barracks for

Marko. The barracks without a war. He used to tell himself he would have stayed if there was a prospect of fighting. But the truth? Marko would never be the soldier Kemal was. And he wanted nothing less than to be a soldier in the war that had taken Kemal from him.

The years burn in the dust of the van's cigarette lighter. He barely recognises his own handwriting on the cassette sleeves. The dry tobacco of the Drina crackles through its cheap paper. Kemal's house looks the way it always did. The scrappy garden before the green wooden door. The place Kemal's father and mother had died.

It had been the winter Marko turned fifteen. The village of Kletovo fell and Kemal's mother was taken by the Chetniks. Kemal came to live with the Novaks. Marko's parents found a bunk bed in the apartment of a friend who would not be returning to the town, and put it into their son's bedroom for the boys. Early in the first war, a stalemate of sorts had settled in the hills around Stovnik. The older boys in the apartment block became soldiers. Every two days, the army's Volkswagen camper-vans picked up the boys and drove them out to their positions, as if sitting in a hole with a gun were really no different from sitting in an office or working at the salt-refining factory. Marko was too young to go. Kemal would leave in the middle of the night, quietly closing the apartment door on ears always awake. He was *their* soldier now. The soldier from apartment 67, floor 6, Slatina, Stovnik.

Marko throws the cigarette out of the driver's window. The music wobbles, tape head creaking, a wavering voice and shimmering guitars. Unlistenable. Even before his body was vaporised in the shelling, Kemal was dead. One by one, Marko had seen the lights in the boys' eyes snuffed out like candles. He thought Kemal had survived this living death. But what if he hadn't?

A dirty starling appears on the blue fence of Kemal's front garden, hops along, then disappears like something in a magician's trick. Why did no one but Marko want to know? Not Samir who had spent three years of his life fighting alongside Kemal, not Marko's father, not Marko's mother, the woman who had practically adopted Kemal and given him a home after Kletovo fell!

'Any number of reasons,' his father had said over the phone.

'Meaning?'

'Any number of reasons why a soldier in that war would not want to be found in Bosnia, or anywhere else.'

When they came here, they would put their shoes in the old iron trough on the porch. The trough is still there, but filled with someone else's shoes now; a pair of black clogs and a small pair of pink Nikes that might belong to a woman, or an older child.

'Yes?' It is an old woman's voice answering his knock. 'I'm not expecting visitors.'

'I was just passing—' Marko realises for the first time that he is calling at the house of a man who lived there ten years ago. A dead man. 'My name's Marko, I'm —'

'Who?'

'Marko Novak.'

'What do you want?'

A cricket twitches at his feet, translucent and new. 'Did you know Kemal Lekić?'

'Who?'

'Kemal Lekić.' Marko picks up his foot and flicks the cricket from the toe of his trainer.

'No, I don't know anyone called Kemal,' the voice coughs. 'You're at the wrong place.'

He tells the woman not to worry. The grass in the front garden of the farmhouse used to grow taller than Marko, now a path is beaten through it. Harvestmen scare into the undergrowth as he walks along the fence at the side of the house. He wants to see the back garden. Before Milošević, before the Chetniks dragged Kemal's mother away, this is where their childhood had happened.

'Can I help you?'

He startles.

It is a woman's face, hovering on the other side of the fence, hidden in the hood of a pink tracksuit. A small, sharp chin. He thinks about telling her he is looking for his childhood. *I've lost my childhood, have you seen it anywhere?*

'My name's Marko,' he begins.

The woman pulls her hood back.

'I know who you are,' she says.

Poipet

The skiff's engine had cut out, and they drifted over the coral, the danger of the ocean beneath them, the illusion of movement as a breeze played over its green surface. Anya in her bathing suit – the body which should have been so familiar it was invisible – had become exciting again. She was flirting with him. And yet at the same time she seemed distracted. He wanted to talk to her – to *really* talk to her. He wanted to tell her about the dead end relationships he had been in, about his disappointment with himself, with the school, about things he didn't even realise he was feeling until he had seen her again. How he had thought a clean break was the only way to do it. How even when they made the mutual agreement to split up, he had secretly felt it was more her decision than his. How he had always thought it was her work getting in the way, but that now he realised, it had been his own lack of ambition. Instead, they were making small talk, like two people on a date. She stood up and shuffled down the skiff to try the outboard motor, and although at this moment Anya spoke, he cannot hear her. He cannot hear her through the noise of the Cambodian street.

He has come outside to make the call, but he is standing in front of a man in a kiosk and can't think why. The man in the kiosk is looking at him with expectation, palms up, smile inviting him to choose something. William looks into the frosted glass door. Scarlet bottles of Chinese lager, emerald bottles of Cambodian lager. Frozen bags of grey shellfish.

On the beach, Anya had been with a man. She had introduced him. William had seen the man somewhere before. He is sure of it.

'What do you want?' the man in the street kiosk asks.

'Sorry,' William says. 'I don't know.'

Anthony answers on the third ring. He is not pleased when William tells him he won't make the tennis match.

'I was just walking out the door!'

'I know, but something has come up.'

'God help me, William, I know this is tough. I mean – I know it has been tough. But there comes a point, and maybe this is it, where your friends – an intervention or something. I think we need to stage an intervention. And I say that with absolute respect and out of friendship, dude. Tough love.'

'I understand.'

'Not to mention the fact that there are now going to be three of us on a tennis court. Come on, William. I've half a mind to *really* come round there and *drag* you out.'

'You don't have to.'

'Don't I? How long has it been since we saw you? Or since you went *anywhere*?'

William opens his mouth to speak, but Anthony hasn't finished.

'And I mean apart from the school. Again, William, dude – this is only out of friendship.'

'Anthony, I'm in Cambodia.'

'Oh – oh, well, that's different – good. I think.'

'I was trying to tell you.'

'William – are you *OK*? What are you doing in Cambodia?'

'It was a last minute thing. But I think – this is good for me.'

'William. Are you *alone*?'

There is something so parental in Anthony's tone, William's response is as quick as a child's, 'I'm not actually – I'm with someone.'

'Good. I mean, good that you're with someone – I mean and getting out – even if you have buggered up our match.'

'We're going to Angkor,' William carries on lying, 'I just – double booked.'

'Double booked? Yes. OK. Well, I'm sure we'll find someone.'

William apologises.

'Not to worry. Angkor's incredible, dude. You'll enjoy it.'

William hangs up and holds the phone to his nose. What did she smell? The heated metal and something else, something that is Missy. The phone is one of those fancy things with a picture for a screensaver, a young man, handsome and dark haired, something of the Mediterranean about him. The man is leaning into the picture, and winking with a confidence that seems to William obscene. The phone has all sorts of options:

Internet.

Phone Book.

Call Log.

Camera.

Gallery.

He has never seen a phone with a camera. When he enters the gallery there are pictures Missy has taken of herself. Missy in a nightclub, her hair the way it was last night, the same red vest and ragged denim shorts. She is looking up at the camera as she holds another woman's head to her shoulder and they pout. A picture of a dun street dog sitting next to a corner shrine of Buddha; a picture of Missy at the night market shovelling a chocolate penis-shaped ice-lolly into her mouth; Missy centre of field, standing with military strictness next to a statue of a Thai soldier, and flanked on either side by two more stone soldiers. The same picture, but now she is joined by two men in skateboard shorts who imitate the statue's pose. One of the men is the winking man, and in the next picture, the winking man is waving from a river taxi in front of the Royal Palace in Bangkok. There is a picture of Missy in an apartment somewhere, looking not quite right. Like an older woman using make-up to disguise her age, arms twisted in a traditional Thai dance, and body wrapped in the silk of a lime-green pra-yuk. The winking man has his arm around her waist.

There seem to be hundreds of pictures, and every now and again, the winking man pops up; younger now, a different haircut, Missy with her hair longer but tied back, standing on top of a skateboard ramp in board shorts and a T-shirt, dropping down the ramp on a board, moving out of the frame, ponytail trailing.

William looks up to find he is almost back at the Visa Office. He stops. He doesn't know how to get out of the picture gallery on the phone.

'Hey.' It is Missy.

He gives her the phone and says, 'I don't know if I pressed the right thing to hang up. It's a pretty smart phone you have there.' He feels as if he has been rooting through her things.

But Missy doesn't even glance at the thing before she puts it in her pocket. 'This sucks,' she says, looking back across the street at the Visa Office, 'but they're telling me it might not be ready until quote, "the end of the day".'

She runs her hands over her bob, as if feeling for the missing ponytail. Beneath the shadow of her left armpit is a black mole, shiny like a leech.

'How far is it to Angkor Wat?' William asks.

Kletovo

The young woman is called Sabina. She shows Marko how the steep garden has been transformed from his clearest childhood memory into terraces of vegetable plots, the beds neatly braced with planks of MDF and twisted branches of birch.

'This is impressive – you did this?'

'It was done before we came. Kemal did it for us. But we've planted it up.'

Steps are cut into the slope. Sabina stops to bend down and pick up a snail from a radish leaf. Marko scrapes at the earth with the toe of his trainer. They had buried a time capsule here, before the war: a plastic Coke bottle, Italian football cards, his Expo '86 badge, some old communist party belt buckles, those Sarajevo Winter Games badges made out of felt and some empty PEZ dispensers.

Sabina throws the snail over the stream and into the trees.

'Kemal was a good man,' she says. 'In the camp he looked after my mother.' She smiles at the memory. '*Dime* bars. I don't know where they came from but he must have found them somewhere because he brought Dime bars into the camp. I mean – boxes of them. If you asked me to eat a Dime bar now I think I'd be sick. But then – we hadn't eaten in nearly three days.'

Sabina's family had left her village and taken to the forest. Marko knew about Telovici; it was one of those villages on the wrong side of the river Drina. But it is the first time he has heard anyone except Samir mention the camp.

'It was a factory,' Sabina tells him. 'Aluminium something or other. Near the village of Ladina. We slept in this giant drum of metal sheets.'

She watches the packet of Benson and Hedges he takes out of his pocket.

'What are those?'

'They're English.'

Her eyes flit to the house behind them. She bites her lip. 'Quickly – my mother doesn't like me smoking.'

They turn their backs to the house and walk down to the stream. Marko lights Sabina's cigarette, and when she leans into the flame, he sees beneath the loose tracksuit top; a wrinkled patch of skin where her breast should be.

Sabina zips the top up to her neck. 'So you're Marko? He talked about you. You were good friends.'

'We used to come here,' he explains. 'When we were boys. Before Kemal moved in with us. Our fathers were both policemen, and we used to meet on those holidays in Bečići.'

Yesterday the men at the flat of Vesna's father hadn't wanted to know anything. Now the need to talk comes as a surprise to him. 'You know when we were all happy socialists and state workers holidayed together,' he tells her. 'Then Kemal lost his parents and there was no one else, so he came to live with us.'

Sabina looks over the stream to the fence and the field of wheat. The valley here is flat. Marko's geography teachers had told him how it used to be the bed of the Pannonia Sea. Seabeds this old were extremely fertile. Which was why people had settled here, and why people would always want the valley.

Sabina has closed her eyes against the light. 'My mother always thinks that someone will come and take the house. But I have the paperwork.' She opens her eyes and looks at him like she has just realised her mother might be right. 'His signature, everything. Kemal was really good about it. Did it all properly. Never asked anything of us.'

She drops the half-smoked cigarette, then folding her arms, grinds the end into the soil. 'If you knew your friend you'd know how generous he was. I'd say he saved our lives at least twice.'

Marko holds his hands up. 'It's *your* house,' he says, 'and I do know Kemal. He was a hero in Stovnik.'

'Like an elephant,' she says.

'What?'

'Elephants – they return to the old graves, don't they?'

'Two graves.'

She smiles and moves her hands into the pockets of her hooded top. She has decided she might trust him. 'We saw his name after the shelling – in the paper. We thought he was dead too. We went to the memorial, laid flowers. I don't know why he ran away – I was going to ask you.'

'When did he give you the house?'

'When? Just before the shelling,' Sabina thinks. 'Maybe a few weeks before?'

The weeks before the shelling. He can't even remember whether Kemal was on duty or leave.

She turns to look back at the new vegetable garden, and with one hand idly reaches for the frayed rope that hangs down from the branch of the willow tree. There is no tyre swing any more. Marko looks back up at the garden. He should be sad the old place has gone, but actually, what they have done is beautiful. When he looks down at the brook he expects to see Kemal standing in it.

'Maybe he did have a plan,' Sabina says. 'It was like he was – tying things up. Moving on. Presenting us with this and the garden all new.'

'But he didn't say anything? About the women who went missing at the camp?'

Sabina shakes her head.

They walk back up to the house, to the porch where Marko used to sit and look up the skirts of Kemal's mother when she stood on a ladder and cleared the gutters of leaves. The mystery of her thighs. The thought of what happened to her is a stone in his mouth.

'It's great to see the place looking so good,' he tells Sabina. 'Have you got a pen?'

'A pen?'

'If you need anything – my number – just give me a call.'

'But you live in England?'

Marko hadn't even thought about it. 'I mean, I'll give you my parents' number. And they can call me and,' but he stops. Sabina's smile makes him realise he doesn't know what he is saying, only that if these people meant something to Kemal they should mean something to him. What she has told him is a gift. She has given Kemal back to him and he feels there is something he should give to her.

'It's OK,' she says. 'We know plenty of people here now. The neighbours are good. Well, the *immediate* neighbours.'

They walk back through the house. It is dim, and thick with the smell of her mother's cooking. At the door Sabina grabs his wrist – quick, just enough to stop him.

'At the camp. Kemal rescued people. From the forest. Bringing them back,' she says. 'Not just us. He was going back and meeting them, night after night.'

Her eyes are wet.

'I can believe it,' Marko says.

He needs to get away from the house and out of the valley. He needs to do what Samir says. Pay his regards, bury his friend. Then get out of Stovnik and out of Bosnia. They can build their new lives here. Sabina with her vegetables and Samir with his business. Perhaps Kemal was screwing this woman. Perhaps it was nothing more than a fucked-up relationship which made him run away. He shouldn't have doubted Kemal. What good does it do him? He wants to be on a plane over the Adriatic Sea. He wants to be opening the door on his sleeping Millie.

Sabina lets go of his wrist. 'Kemal never did anything wrong,' she says.

A tsunami should not be thought of as a single wave. It is a series of waves called a 'wave train'. The time period between waves can last between a few minutes and two hours. The later waves are the strongest.

Christmas Day, 2004

Kao Lak

Anya went under, the slap of the skiff's hull a dull punching in her head. She began to count. The cold came up from the depths. She kicked against it. She didn't want to look down until she had reached the main reef. William had already paddled ahead. He hovered over the giant white bloom in the sea; a reef so big it made the tall man look no bigger than a parasitic fish cleaning the mouth of a whale. One, two, three, four kicks and the coral came to meet her. She could feel the water warming. Plucking up the courage to look down, she saw the dead city of white rock like skulls looming from the black depths. A blue fish darted out of one eye and back into another. She reached the spot where Will was, where the coral almost broke the surface. She had to feel her way over the outcrop to reach him. The dead reef was suddenly alive. Beneath them, a shower of yellow fish shot past and turned as one, striking a perfect right angle around a bush of blood-red fingers. The bush projected from a carpet covering the coral in sulphurous orange, pink and green. Feathery nets of sea cucumbers, and banks of rubbery yellow filter-feeders ticked as though in admonishment. A translucent fish hovered in front of her mask, blue streak pulsing through its body like a cardiogram. With a snap the fish disappeared, and she found herself drifting towards a rock covered with bulbous growths the size of large vases, and painted with the blue veins of fine porcelain. She had an urge to touch one of the vases, just as you do the exhibits in a museum, but as soon as her finger made contact, the thing disappeared, setting off a chain reaction, like the folding spines of a frightened hedgehog. The 'vases' were one organism. Far from being solid growth, this was the skin of a living creature. Alarmed, it shrank to a brittle ball of shells clinging to the coral.

As she kicked back, her flipper scraped against something and before she could orientate herself, a cloud of sand ignited and bloomed.

When the cloud cleared, Will had gone.

She turned around and kicked. She was hovering over a plateau, no sign of movement in the water. She turned again, and couldn't remember whether she was facing the direction she had come from, or the direction in which she was going. She broke the surface. The air burned her throat. She pulled the snorkel out of her mouth. The sky wheeled overhead. Ripping the fog of the mask from her eyes, Anya turned, trying to locate the thin black line of the coast. But for a panicked second she couldn't. Then she saw the skiff. It was much farther than she had imagined and there was no one aboard.

She couldn't see the yellow pipe of his snorkel. Nothing but the flat sea. Where was he? And then right in the teeth of her panic a story formed. She would sit at a dinner table, or a gathering of their friends, many years from now, telling the tale of how she believed William lost, and how he had turned up again, on the boat, on the shore, back at the cabin. It would be one of the legends of their relationship. Like the legend of their three years apart. Then something moved in the corner of her eye – maybe twenty metres behind her, a tail disappearing into the water.

Anya kicked for the boat, gathering armfuls of sea, but the flippers were rocks tied to her feet and it was like reeling in an endless sheet—

Something touched her ankle and she couldn't kick it free.

'Anya! Anya – I was waving!' Will said.

Anya had read it somewhere. You make memories of an event even before it happens. Which means in a certain sense, memories exist in the future. But she hadn't really understood it until now. Until in her panic at losing Will, or drowning, or whatever it was she was panicking about, she had turned her loss into the memory she would have. It was like taking out an insurance policy, a way of mitigating the trauma to come. Except this time, the trauma she expected hadn't arrived, and her insurance policy wasn't needed. Anya wasn't at all used to panicking. She was not a panicker.

Will pulled on the cord of the outboard motor, and she felt the exhilaration of being in the present again.

Will. The Indian Ocean. A skiff.

He pulled on the cord, but nothing happened. The boat bobbed on the lagoon, as though the land turned around the sea, not the boat on the water. Leaning back on the cross-bench, Anya closed her eyes. Her disorientation had started not in the ocean but as they walked the smile of beach, through the kelp, broken shells and watermelon rinds, towards the boat-hire hut. With each step, the feeling of déjà vu grew stronger. An elephant stood in the shade of a tall palm tree and a man on a stepladder brushed its neck. Brushing, brushing with a stiff bristled broom. She had remembered her dream from the night before, the elephant, the Bosnian woman she didn't recognise. Scrape. Scrape.

Scrape. How had she ended up in a picture which belonged in a woman's house in Sarajevo? It had been so easy to find Kemal Lekić's girlfriend. Googled once, and there she was on the staff pages of a tourist agency in the capital. And there was Anya, passing through Sarajevo with a couple of hours to kill before her flight out. It was all so easy. Vesna's employers even gave Anya the address. Only when Vesna opened the door did Anya realise she had no idea what she was going to ask the girlfriend of a dead man accused of rape.

'Fucking thing!' Will ripped at the engine. It coughed politely but delivered nothing. Anya rubbed her eyes, she had forgotten to take out her contact lenses.

In the boat-hire hut of the resort, Anya hadn't found the hero of Stovnik alive. They were served by a young New Zealander with dreadlocks. Exactly the kind of young New Zealander with dreadlocks you would expect to find working on a Thai beach.

'Do you want me to try?' she asked William.

'No, no,' William laughed. 'This is personal now.'

He stood with his hands on his hips, staring at the outboard motor like a father staring at an insolent child.

'Are we stranded?'

'I think that might be the word.'

Anya stood up, and walked the tightrope of the skiff, her stomach brushing the rough knot of Will's shorts as they passed. The rear of the boat dipped to the waterline and Will clambered to the front. When she pulled on the cord of the outboard motor, it didn't even cough. She tried again and the cord burned her palms.

'Do you know what I think?' she asked.

'No petrol.'

'I think there's no petrol in it.'

'We are of like mind.'

Shading her eyes, Anya could just about see the beach. The bristle of figures moving in the heat. A red and yellow rash of umbrellas.

'How far, do you think?' she asked.

'Mile and a half?'

'Swimmable.'

'Do you know,' Will said, 'I don't think there are any oars in this boat.' He was on his knees, looking beneath the benches.

'We should have checked.'

'We shouldn't *have* to check.'

Anya looked across the water, 'What about *that* boat?' but even as she pointed along the reef, she knew the next skiff was just as far. Really, what was she *doing* here? It was the question Vesna Knežević had asked her.

What are you doing here?

Perhaps not so angry at first.

I'm sorry, what did you say your research was about?

Anya had picked up the picture in the hall as a distraction. She just needed a moment to think. *This picture*, she asked Vesna. *A holiday? Somewhere nice?*

It was an elephant on a beach, and over its tabard the words, *Kao Lak, Heaven Resort*.

Anya stepped down the hull as Will shuffled along the cross-bench to make room for her. She was glad she had told him nothing. It would confirm his fears that she was nothing but her work. When Vesna had grabbed the picture and ordered Anya out of the house, it was one of the most professionally embarrassing moments in her life. Tell Will one thing, and all the rest would fall out. It would be like opening the cupboard which hides the mess of your house.

'Well,' he said as she sat down next to him. 'This is another fine bollocks.'

'How could he send us out without enough petrol?'

'He's a New Zealander living on a beach in Thailand.'

Anya pushed a drop of water along her thigh with her fingernail, then flicked it off her knee, leaving a white track in her sun-blushed skin.

'Maybe it's a test,' Will said.

'A test?'

'You know, see how long we can survive without eating each other. Or arguing.'

'I think there would be arguments before we ate each other.'

She felt the presence of Will's hand near her own.

He held up her wrist. 'I don't think your Chairman Mao watch was waterproof.'

'Oh shit!' Anya took off the watch. The plastic had misted. She held it up, and tapped at the back. 'To be honest, I don't think it worked in the first place. *And* I forgot to give you *your* present.' She clipped the watch back on her wrist.

'Why didn't we stay in touch?' The question surprised even Anya.

'I don't know,' Will said.

'I did try. You must have known that.'

'I know.'

'And then I find out you've moved to Bangkok!'

'I know.'

'How was I supposed to feel about that?'

Will wasn't looking at her, but down the boat, over the sea. In his silence, the ocean sucked at the hull.

'Do you know how long we were together?' she says.

'Was it thirteen years?'

'Longer than most marriages.'

'You never believed in marriage.'

'Neither did you.'

'Do you remember when I took the coach from London to Kraków?' Will asked.

'I remember you took *a* coach from London to Kraków.'

'And when I reached the place you were staying, you'd run out of those butane gas canisters, and it was absolutely *freezing* in the flat. That flat above the shops by the cemetery.'

'I do remember we were always running out of gas.'

'Yes, but this was the night I arrived. And then the next morning we had to go out and buy a new gas canister, and we ended up looking all over the place for one with the right kind of attachment, because the fires your cousin had were so outdated. And there was this little place somewhere in an estate, Nowa Huta, I think, and the man in the hardware shop had one of those dogs with no back legs but a trolley with wheels somehow attached to the body of the dog – a little Jack Russell.'

Will drew the shape of the biomechanical dog with his hands but Anya had no recollection of it, or of what happened the day after he arrived on the coach from London. Or even of being in Nowa Huta with William.

'I don't remember,' she said.

'I just always remember it.' He sighed and looked out over the water, 'I didn't ever think I would end up managing an English Language school in Bangkok.'

'And?'

'I don't know. How did it happen?'

'Because it's what you're *good* at.'

'What is?'

'Language. That's your thing. Language and art and music and everything. Honestly. You talk like your life is over and you're not even forty. Do you still even draw?'

'Some bits of it are over.'

He stretched his legs out and flexed his feet, like he was testing their function.

'You know what I miss?' Anya said. 'Going to art galleries. And gigs. We used to do that all the time. I don't think I realised, but that was you. You always organised those things. I didn't have a clue. I can't believe you're not still drawing.'

'The problem is I could never commit to anything I was serious about,' Will said. It took her a moment to understand he wasn't talking about art galleries and gigs.

'Oh come on!'

'I *did* call you though,' he added.

'After three fucking years.'

'That's true.'

'And why did you?'

It was only when he turned his head to look at her that she realised quite how close they were sitting. She could feel his breath on her lips.

'Are we going to fail the test?' he asked.

'What test?'

'The stranded-in-a-boat test.'

Anya hung her head, looking down between her legs to the red purse of her swimming suit. 'I thought you'd bloody drowned.'

'What?'

'Just now. In the water.'

'Oh that.'

But she couldn't quite explain it to him. What a drag it was to be discovering she cared for him the way she always had.

Then suddenly William stood up. The boat rocked and a buzz came over the water.

'It's heading our way,' he said.

She looked to where a speedboat dragged the curtain of the lagoon behind it. The swell lifted the flat-bottomed skiff, then at the last second the speedboat turned and circled, unzipping the sea around them. It was the New Zealander from the beach hut. A second man crouched in the back. He was holding something heavy.

'I'm a dufus,' the New Zealander shouted over the dying noise of the engine. 'Realised I sent you out without a full tank. Wrong boat. Should have had the one next to it.'

'And there are no oars in this boat,' William shouted over the water.

'Oh what the fuck! Fatal.' The man slapped his forehead. 'Well, we'll sort you out now.'

Will reached over to help pull in the speedboat. The sounds of the sea were suddenly sharp again; two boats rocking in the lagoon. It was the man with the jerrycan who stood up and bridged the gap between them. He climbed into the rear of the skiff.

'Take a step back,' Will said. 'Balance things out.'

But Anya couldn't move. The things you think of before they happen. The memories you create for yourself in the anticipation of the event. This had happened before. Kemal Lekić knelt down in the hull of the boat, opened the fuel hatch, uncapped the jerrycan and began to pour the golden liquid in.

Before a tsunami strikes, the ocean may appear to drain away. This is called the 'drawback' — the trough of the tsunami reaching the shore. Energy is turning to mass. Within minutes, the wave can reach ten metres in height.

Saturday 9 April 2005

Stovnik

Before they can order, the waiter unloads two green bottles of Tuborg and two shots of šljivovica onto the pressed metal of their uneven table.

'For your friend?' he asks Samir.

'My cousin,' Samir puts his hand on Marko's shoulder, 'has returned to us from exile.'

Marko asks for a Becks, but they don't have it, so he takes a Heineken. It comes with a shot.

Elvis and Samir raise their glasses. They toast Kemal. Elvis has joined them early, still in the shirt and tie of a job which turns out, when Marko asks, to be something to do with insurance. It is still late afternoon, and the street cafés of the Kapija have caught people on their way home from work. Across the square, a table of women in their office clothes gather around a leaving party with helium balloons. Over the fountain, schoolkids flitter. Girls watching boys watching girls.

'How does it feel to be back?' Elvis asks.

Right at this moment, he does not feel like he is back. The last time he was here, he had been one of the schoolkids by the fountain. 'Things are different,' he says.

The lager is too sweet. The šljivovica is a warm head rush.

'To Marko!' Elvis raises his shot glass. When Elvis sits back down, he has to squeeze himself between the plastic arms of the chair. The body-building muscles of his youth have turned to fat.

Beneath the table, Marko holds his stomach with one hand.

'You don't look any different,' Elvis says.

Marko pauses too long to effectively return the compliment. 'I know.'

Through the office shirt, Elvis pinches a roll of his own stomach. 'Look at this fat bastard.'

'Elvis stopped playing football,' Samir says.

'I stopped doing a lot of things.'

'You look fine,' Marko says. 'For a fat bastard.'

'It's kids. My wife looks better than she ever has but I eat too well. I eat my food and then I eat their food, and then I sit down all day in a fucking office.'

It takes Marko's old friends to show him he is not a kid any more. Children! And a wife! They *can't* be fathers and husbands. They are schoolboys by the fountain. They play on the five-a-side pitch. The war never allowed any of them to be fat. English kids are fat. American kids are fat.

Elvis asks about England and English women. They talk about the state of Sloboda Stovnik's defence. They talk about the kids in the square, the war babies who are not like they were, who take more drugs, and of the wrong kind, who don't want to work, who complain because they can't get Wi-Fi, and don't know what it is like not to get water.

Marko watches a gypsy girl in a Rolling Stones tour T-shirt beg the leaving-do women. They shoo her away. Kemal liked to give to the gypsies. He said they might be gypsies, but they were *Stovnik*'s gypsies. He was like that about the refugees too, the people they were taught to call *internally displaced persons*. Once they were here, they belonged to Stovnik. Stovnik would protect them. Everything Kemal said Marko believed.

Although it can't be the same prepubescent girl who would beg in the square when they were kids, this gypsy girl tonight looks in every way like the girl who would come to them with her black eyes and the palms of an old woman. It is not that things have changed. Quite the opposite. Nothing has changed. The pink and yellow paint of Austro-Hungarian buildings, the green paint of the iron clock, the beech trees budding over Marko's head. Every bit of it resembles the town square of his childhood. But it can't be. All this fresh paint is just fresh paint. The Kapija had been blown to pieces by the shell. A heavy Second World War mortar round had picked up the cobbles and sent them flying through the windows of the cafés; a hard rain of stone breaking the plasterwork, shredding the branches of the beech trees, taking the head of the water nymph in the fountain, lifting children up and throwing them down again, grabbing Samir and hurling him against the wall of the bank where he would feel his right leg for the last time.

That day had blown up Kemal, and with Kemal everything in which Marko believed. He had seen what the shell did. He had arrived minutes later to find the small boy, the adolescent with red hair whose screams were silent like a toddler in the first shock of a fall.

What arm belonged to whom? Whose head was this? In the first few seconds Marko had felt nothing. It was just a puzzle to solve.

'I think he had this woman in Kletovo,' Marko says.

'Who?'

'I went out to his old place this morning. Kemal's. There's a woman living there now. He gave her the house.'

'*Gave* it to her?' Samir asks.

'Signed over the deeds, the lot.'

Samir is nodding. Elvis looks confused.

'He was supposed to be marrying Vesna,' Marko says. 'But what if he didn't want to, what if he had something with this woman too?'

Samir claps his hands together. 'Ha! He was running away from his women!'

'Did you know anything about her?'

'Dirty little bastard,' Samir says. 'Nothing.'

Elvis surrenders his hands. 'He never told me about a woman!'

'Well, well, well,' Samir says. 'Now we know.'

A policeman appears behind Elvis, and clasps his raised hands in his.

'Is this man bothering you?'

Marko barely recognises Bogdan in the forest-green Puffa jacket and peaked cap.

'Look who it is!' Bogdan Banović smiles.

Angkor Wat

William reads from the guidebook: '*Built in the 12th century by the Khmer King Surayavarman II, and the largest religious monument in the world, Angkor Wat stood at the heart of one of the world's first hydraulic civilisations . . .*'

'Hydraulic?' Missy says.

William holds the book he bought in Siem Reap. A stone path bisects a flat black reservoir filled with giant lily-pads, the metallic smell of the morning, stored in its cold, stagnant water. When she walks ahead, he can feel the pull of an invisible rope, and when he catches up, the rope slackens.

'Is this the main temple?' Missy asks. 'Jesus, this is crazy big, there's just so much of it.'

The voices of the other tourists are muffled behind stone walls. The book in William's hand is shaking. '*The modern name, Angkor Wat,*' he reads, '*means Temple City or City of Temples. The outer gallery measures 187 by 215 metres, and the walls are 4.5 metres high, with pavilions, rather than gopura towers at the corners.*'

He follows Missy through an arch that leads back into the shade of a ruined colonnade. In among the carved vines, figures of women nest in the sandstone, their breasts smoothed by the hands of tourists and hundreds of monsoon seasons.

'So who are the ladies?' Missy asks.

William flicks through the pages of the book. 'These could be Asparas, or Devetas: *in Hindu mythology Devetas are celestial dancing girls.* It says – *In the Mahabharata, Aspuras are dancing girls employed by Gods to seduce demons.*'

'Strippers?'

'The book says . . . *the figures are ubiquitous at Angkor Wat.*'

He follows as she treads carefully over the broken flagstones, her fingers tracing the reliefs. 'I want to stay here – the stone's so cold,' she whispers. 'It's like natural air conditioning.'

They step through a rectangular stone frame, a place where a door should be, out into the light and back into the dark again. Ahead of them a series of these broken picture-frames extend like one mirror into another. Where the colonnade roof has fallen in silk trees seem to grow out of walls hardly strong enough to take their weight; long, pale fingers of roots curling around and underneath, or shooting straight up to form a slatted canopy above their heads.

'I think if we turn right at the next path, we'll find the central courtyard,' William suggests. But turning right only brings them out into a hot place resembling the one they have just left – a courtyard path around an empty, moss-covered basin. It might have been a bathing pool; flanked by stone gopura, black flames of sandstone where vines have died and left their shadow.

'It's an entire city,' Missy says.

'Like Pompeii.'

The paths from the courtyard extend in four directions, on to farther colonnades, where flashes of pastel colours are tourists passing through.

'You've been there?' Missy asks.

'When I was a kid.'

Missy points at a new statue carved into the stone walls. 'Who are these guys?'

The relief is a man taller than William, stern face beneath elaborate headdress, hands knotted around the hilt of the sword between his legs.

William flicks through the pictures of the guidebook. '*Dvarapala – generally depicted with lances or clubs, their function is to guard the inner temples.*'

'Here,' Missy hands him her phone. 'Take a picture.'

There is no path up to the guardian, only boulders that have fallen out of the temple structure. Missy skips over them, and climbs onto the sandstone lintel beneath the statue. She pushes her chest out, leaning onto an invisible sword and adopting the guardian's stern face.

'How do I get the camera up?'

'Oh – OK.' Missy skips back. He has never been this close to her. Hair sticks to her neck. Sweat pools at the base of her throat. As her fingers manipulate the phone, the small movements of her collarbone are like something slipping just beneath the surface of water.

'Here.' She hands the phone back to him. The screen has become a camera. The first picture he takes is blurred. Missy is a red buzz in front of the green rocks.

'Hang on.' He takes the phone in both hands, and tries to keep her still. How many times had he taken a photograph of Anya like this? How many times had he held her safely in a camera's eye?

William had slept in the taxi from Poipet, waking to the noise of Siem Reap. The coach was entangled in the deadly charm-bracelets of tuk-tuks, the weary fart of mopeds sacked with families, the volleying yelps of street merchants. From an air-conditioned glass cube on the main street, they bought their temple passes and a guidebook. Walking back out into the heat, William was gripped by a headache. At a hole-in-the-wall next to a Western Union, he asked for paracetamol and was handed a Spanish brand of something in a gold box. Missy said it was good. A kind of ibuprofen and paracetamol combined.

'You only need to take one,' she said. And gave him a bottle of Mountain Dew to wash the pill down.

They boarded a bus to the temple. Not one temple, it turned out, but a jungle full of stone ruins and a city bigger than Siem Reap itself. When they disembarked next to the first reservoir, Will's head felt no better, and he slipped himself another of the pills.

Now he feels empty of any other purpose but to follow Missy. To follow her legs as she climbs over the stones, up steps, over walls. At the edges of the main temple, the muffled noise of tourists recedes, and the trilling of cicadas rise where the canopy of palms thickens. They are in a place where great slabs of the sandstone lean together to form some kind of mausoleum, out of which grow the hands of silk trees. Over the dark mouth of the mausoleum's entrance, the stone has been shaped into one of the giant faces of Buddha that are everywhere in the temple city; the beatific smile, never a single variation, as if it is actually the same face magically reappearing in the stone of the temples, always ahead of them, reassuring. Come this way. You are on the right path.

William sits down on a cool boulder before the shallow broken steps of the building, leaving his head hanging somewhere over him. Missy walks into the mausoleum. The darkness claims the upper half of her body first, for a second leaving only those pale, shining legs, before she takes another step, and they too are swallowed.

Magic tricks. Maybe that's how it was for the people who made the Buddha's face. Magic in repetition; the same urge behind our desire to see a Starbucks mermaid in every town. William tries to remember the last thing he ate. The world is retreating from him. The land moves around the sea, not the boat moving on the water.

Juchinar
Cairo
Stoke Newington

Birdsong breaks over the insistent rhythm of cicadas, suggesting the depths of the jungle. He breathes into his hands. A steady rhythm. Sweat prickling the hairs of his thighs.

Stratton
Hula Hoops
Bosnia

He might find Missy in the dark. Find her small mouth. He might kneel, cup her calves and push his hands up her legs, pull off those shorts; the miracle of finding himself inside her. Wasn't that where this was leading? Not a rope. Not the promise of the dead. Sex. How stupidly simple was the answer to grief! Fucking. How easy to make someone disappear again. Fuck it all out of existence.

Stratton
Hula Hoops
Bosnia

Bosnia. Had Anya really been in Kao Lak to work? Or had she made it all up? Had her heart really leapt like his when she received his first call? Wasn't that what he had wanted her to feel? Hadn't he wanted her to be thinking about him when she put the phone down? To be thinking about him until thinking wasn't enough? Hadn't he wanted her to feel the same way he did? And how was that? How did he really feel? He was scared. He was reaching the middle of his life, turning around like the boat on the ocean. But he didn't know whether it was the boat turning, or the ocean turning, and all of a sudden it was better to head for the shore he had come from than the shore he couldn't see. He wasn't thinking about Anya at all. He was thinking about himself. And when Anya had *wanted* him, really wanted him, when she had tried to take him in the bedroom that night, he had failed so desperately to do something *she* wanted. To play *her* game.

William spits into the sand between his feet. He retches. The metallic taste of the painkillers in his mouth. Then something behind him moves. A scratching sound. When he stands up and turns around, his head trails after his body, filling like a kite. It is at his heels. Black and enormous, growing out of the dirt. The red beady head of the chicken reveals itself, and then the feathers shuffle free. Not one, but two black chickens scrabbling in the sand.

Stovnik

'Didn't Samir tell you?' Bogdan smokes and brings his yellow fingertips to his lips. They are walking home drunk in the closing time crowds, Elvis and Samir ahead of them, arm in arm. Teenagers are slipping away to bars in the suburbs with late licences, or heading for the hills to drink homemade vodka from soft-drink bottles. The children are going home to their parents.

'No.'

Bogdan says nothing.

'Why you?' Marko asks.

'The police in Belgrade. I volunteered to co-operate. Why not? Nothing to see here? Move along! Most people who call themselves policemen – they wouldn't do anything. The ICTY. They wouldn't do anything. It wasn't genocide, was it? Not big enough for them. But I thought we should be fair.'

'You investigated?'

'Statements. I took statements. Made a report.'

'What did it say?'

'I did my job.'

Marko watches his feet over the new cobblestones. They have come to the head of the high street where the crowds thin out, but instead of the old fish market he expects to see, they are met by a car park. A small building shaped like a boat is marooned among the parked cars.

'What do you think?' Bogdan asks.

'What is it?'

'*Ta-da!* I give you the Ethnographic Museum of Stovnik.'

The concrete boat is lit with a floodlight. Where the mast of a ship would be, the flag of the canton rests limp from a flagpole.

'Why does it look like a boat?'

'It's supposed to remind us of the old fish market. Personally I preferred the old fish market.'

They follow Elvis and Samir through the cars, back onto the old streets, into the coral white light of ćevapi shops and kebab houses. Men in dirty white coats cut and chop behind the counters. It is Saturday. Marko should be at Husni's.

'It wasn't a problem?' he asks Bogdan, 'your being in the brigade?'

'I interviewed everyone. We'd kept a list of all the people who came through the factory. There were no witnesses.'

'And the missing women?'

'They were there. In the camp. We had their names. They left like everyone else.'

'And you were there?'

'Of course.'

They have reached Stovnik's only roundabout; a hexagon of grass and the old town well at the centre of it. He had forgotten about the game. When a boy at school crossed their path, bullied their friends or offended someone's family, they would bring him here, and hold him by his ankles over the well. It wasn't serious. The well was boarded up and full of trash. The drop wouldn't break a head. It was just a tradition. Just something they did.

They walk single file along the kerb of the ring road, Bogdan ahead. Marko is trying to understand what he is being told.

'So you knew Kemal was innocent, but you investigated?'

He thinks that Bogdan hasn't heard him, but then realises his friend is muttering.

'I had to get a toothbrush and send it to the morgues.'

'Whose?'

'For Emina. She went missing in 1994. They never found her. My brother had to find some of her DNA and send it to the morgues.'

'Who was Emina?'

Bogdan stops to look at him. 'My sister-in-law. She went missing in 1994. You don't remember. Lovely girl. Just fucking lovely.'

Marko is about to speak but Bogdan isn't finished. 'You forgot, didn't you? Trouble with going away. Those women at the camp. Their families. They deserved an answer.'

'What answer?'

'What answer? No answer. We know they were at the camp. Then they left. Same as everyone else. That was all we could tell them. But we had to tell them at least that. Show them we'd tried.'

Bogdan starts to walk again, Marko on the road and at his shoulder.

'You were with Kemal, weren't you? At the camp? Wasn't that some kind of—'

'Conflict of interest?' Bogdan puts his hand against Marko's chest and stops him. 'I was with Kemal at the camp, so I already *knew* he hadn't done anything. No one raped anyone.' He puts his arm around Marko and pulls him close. 'What about England. Don't you like it there?'

'It's all right,' Marko says.

'And what's wrong with here?'

'Nothing's wrong with here.'

'Exactly. Nothing's wrong with here. It's a fucking beautiful country.' Bogdan tightens his grip on Marko's shoulder.

'So there's no way he could have done it?' Marko says.

Bogdan's face is close enough to kiss him. 'What do you think we were doing out there? Playing fucking superman?' He rests his forehead against Marko's and breathes, 'You still a judo champion?'

Suddenly they are grappling, fighting for the kerb. His head in Bogdan's chest. Bogdan's arms around his waist. A car horn blares. Marko grapples back onto the pavement. They come up, faces red and a scarlet scratch across Bogdan's cheek. With one hand, Bogdan grabs the back of Marko's head, the other pressed against his chest, keeping an arm's length, grinning.

In the dark, Marko runs his hand over the wall and finds the switch; the basement of the apartment block under fluorescent strip lights; a room of foil-insulated pipes, and the gunmetal generator sitting against one wall. The room is white again. The murals have gone. In the worst days of Stovnik's siege, families had moved mattresses down here, sofas and televisions. Marko examines the far wall for traces of Chuck Norris and Bruce Lee. They had found some yellow paint and some black paint, and drawn their heroes as large as they felt them to be.

He places a hand on the flanks of the generator. It should be hot, conducting all that electricity, taking it straight from the network and channelling it through the apartments over his head. (132: that's how many families there were.) But the steel is cold. Only this vibration, this low-key hum. Marko closes his eyes.

Empty your cup so that it may be filled; become devoid to gain totality.

In the first winter, Marko had read Kemal's copy of the *Tao of Jeet Kune Do*. Some people found their religion a comfort in the war, others blamed it and turned away. Some protected themselves by protecting others, bringing the elderly and refugees into their homes. One woman gathered all the town's stray cats around her. Kemal looked after everyone. Marko shot dogs. Surviving was one thing. The real trick was to find a reason to live. There had been something prayer-like about Lee's borrowings from Lao-tzu, about the cod Zen bullshit. Precisely because it *was* such bullshit. They were supposed to have other stories. Historical stories. Stories about patriots, stories about communists. If you listened to the wrong story, the Nazi Serbian story, you were a Chetnik bastard. But Bruce Lee was their own. They didn't know anything about Buddhism or Lao-tzu. But it had become something to believe in; the lines they would deliver like actors in their favourite films, before they attempted to kick the shit out of each other.

Samir said not to listen to Bogdan. Bogdan was twisted. Marko didn't know it because Marko hadn't been around. But after the war some people had gone that way. And they weren't always together at the camp. Bogdan hadn't seen everything Kemal did for the refugees. He was angry about being sent out to defend the hills. The brigade had split, taking it in turns to man a line in the forest and defend the perimeter. Kemal sent Bogdan. And did Marko think Samir wouldn't know? Did he think he wouldn't have seen the women? Did he think he wouldn't have seen the *change* in Kemal? Why was he picking at this scab anyway? It was masochistic, that's what it was. Samir said Marko was picking at a scab because he wanted to hurt himself. Because he had his own guilt to deal with. They were burying Kemal tomorrow. They were burying their friend. They owed him that at least. And they owed him their belief.

Marko kneels down in front of the generator. It had been here, through this gap in the piping. This is where he had seen them. Vesna and Kemal. Vesna underneath Kemal. Over in the far corner of the basement room, fucking beneath a ping-pong table looted from the front.

Angkor Wat

It is cold inside the mausoleum. A shiver runs through William's shoulders. There is a stench of urine so strong he feels like he has to step around it. *Visitors should be warned the temple city is home to over 200 species of bat.* Through another stone doorway, the sun is blinding, and the heat a thick curtain. He looks down on a clearing in the jungle, busy with tourists, street sellers beneath sun umbrellas and the barrows of ice-cream refrigerators.

'Hey, William!' He hears Missy's voice but cannot see her. A Chinese family in sanitary face masks stands for a picture. They are lined up in order of size like Russian dolls.

'Hey, William, you have to see this!'

The steps down from the mausoleum are bigger than he anticipates. He stumbles. The orange robes of the monks float past.

'William!'

Her voice through the crowds, through the tourists queuing to buy bottled water. Anya or Missy, he doesn't know.

'Over here!' Past the straw shack selling plastic dioramas of the temples, and back into the shade of the palms. Missy stands on a rope walkway inches above a mould-green swamp. The trees grow out of the water, bark as pale as cold skin.

'Check it out.' She beckons him with her phone.

The planks over the swamp spring beneath his feet.

'Have you ever seen a girl in a bucket with a snake?' Missy asks.

When she steps back he sees. It is what she says. A plastic blue bucket floats on the water. The bucket is about the size of a laundry-day pail. The girl sits in the bucket, and the rippling pale-yellow belly of the snake curls around her neck.

'What does she want?' Missy asks.

'I don't know.'

'I gave her some money just so I could take a picture.'

He sees now, there are notes in the bottom of the girl's bucket. She is looking up at him with smiling black eyes, lifting the snake off her shoulder as if he might want to take it. On the girl's T-shirt there is a picture of the pop-band Steps.

Missy holds the phone out and is pointing it at him.

'William,' she says, 'would you like to introduce yourself?'

He doesn't understand.

'It's video,' Missy says, 'I send these travelogues to my mom.'

He resists the urge to grab the phone and throw it into the swamp. 'Oh.'

'Well?'

'Sorry?'

'Introduce yourself!'

'I'm William.'

Missy motions like he's a car in her way. 'And . . . ?'

'I am – here in Angkor Wat.'

She rolls her eyes. 'Tell her who you are, or she'll think I've just met some guy.'

'I'm Missy's – I manage the school where Missy is going to work.'

'And what are we observing today, William?'

'We're at Angkor Wat. Cambodia.'

'And?'

Missy points at the girl, but William doesn't know what to say to the phone, and she quickly gives up on him, turning the camera on herself.

'On a swamp, Mom. We have a girl in a bucket with a snake. Floating on a swamp. Welcome to Cambodia.'

When they travelled, it was William who read the guide-books. Anya said she just liked to experience a place, not be led around it. When they visited Kraków, they had slept in the living room on a pull-out sofa, and he had read late into the night. William had started to tell Anya about the Soviet history of Nowa Huta. He suggested they visit the Church of the Lord's Ark which, the guidebook said, was unique as a Catholic church built by Soviet architects. But as William began to describe the concept of the building and the artwork it contained, Anya shifted uncomfortably beneath the sheets.

'Are you OK?' It is Missy.

The rice paddies whip by.

Anya had shifted uncomfortably beneath the sheets and she had murmured something into her pillow.

'Do you have 3G?' Missy asks. 'I can never fucking get my 3G to work.'

'I haven't brought my phone,' William says. 'Remember? I had to borrow yours.'

The taxi passes two backpackers walking out of Siem Reap. They disappear behind them like litter caught in the wind. His memory of Anya has gone. An air-freshener depicting Buddha swings from the rear-view mirror of the taxi. Every now and again the mirror is lit by the whites of the driver's eyes, but William can't work out if the driver is looking at him, the traffic behind or Missy's legs. She sits with her back to the passenger door, bare feet on the seat, blackened toes smelling not faintly of trainers. Eventually she puts the phone away, gives up on the business of uploading the video to her mother, and takes a tray of noodles out of the bag of snacks she insisted on buying before they left the temple.

When was the last time he ate?

'. . . not even any freaking chopsticks,' she says, rooting around the bag.

William presses himself up against the door of the old Mercedes, head against the glass. The window speckles with something like a sea mist. The heat coming with the clouds. When they climbed into the taxi, William had thought he heard thunder.

Close beneath the sheets. Anya murmuring into her pillow.

He looks around and Missy is dangling noodles into her mouth.

'Do you mind if my colleague eats?' he asks the driver.

The driver's eyes flash in the rear-view mirror. 'Of course, she's welcome my friend. Mi casa su casa.'

Missy almost spits the noodles. 'My God, are you American?'

'Thank you,' the driver smiles. 'But no, I studied in Minnesota. I have family in St Paul.' He turns and looks at them over the cigarette tucked into the fold of his short-sleeved shirt, 'New Jersey, yes?'

'Asbury Park, my friend. Garden State, baby.'

'I never went to the East Coast, always flew over it – I have to go to New York one day.'

William wonders what would happen if he opened the door and fell out of the car. What difference would it make?

'So what if he's American?' he snaps at Missy and for once she is speechless.

'Excuse me,' she says. 'I'm just interested.'

William feels his face flush. The driver has turned back to the road. The sound of the rain fills their awkward silence. It is a slowly burning tinder, then suddenly, a conflagration. The storm has leapt upon them and the car brakes into red tail-lights which dribble down the glass, windscreen wipers juddering. They halt behind the tall trailer of a truck, and the taxi driver tells them they are better off staying put until it passes. Where his arm rests on the sill of the window, William begins to feel cold water pooling against the glass.

'I love a monsoon,' Missy says to herself.

William opens the door of the car, feet in the crap-coloured topsoil. The rain bites through his clothes and within seconds it has consumed him, in his eyes, filling his shoes. The mud washes in a stream down the sides of the road, washes beneath the tyres of the taxi and pours into the rice paddies. He slams the car door and stands with his hands on his hips, feeling the weight of the rain, its heavy fingers drumming on his scalp, relieving, for the first time that day, his headache. He looks up for one moment and tries to open his eyes, but the rain pokes at them. If he had seen her. If he knew that she was dead. That she was up there somewhere. The power of the dead over the living is that they are watching us.

But what about the missing? What were they doing?

'If you take these people, you are an accomplice to ethnic cleansing. If you don't, you are an accomplice to murder.'

Mme Sadako Ogata, UN High Commissioner for refugees, 1993, on the dilemmas of taking refugees from the Balkans, and of the internal displacement of ethnic populations into designated 'safe havens'

December 1993

Stovnik

The wind picked up the snow and blew it across the window. Marko watched from inside the Hotel Stovnik. In his daydream, the building was flying, breaking from its concrete foundations, hurtling past the school and over the Kapija, over the roadblocks, on down the valley to the border, down to the coast where the sun struck the sea. Flying buildings. He had seen it in some sci-fi movie, in the days when the cinema in Stovnik didn't house refugees. The wind dropped. The falling world of snow returned; the abandoned buses and a yellow post-office Golf in the car park. There was now so little petrol the cars had been abandoned.

A smoke ring broke on Marko's nose. The smell of coffee, chewing gum and tobacco.

Vesna sat opposite on one of the low leather sofas, bored as their employers chatted. She stuck out her tongue and took a handful of pistachio nuts from the ashtray on the glass coffee table.

'What I cannot understand,' the blond-haired Dutchman sitting next to Vesna said, 'is how they get supplies for a night-club when they cannot get the supplies for a hospital.'

The Swede sitting next to Marko murmured his agreement. He was looking at a flier for the disco in the hotel. 'Or run a disco out of a generator when there is not one at the school.'

'Your leg,' Vesna said in the Bosnian they kept for themselves.

Marko looked at his leg. His left knee was pumping like a kid desperate to piss, and he wasn't sure how to make it stop. 'Too much coffee,' he said.

Vesna shifted in her red padded jacket. It was too cold to take off their coats, and the sofas in the Hotel Stovnik were so low, it was hard to move out of them. 'You should smoke one cigarette with every coffee.' Vesna pushed a packet of smuggled Camel Lights across the table. 'A coffee without a cigarette is like a mosque without a minaret.'

Marko took one of the cigarettes.

'Actually, it's biology – coffee raises your blood pressure and nicotine lowers it. So you achieve,' she waved her cigarette like a wand, 'perfect balance.'

Joachim had called an end to his day with Vesna, but Lorens wanted to go back to the school with Marko.

'Maybe we should take them to this disco,' Marko suggested. 'Get Lorens to "*chill the fuck out*".'

'"*Chill out*".' Vesna savoured the recently learned English words. 'Just chill . . . *man*.' She tipped the emptied pistachio shells into a separate ashtray and turned her coffee cup upside down on its saucer. 'You can read my future.'

While the Scandinavians compared notes on the IDPs, Marko and Vesna waited for the grains to mark the sides of her cup. Marko enjoyed these moments. The moments they had learned to share as they worked together. Talking to girls had never been a problem. He knew the things to say. He knew what to do to make girls laugh, to make them mad, to make them look at him in the right way. But Vesna was the first girl with whom he could really share silences.

The jobs were Kemal's idea. He said it was better than killing dogs. During the first ceasefire of 1993, foreigners began to arrive in Stovnik. First, the brusque, grey-suited officials from the United Nations who arrived on a Friday and left on the Monday; then the politicians from Italy and Germany, even an Australian came. No one knew exactly why this particular Australian minister visited Stovnik, but the blond, barrel-chested presence of this small man had been welcomed like an unexpected national holiday: the Australian visiting the schools housing refugees, the Australian toasting with the Mayor, the Australian always laughing, white teeth against tan skin. Perhaps it was his laughter and his tan they loved. The feeling of sunshine he brought to the town. The Australian declared Stovnik should be a 'safe haven' and a 'shining light of multi-ethnic harmony' in dark times. He said they should be proud that here, Bosnian Muslims, Bosnian Croats and Bosnian Serbs had defeated the evil of ethnic cleansing.

And then the first road convoys appeared; trucks that had been expected months earlier, their canvas sides black with the dirt of the road, and the metal of their cabs chipped with bullet holes. This was the 'aid' they had heard about on the news; lorries driven by dreadlocked British men with tattoos and two-week beards, women in vests who hadn't shaved under their arms. These were the trucks they had seen on the television, backed up in fields on the other side of the Sava, stopped before the blown bridges. With the lorries came whole fleets of battered transits and bent camper-vans, and then, a few weeks later, a different class of foreigner; the sensible Volkswagens and Land Cruisers of the Dutch and bespectacled Swedish; young, serious-looking men and women, in new but sensible outdoor clothes, who would stay and pay good rent for houses that had already been abandoned by those families who left before the war and would never return. This was Europe in action. Europe in all its glory. A scruffy army of technocrats, of the unemployed, of students and the politically disaffected.

Maybe it was because Kemal had no real family left; maybe the same qualities that made him a brother for Marko and a second son for Marko's mother made him the natural head of this new family of foreigners. There were others who were supposed to do the job – the pallid politicians and their sons. But no one else had Kemal's gift for getting things done. No one else seemed to enjoy the war as much as Kemal. When he wasn't out with the army, Kemal was at the tables of the Kapija, tables which were pulled together to accommodate an ever deepening pool of foreigners, none of whom conformed to their stereotype. The Scandinavians were irreverent. The French were not at all patriotic. The Italians were cool intellectuals, not warmhearted peasants. And the Germans were hard drinking and fun. Whatever they were, Kemal could accommodate them. With no family of his own, he could fit into anyone else's. He could also introduce them to Marko's father and the other important men of the town. Like Marko, Kemal had always been good with English, the language all the foreigners used to communicate, and when the foreigners' needs became too many, Kemal introduced them to Marko, and then to Vesna.

Marko and Vesna were both sixteen in that first year of foreigners, but when they learned how much the

Scandinavians were willing to pay them as interpreters, they didn't mind being eighteen on paper.

The snow rushed at the windscreen of Lorens's car, and Marko thought about how cold it had been in the school. About the dirt under the fingernails of their last interviewee. They had returned to the school because Lorens had forgotten to ask the woman two of the pro-forma questions on his spreadsheet.

Could she give a physical description of the soldiers who entered her village?

Did she know any of the names of the soldiers who had met her party in the forest?

The din of the Toyota's heater filled his ears. The familiar streets of the town had been made new with snow; car pushing through the ring-road blizzard of snow, Marko trying to look to the peaks of Majevica where the edge of the known world had grown with snow.

'The pattern is getting stronger, especially around this town we heard about today,' Lorens said. 'And the evidence is getting stronger. We're getting names.'

Lorens was full of it. Excited. He got like this sometimes, despite his attempts to remain sombre.

'But we know what was happening,' Marko said. 'All of them tell us the same thing. They have told us the same things for months.'

'These names – they mean that in the future someone can be punished for these crimes. And you're going to be a part of it!'

Punished for war. Marko didn't know what he thought about that.

The freezing glass of the passenger window numbed the tips of his fingers. He understood the Swede's logic. It wasn't their job to intervene; it was their job to gather evidence and persuade people who *could* intervene. In the end, people would be punished. The world would be held to account. History would be written. But the more Marko heard about what was happening, the less he understood what the punishment was for. It was a civil war. There was no wrong or right any more. And it was happening now. Not in the future. Sometimes, Marko felt secretly relieved he was too young to fight. He watched the news of the villages burning in the plains and thanked God for the mountains surrounding them, for the siege which had turned into a stalemate no one wanted to break. Then on days like this one, with the woman who had watched her children burn in a house, he wanted to be out there with Kemal, in the mountains and the snow, killing people. Anyone could kill a man.

Lorens turned onto the estate and Marko jumped down from the car, ankle deep into the pavement snow. The Land Cruiser's fan blew hard, tyres scrabbling for purchase, the whining sound of the engine's heater disappearing in the drifting snow. The quiet of the estate was so sudden it was like a fall – an endless white fall. The snow was virgin; not white now he walked into it, but sparkling blue beneath the dim evening sky. Over the playground in front of the flats, Marko crumped through the snow. There should have been snowmen, and rolled carpets of snow, but no one had been out today. The seats of the kids' swings were tall with snow, the basketball hoops wore hats of snow. On the other side of the playground, no one had cleared the steps to Marko's block, but someone's feet had been here; small footprints trailing back along the pavement by the flats. He found the door to the stairwell wedged in the groove it had made in the concrete floor.

Vesna sat on Marko's step. 'They don't stop coming – do they?' she said.

She meant the refugees. He sat next to her, and the sleeves of their padded jackets rubbed together. Feeling in his pockets, he found the new packet of Camel Lights that Lorens had given him. Vesna told him she had come to see his father but no one was home.

'They've gone to Živinice,' he told her. 'You should have asked me. They're bringing my uncle in.'

Vesna wanted Marko's father because he was one of the few in the civilian population with a military handset. If Kemal could call, it would be on the field phone Marko's father kept. But Kemal hadn't phoned in a week and Marko had been trying to avoid telling Vesna this.

He sat down on the step next to her.

'Three weeks! No fucking phones.'

He told her everything would be fine.

'How do you know that?'

The lie left Marko's mouth before he even knew it was there: 'He did phone – this morning.'

'Why didn't you tell me!'

'I forgot.'

'You forgot!'

'Sorry.' Marko put his arm around her.

'I don't want to fucking,' she started, 'I don't want to fucking sit at home waiting for someone to call.'

With his hand on Vesna's back, Marko felt he was touching the very centre of the world. He could feel her breathing beneath the cold material of the padded jacket. But every time he came this close, he could only think of her in the basement with Kemal.

He had seen something like it before, after school, in the concrete pipes by the waste ground of the old railway station where the older girls lined up and did it with younger boys as if the whole business was some kind of co-ordinated exercise routine in a gym class. There had been an intense kind of quiet disturbed only by a sound like men trying to walk quietly through mud. Hands up skirts. Before the war, Senka Janković from year seven had allowed Marko to get his fingers wet. But that was as far as he had got.

In the basement, Kemal and Vesna weren't standing up like the boys and girls in the pipes, they were lying down. Vesna's vest had been pulled up over her breasts. Vesna's breasts! Was there anything in the world he wouldn't have given to see them? How many times had he taken the outline suggested by her clothes and revealed them in his imagination? But when they appeared to him, Marko had found himself numb with shock. As she lay on the floor of the basement, Vesna's breasts trembled, no more shape than his mother's lemon mousse. Her skirt had rucked up, rolled into a rope around her waist, her back on the concrete floor, and the bone of her hip showing like the bodies thrown into shallow graves. Watching Vesna and Kemal, Marko had wanted to jump out from his hiding place and make it stop.

Against his shoulder, Vesna sobbed, their jackets rubbing like two sleeping bags. 'What did he say? When did he call?'

To Marko's disappointment she sat up, wiped her tears and abruptly ended her crying in that shocking way girls can.

'Who?'

'Kemal – when he spoke to your father, what did he say?'

'I don't know.' Marko felt his face flush. 'He said they were digging in. And it was quiet. And they hoped to be returning when the road was clear.' From the conversations his father had with other policemen, Marko felt this last part stood a decent chance of being true.

'Good,' Vesna said. 'Good.'

She took a hold of Marko's knee and squeezed it hard. He felt every muscle in his body come alive. 'Sometimes I forget you aren't his little brother.'

Christmas Night, 2004

Kao Lak

'Doesn't this place combine some of your worst fears?' William asked.

They sat at an upturned wine barrel on the last available stools, plastic crabs caught in fishing nets over their heads. Anya scrutinised the room. It was popular enough. Full of expat Christmas parties. The bar itself seemed to be fashioned from the hull of an upturned boat.

'I mean, expats – *tick*,' William said. 'Nautical theme – *tick*.'

'Maybe I'm confronting my fears,' Anya said.

'Are they actually playing E17?'

Somewhere, in the fairy lights and Christmas twinkle, she heard a familiar chorus.

'I could do that again.' Anya held up her empty cocktail glass. All the alcohol seemed to sweat out anyway.

'All right.' Will got up for the bar. 'Then you shall.'

She watched William being served by a Thai man, or boy – telling the boys from the men in this country was difficult. So far, there was no sign of Kemal Lekić, although according to the New Zealander, the bar was where Kemal Lekić was most likely to be. In the boat-hire hut, he had told Anya if she did recognise his colleague, she'd probably seen him at *Chuck's Place*. Because his colleague was called Chuck. And this was Chuck's place. Now she was beginning to doubt what she had seen on the skiff. Kemal standing up, capping the petrol can and stepping back over to the speedboat. The smell of petrol, an unwashed vest and unwashed skin. When she tried to recall the moment, Anya couldn't quite see Kemal's face. She had been unable to move, unable to even speak; the speedboat disappearing, the curtain of the lagoon closing behind it. Afterwards, they had chugged back to the shore, William complaining and Anya unable to explain to him her haste. On the beach, William was busy tying up the boat. She told him she would go ahead and retrieve the deposit from the hire hut. Anya didn't want William there. She wasn't yet sure of what had just happened. When the New Zealander appeared from behind the bead curtains, she discovered she had no clue what she was going to ask. She couldn't very well ask where his colleague was. Even worse to ask him directly *who* his colleague was. Then she remembered Bogdan, the uncomfortable man in Stovnik. And how far instinct had taken her then.

'Did I recognise your friend from somewhere?' she finally said.

In a booth at the windows, a group of expats wearing Santa hats raised a toast. A couple with snow-white hair slow-danced by the saloon doors to the toilets. The place was a local favourite apparently, big with the expats, especially the English and Germans. But if Kemal Lekić owned the bar,

Anya suddenly thought – rather than just *working* here – it didn't necessarily mean he would *be* here.

When Will returned with the blue cocktails, he placed a packet of Camel Lights on the barrel top.

'Oh my God, I haven't smoked in years,' Anya said.

'Me neither.'

She picked up the packet and turned it in her hands. It seemed smaller than she remembered cigarette packets to be.

'They don't put the warning messages about a "slow and painful death" on the packets here,' Will said, 'so they can't be too bad for you.'

Anya pushed the cigarettes across the table. 'You're really going to?'

Will took a deep breath. 'I don't know now,' he said. 'They just seemed to call to me from behind the bar.'

'I always associate smoking with Kraków,' she said.

'Me too!'

'Walking through the botanical gardens in the middle of winter and trying to take arty photographs. Do you remember I took a whole series of photos just of feet?'

'I remember you developing them back at university.'

'Actually *developing* film!'

'When I think of smoking, I think of the apartment – your cousin's place.'

A silence fell as they shared the memory. His head at one end of a pillow, hers at the other. It could have been any number of pillows in any number of places they lived.

'It's good to see you, Will,' she said. And she thought of telling him everything then; of telling him about Ljuba Crvenović, and the policeman in Stovnik, and her visit to Vesna Knežević, her bumbling mistakes, and how they nearly put a man's life in danger. But that was her work. And wasn't it her work which had come between them? Instead, she excused herself, and stepped around the dancing couple on her way to the toilet.

Anya slipped off the holiday Havaianas, felt the cool tiles beneath her feet, found her posture and focused on the centring technique she had been taught in a class Dignity Monitor provided for employees on an away weekend. It hadn't been long after the split with Will when the stress started to show. They said she was working too hard. She shouldn't have allowed herself to take on too much. The incredible thing was she hadn't connected it to William. The split itself had been something they both decided on, a decision *she* had partly made (although she suspected it was more his). They agreed on much. They had been together as long as many a married couple, and from such a young age too. They had *changed* so much in that time. They were not the same people they were when they were eighteen. The year of their break-up had been the same summer she visited Bosnia. The same summer she visited Ljuba and began to fuck things up. Anya was a researcher, not an investigator. But her country expertise had begun (somewhat serendipitously) with a master's dissertation entitled: 'Rape as a Weapon of War: The Balkan Conflicts – 1992–5'. She had intended to study child soldiers in Angola, but the Conflict Resolution professor at Cardiff had a research project plugged into the war-crimes tribunals at The Hague, and said he felt better qualified to assess something with a Balkan orientation. As the trials at The Hague began to unfold, there had been an urgency in studying the social psychology of specific war-crimes. 'The systemisation of rape in brigade cultures and their impact upon strategic military success in war. Case studies from the Bosnian conflict, 1992–5.'

It was a PhD title she had spent endless tutorials refining. Towards the end of her study, she had made her first field trip to Bosnia, to the site of a 'rape camp' which turned out to be an unremarkable-looking home in the coal-mining hills outside Foča. Weeds grew tall in the slopes of the garden and the noonday sun made mirrors of the windows. Sitting in a small field above a farm road, the house looked like any one of the hundreds-of-thousands of homes dotting the slopes of Bosnia, but as she reached the end of the path beaten in the grass, Anya noticed the glass in the windows was cracked, the 'curtains' no more than cloth and rags, strung up as if to hide a shame. The black marks of a recent fire licked the frame of the front door. Someone had made a pathetic attempt to burn the place down.

In 1992, the Muslim owner of the house had lived in Germany. When the Serbs of the village organised to kill and expel the Muslim population, Nusret Karaman's home was one of the many properties appropriated by Chetnik soldiers who ran their operations from the motel just down the road.

Anya would never forget being in the house. She would always be able to smell the bad breath of the fire's destruction, the air which felt as if it had most of the oxygen sucked out of it. Beyond the ground floor, the walls and floors had survived. An abandoned fridge against the unplastered walls. A room of broken parquet where tartan rugs and Turkish carpets were lined up in military fashion over the floor, as if the bodies sleeping on them had only just left. A kitchen unit covered with vinyl table cloth, and empty plastic bottles knitted together with spider's webs. A frying pan on the floor.

The women had been forced to cook and clean. When there were jobs in the village to be done, a room to be painted, sheets to be washed, they were taken from the house under supervision, and returned again at night. If they did not follow their orders they were beaten. Some of the women were not women. They were twelve-year-old girls, taken from the local school and shared among the soldiers. Testimony at The Hague told of how the soldiers liked in particular to identify mothers and their daughters – how they liked to swap them between each other.

When Anya stepped out of Karaman's house, the sloping field seemed to scroll beneath her feet. She thought she would never reach the road. When she did, she doubled over, hands on her knees, waiting for her balance to return. The sun burned on her neck. When she could stand straight again, the house was still standing. It was just another house in white plaster, three floors and a red tile roof. Like the one no more than fifty metres away. People lived next door to this house and knew. It was the silence that had spooked her. Inside the house was a terrible silence. Inside the house nothing but her own breathing.

There were plenty of witnesses at The Hague. The UN staff working in the region had called Karaman's house the 'Miljevina Bordello'. The women here, the women at the Partisan Sports Hall right next to Miljevina's police station, and the women kept at a number of other houses in these hills – what happened to them had happened beneath the same bright sun hanging over the village that day of Anya's visit. Before then, Bosnia had only existed in the shimmering and colourless images of deteriorated video-cam footage viewed in a library. Footage which made another world of a place which belonged to this. It had taken Anya four hours to get to Miljevina from Heathrow. The taxi driver from Sarajevo had asked her whether she knew the Spice Girls. It had all happened four hours away. And as the taxi drove her back to

Sarajevo through Bosnia's green and beautiful hills, every white plaster house with a red tile roof seemed to look at her with the same black silence.

A toilet flushed. Anya opened her eyes to the clam shells stuck in the flimsy planks of the toilet stall. Taps running. The washing of hands. She shouldn't have interfered. It was not her job to pursue allegations of war crimes. In Bosnia, every town, even Sarajevo, was a small place. Everyone knew everyone's business. Ljuba had been through the channels available. She had reported the crime to the Serbian police, and the Serbian police had requested the assistance of Stovnik's police. Stovnik's police had returned no evidence for indictment, the missing persons' case had been logged and there it was. Done. If Anya could do anything more, it was to report Ljuba's story, with her consent, to an organisation compiling data on such events. There had been no need for Anya to drop in on the investigating policeman, and the first conversation she had with Bogdan Banović should have persuaded anyone, with any sense, to steer clear of the whole mess. She did not doubt Bogdan's sympathy for Ljuba's situation. He had explained how Emina, his sister-in-law, was herself registered missing, his cousin's wife too. Bogdan told Anya he had offered every assistance to the Serbian police, and interviewed all the members of the brigade who had been at the aluminium factory where Ljuba alleged the offences took place. The brigade had even kept a list of all the displaced individuals who passed through and entered into their protection over those four days, and Ljuba, along with the missing women, was on that list. But Bogdan was a deeply uncomfortable-looking man. Everything about him seemed to resist what he was saying.

'You don't keep lists of the women you rape,' Bogdan said. He had chain-smoked Camel cigarettes, screwing them into the ashtray with his yellow fingers. He had arranged to meet outside of his workplace, in a café on one of the estates in the upper town.

'Even if Kemal had done these things he is dead,' Bogdan said.

She found him hard to look at. His discomfort catching. On the wall behind him, the face of Tito grinned over the wide lapels of a white suit, teeth biting down on the end of a pipe.

'Even if he had?'

To Anya's surprise, Bogdan had only shrugged and told her you could never be sure.

Washing her hands in Kemal Lekić's sinks, Anya tried to remember exactly how Bogdan had said this. Exactly what made her think he *believed* Kemal was guilty. But the moment escaped her. She remembered more clearly how Bogdan had been staring over her shoulder when he told her he had to leave. She had looked to the street outside but seen no one. She didn't have to see anyone to know he was a frightened man.

The hand dryer startled her. It was one of the expat women, tipsy in a Santa Claus hat.

'This is a great place,' Anya said.

The woman smiled. Ruddy cheeks. In her fifties perhaps.

'We're on holiday. Are you local?'

'Nurse.' The woman had a northern English accent that twisted Anya's nerve for home. 'Local hospital.'

'Is this place run by expats then?'

The woman held her wet hands out in front of her like a surgeon waiting for scrubs. 'Sort of,' she said. 'Owner's from – Balkans or somewhere, I think. Croatia, is that the place?'

The bathroom door opened, and someone disappeared into the stall behind them.

'Chuck's place.' Anya smiled. 'Which one's Chuck?'

'Oh, he'll be out doing the fireworks. For after.' The woman wiped her hands on her skirt, head down and feet planted apart to keep herself upright. 'You have a good one.'

'Thanks,' Anya said. But she was already beginning to feel like none of this was her business. She shouldn't be there unbidden, doing the work of an investigator. The emptiness of the rape-camp house again, telling her she was just a voyeur in all this, a tourist in other people's lives. When Anya stepped up to the hand dryer, the nurse stopped, and turned at the bathroom door.

'The fireworks are always great,' she said. 'If you're on holiday. Up the beach. You know – I mean, you don't know. But in front of Chuck's house. You'll find it. Follow the crowd.'

Another couple were sitting at the barrel she had occupied with Will. Will was outside, his face pressed up against the window. He mugged, squashing his nose against the glass, and puffing out his cheeks. Miming drunkenness, Will swayed on his feet, waving the unlit cigarette like a magician's wand.

It was almost as warm outside as inside. Beneath the moon and the fairy lights, a choir sang on the beach. Not a bad choir at all but a good choir; expats and local faces, three-part harmony filling 'Good King Wenceslas' like a sail. Anya sat down next to William on the top step. Over a black sea, the moon rolled a flickering ribbon of light.

'Go on,' Anya said to William. 'You've gone to the trouble of buying a lighter.' He had the cigarette in one hand, the brand-new lighter in the other. She watched as he put the cigarette between his lips and brought the flame to its tip.

He didn't cough. He sat up and pulled his chin into his chest. 'Jesus,' he finally exhaled, 'that is *not* what I remember.'

Anya took the cigarette. It felt too big between her fingers, and the filter unpleasantly dry between her lips. The smoke was hot. She kept it in her mouth, afraid to take it in. Then she found it coming out of her nose, her eyes stinging.

'I used to do this like, twenty times a day,' William said, taking the cigarette.

'I don't think it's doing it for me.'

To her surprise, he took another long drag.

The aftertaste did recall something of her cousin's flat, the place they had stayed on a pull-out sofa. Her cousin had gone to Warsaw to take an intensive English course. William and Anya had spent long mornings on the sofa-bed. They had curled up through the winter beneath heavy blankets, the cigarette smoke and heat of a portable gas fire.

'That dog!' She sat up.

'What?'

'That dog you were talking about. The Jack Russell with the wheels. I do remember now! We went out into Nowa Huta! For the gas fire!'

'Yes.' He put his arm over her shoulders and it seemed to draw a silence around them. For a moment she was too nervous to look at him. She looked at the choir, at the sea, then slowly let her head rest against his shoulder.

'I was in Kosovo this year,' she told him. 'We're producing a report on the Serb returnees.'

'Like you did in Bosnia?'

'Did you hear about the riots?'

'No.' William held the cigarette out in front of him, the filter pinched in his fingertips, the butt pointing straight up.

He turned it like a botanist holding some rare flower; idle and happy, full of wonder.

'I wonder what it's all for sometimes,' she said. 'We're all over the place but when it comes down to it – when it came to the riots no one could actually DO anything.'

'You're not supposed to do anything, are you?' William asked. 'Isn't that the point? You're neutral.'

'We report things that have happened, *after* they have happened. Sometimes I think that's no good to anyone at all. It doesn't seem to stop people.'

'Lessons learned,' William said. 'At least that's what you always told me. You help people learn the lessons of things.'

'Sometimes I think they should just sort out their own fucking mess and we should all go back to minding our own business.'

'This is not the woman who lectured me on the global interdependence of our economies and the declining powers of sovereign governments.' William's hand had found the small of her back. 'You haven't changed, have you?' he said.

'It's like Poland. I so desperately wanted to be where it was happening. To be there while history was being made. Anyone who actually *lived* there wanted to get out. That's a kind of disaster tourism, isn't it?'

'It's getting involved. Getting yourself *involved* with people. I think it's brilliant.'

'I think I must be sick. A bit twisted.'

'But that's the worst kind of liberal bleeding heart right there,' William said. 'You do a job. I think you should just get on with it. Get stuck in. Doesn't matter what your motivations are.'

She had certainly been *stuck in* with Bogdan Banović. After Stovnik she had heard from him one more time. Her mobile had rung in the taxi between Vesna Knežević's house and

Sarajevo airport. Her head was already filling with the consequences of her amateurism. *You were seen with Vesna Knežević*, Bogdan said. The fear in his voice. Didn't Anya realise how difficult this could make things? Didn't she realise people would connect her visit to Vesna with her visit to him?

Anya had known Banović was jumpy. She knew policemen charged with investigating war crimes could be put in a very difficult position. But in her ignorance, she hadn't realised the danger might spread to her. Who had seen her in Sarajevo? How? She had always suspected it might have been Banović himself. If he were really so nervous, it would make sense to follow her, just to make sure she left the country without causing any more trouble.

Her eyes walked up the path laid by the moon. The more she stared, the more the flickering slowed, like a strip of film spooling to its end. They had their arms around each other again. William and Anya. It was how it always had been. Her fingers hovered with uncertainty above the cotton T-shirt hanging over his hip bone. It seemed too forward to hold his hand.

'William?'

'I used to feel sometimes you forgot about me though. When you were off working. On one of your foreign trips.'

He rubbed her hair with his knuckles, like a father who can't quite express their love for a child. This, instead of a kiss. He didn't sound angry. He didn't even sound sad. Just sort of wistful, and nostalgic. Anya closed her eyes. The voices of the choir were so round, so full, she could lean against the sound. *When the snow lay round about, deep and crisp and even.*

Saturday 9 April 2005

Poipet

In keeping with the intimate scale of the Holiday Poipet, our casino is both comfortable and compact. William reads this on a poster in the hotel lift. *You'll find its oval layout convenient and cosy. The central area gives way to tables where popular card games are played. The type of slot machines changes regularly, and we offer both the classic fruit machines types and the new cutting-edge machines with sophisticated LED displays and sound effects.* He drinks up, and in the elevator bin, disposes of the last minibar bottle. There were no trousers his length, but William has bought new underwear, and a new shirt. When the doors open, he walks into a room of soft carpet and muzak. At the desk he asks for the restaurant. The woman tells him there are three restaurants along the corridor. He can choose from Japanese, Thai and Korean. Missy had said she would meet him in the Japanese restaurant.

'Do you have a pen and paper?' he asks. The receptionist passes him a notepad with the hotel's letterhead, and he writes:

'The type of slot machines changes'

Change to: 'The type of slot machine changes'

'Your copywriters can change this.' He underlines the incorrect noun, 'so that the singular form of "machine", agrees with the singular "type". And then, keep the plural form of "changes" and "machines", after the words "cutting-edge".'

In the hotel corridor, William passes a hairdresser's where two Thai women in coral-pink pyjama suits perch on stools. He walks on past an Internet lounge, a convenience store and the doors to the casino. The corridor splits in two, the sign for the restaurants pointing right. When he reaches it, the Japanese restaurant is a large, low-ceilinged hall, with marble floors. Beneath bright chandeliers, an island buffet of gleaming silver domes sparkles next to perfectly set tables.

'Welcome, sir.' It is a woman who looks exactly like the woman at the reception desk. 'Please to help you dining this evening?'

'I'm expecting someone.'

William looks over the empty restaurant and assumes he must be early.

'How many so, sir?'

'Just two of us.'

The woman seats him at a table facing a Japanese mural of old men in pastel robes. *Sensei*, William thinks (although he does not know whether they are, or even exactly what the word sensei means). The sensei kneel among mountain boulders, holding out their hands to a sun represented by a balled-up fish hanging over temple walls. Now he is sitting still, William has a feeling everything is moving around him.

It is the rain streaming down the wall of glass.

'A drink?' Another woman who looks like the last.

'I would, yes – maybe a beer. A Tiger?'

She leaves him. He closes his eyes for a second. It had all seemed like a nightmare, but now he can count it as an achievement. Something he has survived. The drive, the border, Angkor Wat, the taxi and the rain. Today he left Thailand and visited one of the great wonders of the world. He walked among thousands of strangers. He allowed himself to be driven through a monsoon. All thanks to an American woman without a visa. Perhaps he even made the clerical mistake deliberately, left something undone in his work, some loose end to trip himself up; his subconscious looking desperately for a means of slapping him in the face. William is drunk. And it feels just marvellous. He opens his eyes. The window of the restaurant looks on to a courtyard of some kind. Soft lights spot a limestone path and the branches of a small tree rock in the wind. Across the courtyard, he can see the glass wall of another room, not empty but full; a bar, coffee tables, sofas, sulphurous light. The rain on the glass keeps rearranging what he sees, dribbles people, drops them, runs them together. He has always found comfort in rain. Because of the rain, they are still in Cambodia; the road was a rapid and the cars crawling. Something had come over him afterwards, in the back of the taxi, his clothes sticking to him. Something had mysteriously left him, like it had on the beach that first day after the wave. Not a moment of horror, but a moment of wonder.

The rain had lifted and given them some hope of reaching the Visa Office on time; traffic gathering speed as they reached the shacks and boathouses on the edge of Poipet. But as they neared the Visa Office the taxi stopped. There was a wide load ahead. A long white bone on the truck bed. Like a dinosaur find. A mammoth's tusk. Although no mammoth was ever this big. When it eventually turned off the main road, the vehicle became stuck on the turn. Not a truck, but a long, open trailer bed. Three, six, nine – William counted – twelve sets of wheels.

'Wind turbine,' Missy said. 'You see them going through Jersey to the coast.'

When the turbine finally resolved the turn, the rain started again, and by the time they reached the town, the Visa Office had closed. They would not be returning to Bangkok tonight. In his room, William had started drinking.

He wipes at the window with the back of his arm. But of course, all the water is on the other side of the glass and he can make things no clearer. Where is Missy? They are supposed to be meeting for dinner. He had finished three bottles from the minibar to get himself through it.

'Your beer, sir.' The woman places a paper napkin on the table, and the cold beer on top of it. 'To buffet please help yourself.'

William stops himself from correcting her. 'What's that?' He points across the courtyard. 'Is that another restaurant?'

'The bar. The restaurant is closing twenty minutes sir – last service only.'

William touches his wrist but there is no watch. No mobile phone in his pocket either.

'But what time is it?' he asks the woman.

'Nearly twelve, sir,' the woman says. 'We close at midnight.'

Sunday 10 April 2005

Sarajevo

While waiting on the street in Sarajevo, Marko turns on his phone for the first time in two days. Texts from Emeka. Cover to be arranged for tomorrow. T-Mobile roaming charges. Three missed calls from Millie.

He watches the windows of the travel company across the street, and dials her.

'There you are,' Millie says. 'I thought you'd gone AWOL.'

Her voice is perfectly clear, no distance, just as if he were calling her from the other side of town.

'Sorry.'

'OK. I know you can look after yourself.' He can hear her breathe. She is walking.

Over the road, something catches Marko's eye. He has been here for twenty minutes, and now he sees her. It is a woman in the tourist office. She has dyed red hair. She is working a photocopy machine.

'So how is it?' Millie says. 'Bosnia? Like you remember?'

'Not really.'

'It's the first time you've been back, isn't it? What about your friends? Your cousin – did he meet you?'

'Samir.'

'The hero's return!'

'I'm not a hero.'

'No – I don't mean it like that. You know what I mean.'

'Where are you going?' he asks.

'What?'

'You're walking somewhere.'

'I'm just along the Backs.' She has stopped. He imagines her beneath the long avenue of tall trees past King's field, the walk from the English library to the bridge at the College. The iron gates thick with coats of black paint that have been applied one over the other, year after year after year.

Across the street, the woman with dyed red hair has finished with the photocopier. It might be her. It is definitely the right company, the one on the website. BH Tourism. It had taken him a moment to realise the hoardings are in English, not Bosnian.

Bosnia, The Heart-Shaped Land.

'Guess who I saw today,' Millie is saying.

'The funeral's tomorrow,' Marko says. 'I should be coming back after that.'

'Should be? Tempted to become a fully paid up Bosnian again?' She is joking, but there is a nervousness too.

'Of course not!'

'I'm only joking,' Millie says. 'The chicken we bought last week goes off on Tuesday, I wanted to do a proper dinner with it. I hate cooking for myself.'

He could kiss her. 'And I can't miss my Tuesday class,' he says.

'It's only two hours, isn't it? I keep telling myself that. And it's not dangerous any more. Is it?'

But Marko isn't listening. The woman at the photocopying machine is staring out of the window as the papers spit out. She is staring at him.

Poipet

It is past midnight. William is hopelessly late. Missy has already eaten. He finds her not in the restaurant, but in the bar, sitting down with her bare knees pointing towards a youthful-looking western man, who sits on the low sofa next to her.

'They have bar snacks,' Missy shouts over the music. 'It's not so bad here!' She hands him a menu. He tries to read, but the letters keep getting up and marching around on the page.

'So you're the boss?' The man who stands up and holds out his hand is English.

'This is Henry,' Missy says.

Henry's shake is firm.

'I manage the school where Missy works.'

'Try this.' Missy hands him a glass of something tall and purple. He sits down on the sofa opposite.

He can do this.

The drink has a bitter, gingery taste. 'How do you find yourself in Cambodia?' William asks.

'I work at Angkor Wat.'

'We were there today!' William says.

'Henry gets to stay out there overnight!' Missy says.

William maintains his smile. 'That must be wonderful. When all the visitors have gone.'

Missy reclaims her cocktail from the table. 'Henry works in conservation.'

'We help organise some of the restoration work.' He holds up his hands as if in apology.

'What a wonderful job,' William says.

'I'm very lucky.'

'It must be incredibly difficult,' William continues, 'because it's all made out of sandstone, isn't it? Who do you work for? Is it the WMF?'

Henry smiles. The English man is glad to have met someone who knows at least a little about his work. William nods enthusiastically as Henry begins to explain how the World Monument Fund works with local sculptors, many of them retrained soldiers, some of them disabled veterans who carve on site making new Aspara figures for the broken reliefs.

'I read somewhere there were two million visitors last year,' William says, 'all those footsteps, all those hands . . .' And he remembers he is good at this, at making people feel they are being listened to. It is what makes him a good teacher; not the ability to talk *at* people, to *deliver* information, but the ability to *listen*, to ask the right question. It is coming back to him now. He *can* do this. It is one of the things Anya loved about him.

'Now I feel guilty,' Missy says. 'I just washed off a ton of sandstone in the shower.'

'It's a catch-22,' Henry confesses. 'The tourism helps pay for the restoration.'

'You were trained as a sculptor?' William asks.

Missy grabs Henry's wrist and presents his hand. 'Look at these sculpting mitts!' she says.

William claps his own hands together. 'Your drink?' He points at Henry's empty glass. 'Let me get you a drink.'

The bar is busy. The Thai man who stands next to William nods in courtesy and offers his place. The Cambodian woman who serves has a flat face, as polished as a porcelain plate. Looking at the artfully chalked board behind her, he has a sudden urge to order cocktails with rude names just so that he can say the words out loud (although he avoids the one inexplicably named *Sexpoo*). As she assembles the drinks, the girl's movements appear to be choreographed with the music, and William understands for a second why men hire private dancers.

'I love this track,' he blurts when the girl serves him, but her serving smile and her serving eyes are impenetrable.

'A game!' William returns with the drinks. 'Do you know that you can put the word "poo" into the name of any Bond film, and it works?'

'*Any* Bond film?' Henry asks.

'Any Bond film.'

'What,' Missy says, 'like, *Moonpoo*?'

'I prefer *Pooraker*,' William says.

Missy laughs.

'I get it,' Henry takes the straw out of his cocktail. '*You only Poo Twice*.'

'Excellent work.'

'Oh my God,' Missy says, 'it's true, like – *Thunderpoo*.'

'I love *Thunderpoo*!'

'*Thunderpoo* is very good,' William confirms. 'But not as good as *The Man with the Golden Poo*.'

Missy snorts through her straw. William hides his smile by bringing his glass to his lips.

'What about *From Russia with Poo*?' Henry says.

'Now you're talking.'

'Talking of poo,' Henry says, 'although actually, that's not what I'm going to do, did either of you see the toilet on the way in?'

When Henry is gone, Missy relaxes, and spreads her arms across the back of the sofa. He notices for the first time she is wearing a New York Yankees T-shirt, and not her red vest.

'Well, you turn out to be fun,' she says.

'You didn't think I would be?'

Missy shrugs and smiles.

'You managed to buy some new clothes?'

'There's a store in here. Sells a lot of baseball merchandise for some reason.'

'I like it.'

'Anyone in New Jersey ever saw me wearing a Yankees shirt I'd die. But the Mets clearly don't merchandise in Cambodia.'

At a booth next to them, European men are toasting each other. At another table, a Thai man brings his chair around to sit next to his pregnant lover. The couple press their foreheads together, laying their hands on the table, one on top of the other.

'Well, you look good,' William tells Missy.

'Why thank you.'

He turns the cold glass in his hands and pokes at the ice with his straw. He doesn't need to be anywhere else. He doesn't need to be *with* anyone else. He just needs this.

'Truth is, I was starting to honk,' Missy says. 'In fact I think I still do, despite a shower – here—' She shuffles onto the edge of the seat and presents him with the left armpit, 'truthfully, does this smell strange to you?'

William leans over the table. It is the smell of body odour disguised by soap. 'You smell perfectly normal.'

'I think I smell weird.'

'Missy tells me you rescued her?' It is Henry. He has returned from the toilet and hovers until Missy shuffles up.

'I told him about the visa,' she tells William.

'I rescued her from my own mistake.'

'I'm glad you did,' Missy says. 'Make a mistake, I mean. Or we wouldn't be having this adventure.' Putting her hand on Henry's knee, she says, 'Hey – Henry's a hero too. Henry volunteered to go down to the beaches, after the tsunami, to help with the clear up. Henry – tell William that story.'

Sarajevo

Vesna's hair isn't long any more. It is cut into a plum-red bob so neat it looks like a wig. From beneath this wig, someone, who occasionally resembles the girl Marko knew, is talking about the burgeoning travel industry in Bosnia, how the company she works for isn't really a travel company, but a department of the government's tourist board. Eco-tourism. Heritage tourism. And something to do with combatting the work of illegal logging companies.

They are in the café opposite her work. Over Vesna's head in a slick suit and leather gloves, Justin Timberlake dances across a widescreen TV. The sound on the television has been turned down, and the stereo behind the bar plays a Dino Merlin track. Nothing about any of this seems to quite fit together. He doesn't know what he expected by surprising Vesna, but perhaps he had imagined she would be more – *surprised*. Instead, Vesna greeted Marko like a man she hadn't seen in a few months. Someone who had been on a long holiday, not a ghost of ten years. She hugged him, and held him at arm's length like a relative who remarks how much a child has grown, her beaming greeting more for the benefit of her colleagues than any expression of true feeling. *This is Marko! Marko from Stovnik!* As if they had only just been talking about him.

In the café, Marko expects the stiff smile to loosen, but Vesna keeps it up.

'I really hoped I would see you,' she is saying. 'But I couldn't come and I lost your parents' phone numbers and then we had all these things going on at work.'

She divides a tiramisu cake with a small fork. Marko pours another packet of sugar into his coffee. She is just like the others. Acting as if Kemal's resurrection and death were nothing remarkable at all.

'You still have a sweet tooth?' she asks.

'It's good to be back in a country where they make proper Bosnian coffee.'

'But you're drinking latte,' she says. 'And in England they only drink tea, right?'

Marko asks her if she has been there.

'Are you kidding?' She pulls a face. 'I'd love to go to England. When are you going to invite me? The only time I get to travel is with work. Which isn't so bad. Italy, Turkey, mainly our neighbours. But I still love Italy.' She stops and looks at her fingernails. 'Am I complaining? I shouldn't be complaining. I have a great job.'

'Where else have you been to?'

'Hmm?'

'With your job?'

'Oh, I don't know – not so many places. It's only if there's some marketing work. I try to get myself those gigs.'

'Just Europe?'

She presses down on the sponge with her fork. 'Yes, just Europe. But who gives a shit, right? Wow. Marko.'

When she shakes her head, the straightened bob doesn't appear to move.

'I like my job.'

'What do you do?'

He tells her about the security company. About working as a doorman. How he began to employ his own doormen. He is about to tell her about the philosophy classes he started this year, but has lost interest in himself already.

'And you married an English girl?'

'No! What makes you think I would do that?'

'Why not? How old are you now, Marko? Twenty-eight? What are you doing? Come on. You won't be beautiful for ever. And neither will they.'

'Twenty-seven, I still have a month. And I'll marry a younger woman.'

'Of course you will.' Vesna rests her fork on the plate. In the silence between them, Marko realises one thing hasn't changed. He will play whatever game Vesna wants to play. She has always had this power over him.

'You remember the Hotel Stovnik?' he asks.

She nods, but not out of interest. She is looking through the window as though she has lost her smile on the street somewhere.

'Lorens,' Marko says, 'and what was the guy's name, Joachim?'

She finds her little plastic smile again. 'Sometimes I think, why didn't I do what Marko did? They offered me the same deal. Come and study for six months, try to claim asylum if that's what you want.'

'Why didn't you?'

'Maybe I love my country,' she bites, and excusing herself for the bathroom, leaves Marko to watch her walk across the tiled floor of the empty café in her heels.

'We were just helping to move the debris from a few of the villages—'

'But tell Will that thing you told me about.'

'The dugong?'

'Show him!'

Henry digs in his pocket and pulls out his phone. 'We were in a village down on Koh Lanta, you know? They had these apartments, badly built – that were flattened. But the funny thing was, generally the bathrooms, if they had good bathrooms, had stayed intact. And swimming pools too. Anything plumbed in, or rooted in the ground I suppose.' He thumbs through his pictures. 'So we were working on this place all morning, shifting great piles of glass and brick, and suddenly we find there's a swimming pool under it.' He hands William the phone.

'Does everyone have a camera in their phone now?' William jokes.

'It looks like a manatee,' Missy says.

William is looking at a picture of something lying in a swimming pool.

'It's a dug*ong*,' Henry says. 'From the same family.'

'And it was still alive!' Missy says.

William watches Missy's hand drift over to Henry's knee. Henry starts to explain how there had been enough water in the pool to keep the animal hydrated.

'So they lifted it back down to the *sea*!' Missy says.

'You have no idea how fucking heavy a dugong is – it took, like, twenty of us.'

The dugong sits in a pool of green water, anvil of its trunk flat on the floor, flippers useless. If anything, it looks mildly pissed off.

When William hands back the phone, Henry sighs. 'You really had to be there just to get the madness of it.'

'I was.' William is grinning, he doesn't know why.

Only when there is no response does William realise what he has said. Missy looks confused. Henry's mouth has opened, but no words have come out. It seems they expect him to keep talking. 'The tsunami. At Kao Lak.' William adds the facts. 'On Boxing Day. In the first wave.' He feels as though his grinning face no longer belongs to him.

'Dude.' Missy slumps back in the sofa.

'In it?' Henry leans forward.

'I got washed into the mangroves.' He is not sure what they want to hear. It has left him: the man he was a second before, the man sure he was in the right place. Whatever lightness entered William on the way back from Bangkok, whatever sense of wonder for the world, it has stepped out of him, and is walking away, leaving only the noise of the room swelling in his ears.

Sarajevo

Her manicured fingernails are painted a bright canary yellow and stand to attention on the coffee glass.

'How many years have you been in England?' she asks.

'Nine, nearly ten years.'

'Do you think things have changed? Around here? From what you've seen?'

'It's been two days.'

'Still.'

Even though it is noon, they are the only customers in the café. The barman is using a napkin to work his way through the cutlery lined up along the bar.

'Widescreen TVs in bars,' Marko tells Vesna. 'There's an Audi TT parked right there. And you can walk down Mustafa without getting shot at.'

Vesna raises an eyebrow. Since she came back from the toilet, there is something different about her. She has reapplied her eyeliner, freshened her face. Her cheeks have some blood in them.

'Some people miss the war.' A cigarette appears between her fingers. Marko digs in his pocket before realising he doesn't carry a lighter any more.

She lights it herself. 'People our age miss the war because at least during the war they had a job to do. There are children – fifteen, sixteen – who don't remember it, and think it might have been some kind of adventure. Either that, or they do remember, and they want to leave the country.'

'What do you think?'

'I don't,' Vesna says. 'I don't think. I still don't watch the news.' She straightens up and tucks one curtain of the bob behind an ear.

'But you heard about Kemal?'

'People told me. My neighbour showed me the newspaper.'

She looks out of the window. A refuse truck is backing onto the pavement, orange lights spinning. A man in green overalls wheels the dumpster and, with another man, positions it against the piston arms of the truck.

'You don't want to come to the funeral?'

'Isn't it enough to bury a man once?'

'I have to do this thing. This ghusl ceremony. Muslim bullshit. He'd have hated it.'

'Why you?'

'Because there was no one else.'

She places her hand over her mouth, and for a moment he thinks this is finally it. Finally they are going to say something real to each other. But she just pulls on her nose and says, 'I really should be getting back to work.'

'You didn't know he was still alive?'

'What kind of a question is that?'

'I don't know. Maybe you'd been to Thailand.'

'We buried him *together*, Marko. We thought he was dead.'

She reaches across with these words, tapping them on the tabletop with her finger.

Marko wants to cup her hand in his.

'It's supposed to wash away his sins.' Marko tries to change the subject. 'This ceremony.'

'I know what ghusl is.'

'Why did he run away?'

'Why did *you* run away?'

The channels change on the television above Vesna's head. The screen flicks through an Italian shopping channel, a South American soap opera, a Turkish game show, a Serbian news channel. It rests on *Eurosport* and a German football match.

'*Did I know he was still alive*,' Vesna tuts.

'You might have done. What do I know? I haven't been here.'

'That's right,' she says. 'You haven't been here. You know why I don't watch the television? Why I don't read the newspapers? Because every time you look at anything, there it is. Having the old arguments. Digging up old graves. They don't let anyone stay dead around here.'

He takes a cigarette from her packet. Dunhill. A luxury brand in the war. She had always wanted Dunhills. 'You aren't offended? He was your boyfriend!'

'Total amnesia,' Vesna says. She is not answering him. She is still talking about herself. He reaches for her lighter.

'That's my policy. Keep moving forward. I thought you'd appreciate that. I thought: Marko's made it. Made a life for himself. I *want* you to have a life for yourself. OK? I'm *envious*.'

He cones the burning end of the cigarette on the edge of a glass ashtray with a photograph of Tito's face printed on it. Tito in his prime; the solid, square head beneath a Partisan beret; the brow furrowed in a victorious V. The same Tito who cut the ribbon on the opening of new schools. Tito looking straight through the camera and into his eyes with a stare that, as a boy, had always reminded Marko he could try harder.

'I really need a swim.'

'Is that your old van, Marko?' Vesna is looking out of the window again, across the road where he had ramped the van up a kerb.

'Did Kemal,' Marko begins but doesn't know how to finish.

She raises the question in her eyes. 'What?'

Vesna and Kemal in the basement of the apartment block. She doesn't know he was there. She has never known he was there. How can he ask her now? The girl who wants to forget everything? Did Kemal rape those women? *Did Kemal rape you? Was everything about our war a lie?*

'Marko?'

'I saw the guys last night,' he begins again. 'Samir, Elvis, Bogdan.'

'Oh.'

'Apparently there was an English woman. Some investigation into crimes committed at a camp in Ladina.'

Vesna is shaking her head. She leans forward to crush her cigarette into Tito's face. 'And you believe that?' she says. 'God, Marko. I would have thought it was a relief to know he didn't die in the shelling. At least you can stop feeling responsible. He didn't die in the shelling. Therefore it wasn't your fault. That's what you want to know, isn't it?'

'It was never my fault.'

'Because you were such a good *friend* to him.'

Her wrist is in his hand. He is holding it over the table.

'Do you know what happened?'

'Let go of me, Marko.'

He can feel her pulse at his fingers. 'I can't believe you aren't even going to the funeral.'

She pulls again. 'I already buried him. So did you.'

Marko lets go. She holds her wrist like someone stung.

'You still have that temper!'

Marko places his hands on his lap.

'Well, tell everyone I love them.' Vesna stands up and gathers her bag. And before Marko can think of what to say, she is standing at the kerb outside of the café, waiting for the traffic to pass.

Poipet

In the hotel bedroom, William flicks through television channels. *EuroNews.* Stock exchanges. CNN. A pack of hyenas. The screen unwinds a rope of images he can't quite grasp. He wants something to stop and enter him, to take him over. Whatever it was in the taxi. But nothing is enough. And Anya still isn't speaking to him.

The dugong. That is what William had been. A cold, heavy mammal, lying in the red earth of the mangrove roots. Except it had taken only one man to pull William out. They had run from the bar. Breathless in the street. Swimming in the street.

Drowning. Afterwards, the man picked William out of the mud. He had a bike, a lime-green moped, and when William climbed onto the back of the bike, he was practically naked. They switched around the tears in the road, around refrigerators, the mess of surfboards, the broken hull of a boat. William thought his leg broken, or deeply cut, but would later learn he'd escaped the wave with only scratches. The sensation of pain in his leg was the skin of his calf burning on the hot metal tank of the bike's engine.

Just a burn, the doctor told him in the hospital. Superficial. You seem to be fine.

Just a burn.

The man who rescued William was taken away on the arm of a male nurse. He had driven the bike thirty-two kilometres down the broken coast road with a straight back and straight arms, and now he seemed incapable of even standing up. A nurse bandaged William's calf, and gave him antibiotics and painkillers. When he woke on the floor of the hospital corridor, he was only one of many patients sleeping there. A woman came and gave William a pair of tracksuit bottoms – Fila, black with a white stripe down the seam. *St Mary's Immaculate Phuket.* Blue words across her yellow T-shirt. William couldn't move his leg. He couldn't *move.* He sat on the floor of the hospital corridor watching the photocopied pictures go up on the walls. ZOLTAN MOLL. *33 years old. 1.89 metres. Hungarian. Khao Lak Resort.* The pixelated Hungarian man, already disappearing in his own picture.

It had slowly dawned on William that Anya might become a picture too.

In the bathroom of the hotel, William kneels on the cold floor. *Casino Poipet.* The words crawling across the tiles. He heaves before he reaches the toilet bowl, steps around the vomit and splashes water over his face.

When he knocks on the door in the hotel corridor, it is not Missy who answers. It is a very short man with pink skin, a monk's pate and rectangular spectacles over a drunk's strawberry nose.

The wrong door. Not the door down, but the door up.

William knocks again and Missy opens it, just a crack at first.

'William?'

'Would it be possible to talk to you?'

'Yes,' she says. She winces in the light. He has woken her. 'Give me a minute.'

The door closes, leaving him with only the buzz of a soft-drinks machine. When Missy opens the door again, she shuts it behind her and stands in the corridor doing up the buttons of her shorts.

This is not what he meant. Not here.

'I haven't talked to anyone before,' he says.

'Right. You want to go to your room?'

He thinks about the mess in the bathroom. 'What about yours?'

She looks at him. 'OK,' she says. 'Wait right there.'

She closes the bedroom door again, and for a moment there is still a chance to walk away, but then the door opens and he is stepping in. The bed is neatly made, as if the place had never been occupied. There is a faint smell of sick in the air. When he sits on the dressing-table chair, William realises the smell of sick is him.

In one swift knotting, Missy climbs onto the end of the bed, bare feet on the purple duvet, and knees beneath her chin. The knees are distractingly pink.

'About the tsunami?' she says.

'It took me by surprise.' William finds himself smiling at the mistake. 'Not the tsunami, I mean, obviously that. But I mean I hadn't spoken to anyone about it until tonight. It took me by surprise.'

'Right,' Missy says.

He looks at her toes, how long they are. Her strangeness. How utterly alien she is. Her *otherness*.

He doesn't know this woman at all.

'It feels like—' He pushes his eyes into the heels of his palms. 'There are things I don't want to forget.'

'You didn't tell us much – I mean, you talked about the man rescuing you but you also mentioned your girlfriend. And you didn't really – *talk* about that.'

William shakes his head. 'I couldn't find her, afterwards. I think I fell asleep in the hospital, for almost twelve hours. Apparently it was the shock.'

'She wasn't in the hospital?'

'I thought the man who found me might have seen her. But it only occurred to me afterwards, after I'd been back to the resort and to the temples. You see, I think the guy who rescued me was this guy Anya had *been* with on the beach. This guy at the bar. But I never went to the hospital to find him. I should have done that. Maybe he knew what happened to her.'

'You said you went to look for her, at the temples?'

'That's where they were keeping the bodies they found.'

'And the man wasn't in the hospital?'

'No.'

William is about to explain when something shatters. Glass falling on a hard floor. He startles, but it is nothing in the room. The noise has come from the bathroom. Missy's eyes are pinned on William, unsure whether to acknowledge the sound. Then her face screws up, a child who knows she has done wrong. 'Sorry . . .'

The bathroom door opens. It is Henry.

'Sorry.' Henry tiptoes around the bed, naked from the waist up, holding his hands in the air like a surrendering cowboy. When he has closed the bedroom door, Missy apologises again.

'What is everyone saying sorry for?'

'Just go on,' she pleads.

But he can't.

On official visits Tito was known for asking children, 'do you work hard in school?' Born into communism, the children of Yugoslavia were its new people, unburdened by the past.

'It is only the dead who do not lie, but they have no credibility.'

Dubravka Ugrešić, *The Culture of Lies*,
translated by Celia Hawkesworth

14 September 1994

Stovnik

At the roadblock in Upper Stovnik, soldiers waved the coach through and the boys of the judo team were silenced. It had been three years since they had seen this road; into the pine forest, through the hairpins, the sound of the engine whining up, and up, as the coach geared down. The chatter returned as they climbed the road above the town. Bureks made by mothers for lunch were opened and eaten for breakfast, and there was a much anticipated fight between two boys who had insulted each other's girlfriends. But at the crest of the road, the boys fell silent again.

Most of them knew the Panorama Bistro from childhood weekends spent walking in the hills. They remembered ice cream in tall glasses, and mutton sandwiches from a roasting spit. The restaurant marked the closest to Stovnik the Chetniks had ever come. But none of them had seen what the Chetniks had done. They saw it now, as the coach slowly rounded the hairpin curve in which the restaurant was caught.

Only a single concrete wall remained, bones of twisted steel breaking from the top. The wall stood on the concrete foundations where the restaurant used to be. All that remained now – an oven door, broken chairs and the frames of windows scattered in the surrounding trees, as if a giant's hand had reached out of the forest, and dragged the building away.

The graffiti on the wall read:

ROAST THE MUSLIM PIGS

The boys sat back in their seats, Marko next to Vesna. The radio squealed between frequencies. It was the first time Marko wondered whether it was all a good idea. They had come to know what a ceasefire was. Ceasefires were not a silence on the battlefield. Ceasefires were not still moments in which people took stock. Ceasefires were a break in play, the clock still ticking on the ceasefire business to be done. Ceasefires were a time when coaches huddled around to devise new strategies, when subs limbered up, and prepared to take the field. Troops moved in the hills, and reinforced their positions. Politicians, and international peaceniks, used ceasefires to show the world the country was capable of supporting 'normal life'. The more 'normal' a life they could demonstrate, the more the Americans and Europeans pushed for the ceasefire to be maintained. In this particular ceasefire, Bosnia's district judo tournament would take place. Moreover, it would take place in Sarajevo. The big idea was this: for the first time in three years, teenagers from all over Bosnia would come together, united by the spirit of sport, in the country's threatened capital. Except so far, for the boys from Stovnik, a journey which should have taken twenty minutes, had taken two hours.

'Look,' Vesna pointed out of the window. The forests were suddenly beneath them, mountain peaks flat and unremarkable against a white morning sky. Marko didn't know what he was supposed to be looking at. Then he saw what Vesna saw. Nothing and everything: Majevica. Their mountain. The humpback whale and foothill tail they had lived and slept and dreamed under. Only now the whale appeared to be turning and swimming away. Staring at the other side of the mountain, the side they hadn't seen in more than two years, Marko felt Vesna's breath on the back of his neck, and wanted to kiss her.

'When you get there, you don't lose sight of her.' Kemal had put his hands on Marko's shoulders and held him at arm's length. He had called his friend a Croat cunt, and Marko had called him a Muslim pussy. There was something about Kemal these days. His fingers too deep in the tendons of Marko's shoulders, the jokes with a sharper edge. Kemal had not been himself since he returned from the front that summer. He had shaved his head, lost weight, developed a habit of sniffing and pulling on his nose between every sentence. At first Marko had wondered whether it was drugs. He'd even *hoped* it was drugs, and not the other thing. Not the thing happening to so many of the older boys he knew. Not the light going out. It was a great sadness to admit to himself. Some small part of him was relieved to be getting out of the same room as Kemal, if only for a few days.

'Fuck off then.' As the coach engine started up, Kemal had put his hand on Marko's head and turned him towards the boy with the camera.

The radio finally found Dino Merlin singing '*Šta ti značim ja*' and at the front of the bus, the team's coach joined in. Out of tune, the boys began to follow. When they hit the straight road across the floor of the next valley, the clouds broke, and fields of tall corn opened up on either side of them. These were the valleys where fighting was easy. In the village of Kosočić, the burned-out farmhouses and holiday homes of Bosnian Muslims stood next to the untouched homes of Bosnian Serbs. In Edrava, the burned-out homes of Bosnian Serbs stood next to the untouched homes of Muslims.

'*Sta ti znacim ja!*' The boys in the coach sang, '*Sta ti znacim ja!*'

In the village of Zabor, on every remaining wall, someone had scrawled:

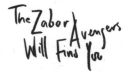

The village of Boronca had been plagued with swastikas, and on the side of the school building, someone had written:

KILL THE JEWS

On the flats in Isidor, in surprisingly educated handwriting, the graffiti delivered its joke, on each successive building:

THE SERBS   NOW

WERE ALWAYS   THEY ARE

COCKS   ONLY

BUT   BALLS

'*Sarajevo!*' the boys sang. '*Ljubavi moja!*'

When they came to the Losa River, the paved road ended in a pile of broken tarmac where the coach turned onto a dirt track, no more than a widened path clinging to the side of a gorge. Around the town of Kacko, the fields were taped off with black skulls and crossbones, warning landmines had been laid in the area.

'*Ljubavi moja!*' the boys sang. '*Sarajevo!*'

The singing in the coach only stopped when they reached a roadblock outside Vilnik, the boys struck by the sight of a tank not in a convoy heading out of Stovnik, or parked at a barracks, but actually standing in the road with the long, dark tunnel of its gun barrel pointed directly at them. UNPROFOR.

Coach Edo told the boys to stay in their seats, and climbed down to talk to one of the blue helmets at the side of the road.

'We're only at Vilnik,' Vesna whispered to Marko. 'My father said he'd be at the airport from three o'clock.'

'He'll wait,' Marko whispered.

'What if it isn't safe to wait?'

'Don't worry. I'll sort things out.' Marko knew this is what Kemal would say.

Vesna grinned. 'How will *you* sort things out?'

Marko smiled. 'I don't know!'

And suddenly they were both giggling.

'Why are we whispering?'

'I don't know!'

The doors opened, and Coach Edo climbed back on, to the applause of the boys. The barrel of the gun swung to the side of the road and pointed at the empty fields.

At Vilnik bus station, the boys lined up to relieve themselves in the overgrown grass next to a basketball court in which a Yugo sat, upside down, slam-dunked onto its roof. 'First one to hit a landmine!' one of the boys said. Another set the challenge of using their streams to spell *Fuck the Chetniks* in the air, each boy a different letter.

After peeing, the boys ran to buy chocolate from the stalls in front of the bus station, and Marko sat down at a picnic table to wait for Vesna. The only girl in the group, she had disappeared into the clearing behind the kiosk that used to sell ice creams in the times when day-trippers stopped here. He wouldn't have noticed this particular graffiti, if he wasn't waiting. It wasn't painted three metres high on apartment blocks or sprayed in giant letters across the walls of farmhouses. It was scratched into the edges of the picnic table, among the names of football teams and young lovers:

Lado loves Mirka, Enis loves Edita, FADILA 4 ADAM,

Slobodna Tuzla 4 EVER and

THEY ARE
TRYING
TO BREAK
YOUR
HEART

'Where's Vesna?' It was Coach Edo at the door of the bus. Marko was the only boy not yet on.

'I saw where she went,' Marko told him.

The wooden kiosk stood at the edge of the picnic clearing, sides plastered with stickers for Ledo Bears and Sputnik Rockets and strawberry-milk mice. At first sight, the kiosk looked open for business, and as Marko approached, he heard a buzzing sound, as though inside the hut there were some loose electric connection. The glass in the hatch of the kiosk had been smashed, and the sides were splintered with the kind of holes made by a sniper's rifle.

'Vesna?'

A breeze twitched the ears of long grass around his shins. 'Vesna, the coach is leaving!'

'Marko?' Vesna's voice came. 'I can't move.'

Marko stepped into the grass. He had heard enough of Kemal's stories to know a person who steps on a landmine is dead not when they put their foot on the pressure plate, but when they take their foot off.

Her voice sounded distant. 'Can you come here?'

Marko looked at the foot he had just planted in the grass. He pressed down. The ground beneath felt solid. He could see a clear patch of soil and placed his left foot into it. There had been none of the tape with the skulls and crossbones they had seen at the side of the road, but it didn't mean he trusted the earth.

'What do you mean you can't move?' he said.

'Just come here!'

He couldn't place it. There was something wrong with the sound of her voice. It was smaller somehow, farther away than it should have been.

'Now, Marko!'

Marko took another step, and turned the corner at the back of the kiosk.

She was a good twenty metres away, crouched down in the overgrown grass.

'Have you finished?'

'Could you come here?' Vesna wasn't looking at him. She was looking at the back of the kiosk. The grass had been beaten into a path but Marko still took delicate steps.

'What's up?'

'I know I *can* move,' Vesna said. 'But I can't.'

The breeze picked up again, and the tops of the trees behind Vesna trembled. Marko smelled the vomit, still steaming next to her.

'You feel sick?'

Then he turned to see what she saw. He saw the woman's face first. It was sliced by the light through the half-open door of the kiosk; her head resting on her shoulder and her eyes frozen in fear. His first instinct was to hold out a conciliatory palm. He did not want her to be afraid. But he stopped before the words left his mouth. And then the small hand of a breeze pushed open the kiosk door.

She was sitting on the concrete floor, back against the ice-cream refrigerator, and head bent beneath the hatch. Naked from the waist down, the woman held her knees, pulling her legs open as if she had been asked to show herself. The breeze dropped, and the door cast its shadow again.

The woman's eyes didn't move. They were fixed on the space between her legs. Her mouth hung open and her lips were black. Her skin was as white as flour. The baby's head had split her in two, its face closed as tight as a fist, one shoulder loose, black with dried blood. The floor danced in neat, sudden squares. Flies. Marko sank down until he squatted in the grass next to Vesna, his eyes level with the woman. No woman at all. Little more than a village girl, a faint moustache of puberty on her upper lip.

Marko took Vesna's hand and pulled her up. Stumbling back to the coach he was falling; falling and Vesna trailing after him. The feeling he had diving off the cliffs at Lake Borače.

They would tell Coach Edo. There was nothing to be done for the girl but someone should be told. Tripping onto the steps of the bus, Marko opened his mouth but instead of anything coming out, his ears were filled with the din of wolf whistles and whooping.

'Nice move, Marko!' One of the boys led the calls.

They clapped him on the back and pushed him down the aisle.

'You guys deserve the back seat!'

'Hey – Marko – Kemal's going to cut your dick off.'

A wave of arms pushed them to the rear of the coach, the team crowding in and clapping, stomping a rhythm until Edo told them all to sit down and shut up. Marko tried to swallow what he had just seen but it kept coming back. Vesna shuffled to the end of the rear seat and pressed her face up against the window. He stared at the seat in front of him. Zurab's eyes appeared between the headrests, offering a fraternal look of sympathy. Marko turned away.

The engine shuddered, and the coach turned around. They were back on the road, the hills moving like slow ships, taking the dead woman away.

'The radio!' one of the boys shouted. 'Music! Give us music!'

Christmas Night, 2004

Kao Lak

Anya sat in the sand. A firework glittered across the sky and popped, falling flashbulbs turning to smoke and drizzling into the sea. The last time she was at a fireworks night, it had been an English November, where explosions lit the bellies of grey clouds. Had she been with William then? She couldn't remember. So much of her life had been with William, and being with him again seemed to erase the years alone. Time didn't go forward, it concertinaed. All those years without William drawn out, and then pushed together. Anya was rushing to meet her past. No wonder it had ended in a collision. She had been in the kitchen filling a glass with water when he kissed her neck. She dropped the glass and it shattered in the sink.

What are you doing?

It didn't seem to matter that it was what she wanted. These were the words which came out of her mouth. She didn't move. He grabbed a handful of her hair and pulled. His hand slipped into her shorts but she stopped him.

You don't get to have this.

His mouth felt like the mouth of a stranger. His neck a stranger's neck. She turned around. It was the look on his face she wanted to see. She wanted his anger. She thought about walking out, telling him she needed to shower. He knelt down in front of her.

What do you think you're doing?

On the beach, Anya sat up and held her knees. Colours shimmered on the water, magnifying the light in the sky. The night turned red. Then yellow. Then orange. Then a white so bright she had to shade her eyes.

She didn't quite have the willpower to hold him off. He bent her over the bed, face down. But something was wrong. He was fumbling between her legs, he was taking too long. She turned over and pulled him on top of her, determined if it was going to happen, it would happen on *her* terms. Then it had all gone wrong. When she pulled his cock from his trousers, it had flopped out like something shy of the light, some nervous creature disturbed from its sleep beneath a rock. The life went out of their kissing. He made an excuse to go to the bathroom. He took so long she almost thought it might be more polite to *leave* the bedroom.

When he came out, he asked if she wanted a drink, and eventually she found him sitting in the lounge area, both glasses made up on the wicker coffee table, flicking through her copy of the *New Republic*.

'I've lost touch with what's going on in the world,' he said. 'You used to keep me up with current affairs.'

Anya really didn't mean to, but the innuendo was standing right there in front of them, bold as a naked man. *Keeping him up*. She held her hand over her mouth to stifle the laugh.

'What?'

'Nothing. Really. It's nothing.'

She told William she was going to the fireworks display, but he said he didn't fancy it. The way he turned the pages of the magazine was a mark of disapproval, and the perfect example of everything that had started to go wrong with their relationship. Not the beginning, but the end. The William who assumed his decisions would also be hers.

'I'll see you later,' she said. 'If you're still up.'

A young couple lay among flares stuck in the sand like some ridiculous advertisement for mobile phone networks; the boy handsomely bare-chested, the girl wearing just a light shift over her bikini. Anya wrapped her arms around herself. She was cold, and old. A small fishing boat floated in the bay, disappearing in the dark, appearing again, curtained and then reborn as the smoke died over the water; Kemal Lekić lit the fireworks from its prow. Every now and then, Anya saw him stand up, bend down or walk aft, presumably to unbox another rocket. A lopsided yellow ring exploded above the bay. Another bigger, bigger still. Something dark passed through the circles, crackled into a white spray and left the glowing embers falling over their heads.

Anya stood up and stepped back in the sand, upsetting her ankle on something. Someone's leg.

'Sorry!'

There could have been thirty, perhaps forty people on the beach, all lying on a narrow strip of sand between the shallows and a pitch-roofed beach house on stilts. She recognised a man with a white beard from the bar, and the English nurse from the bathroom. Most of the crowd were expats, but some local boys sat in the sand on the edges of the group, and farther down, along the curve of the bay, an older Thai couple drank something steaming in paper cups. She wandered over to the steps, leaned against the wooden banisters and found herself standing over a dark-haired man in combat shorts and an orange cycling mac. A rocket whistled up. The crowd oohed. In the blue flash, Anya looked back along the beach for any sign of William. But the only silhouettes belonged to the shock-headed figures of coconut trees. When the sky darkened again, the lights of the hotel resort on the headland seemed farther away than the fifteen minutes it had taken her to walk.

'Are you English?' It was the man sitting on the step, the one in the orange cycling mac. He sounded German. 'Do you want to sit down?'

Anya shook her head. The sign on the banister pointed up the steps. 'Toilet', and next to it a sketch of the item in case there should be any confusion.

Kemal Lekić's toilet was in a shed on the veranda behind the house. Anya closed the door behind her, and had to open it again to find the light switch on the end of a cord. In the dim light of the naked bulb, she locked the door, sat down on the closed lid and felt her heart beating big in the small room. It all belonged to him: a toilet-paper holder, an air-freshener Buddha hanging over a small stone sink, a broken shard of mirror. She sat and listened to the fireworks shudder, the booms ricocheting through the mangroves at the back of the house. When she was a schoolgirl, Anya had trespassed on the playing fields, on a Sunday. She had climbed onto the roof of the school with a boy called James, who was from the Catholic secondary. She had always retained an absolutely perfect memory of climbing the fire escape at the side of the school building with James, before realising they would be completely visible to anyone walking down School Road or the great number of people who walked their dogs on the playing fields. On the roof, she had been using James's penknife to scratch her name into one of the air-conditioning units when the caretaker had discovered them. This was no schoolgirl prank, but when she tried the door handle at the back of Kemal's beach house, she almost expected the caretaker to catch her again.

The door to Kemal Lekić's house opened. Anya was entering, if not quite breaking.

For what felt like a long time, she stood, pressing her back to the door. She watched the fireworks light the walls of the room. A red flash of bookshelves, yellow flash of a surfboard, blue flash of the beaded curtain on to a kitchen. She knew the plausibility of her excuses diminished with every step, but her feet were moving, and had found a deep-pile rug between the sofa and the chairs of a lounge. A door to her right opened on to another pitch-black room. It sounded as though the fireworks were in the house, and even when they stopped, the echo fooled her ears.

'Hello?' she called out. 'I'm looking for the toilet – I may well be completely lost. Hello?'

A firework cracked in response. The new room flashed green: a double bed behind a mosquito curtain, white sheets rolled back, but no other covers. Shelves ran the length of the wall to her right. No books, just CD cases. She walked along them, reading the spines: Def Leppard, Metallica, Michael Jackson, Bon Jovi, Ministry of Sound. Nothing particular or identifying. None of the music she had learned about on her trips to the Balkans. No Dino Merlin or Bijelo Dugme. No nice, corroborating collection of Bosnian folk music. Any farther into the room, and Anya knew she would find the pretence of being lost very hard to keep up. But she was doing this for Ljuba. It was really Ljuba's right to be here. Ljuba's right to walk into the home of the man who had raped her, and take whatever she needed. It was not a violation. The violation had already been committed. This man was supposed to be dead.

Anya did not know exactly what she was looking for – some evidence to verify who 'Chuck' really was perhaps – but it seemed to her the man whose house this was had no real right to it.

The room came to life in a bright, white light and when it fell dark, Anya was absolutely certain the ghost at her back had turned into someone real. Someone standing behind her.

She spun around to face a girl.

Cheers and applause rose from the beach. It was her reflection in a mirrored wardrobe. Next to the wardrobe, a desk, and a computer, and the Windows screensaver bouncing slowly from one edge of the monitor to another. She turned around. There were no drawers and no paper in the printer; nothing in Serbo-Croat. She tapped the space bar on the computer keyboard. A photograph unrolled over the screen. A group of men standing in front of a coach. The men wore the white robes of a martial arts team. Four wore the fatigues of a brigade. It startled her to see it. The detail which Ljuba had given her. One of the horrible details which until now, had only been in her imagination. But here it was. The red sash around Kemal Lekić's arm.

The background of the picture told Anya almost as much as the subject; the front half of a dirty coach in the Stovnik district. The white and yellow buses she had travelled on herself, and the wooden destination plate by its door.

Stovnik – Vilnik – Sarajevo.

Anya tapped the space bar again. A password box appeared.

She had been too absorbed to notice the fireworks had stopped. But stopped they had. On the beach, people were standing up, some already heading off along the shore, marching with their stakes of fire; at the water's edge, the beached boat was empty.

Anya sprinted to the bedroom door, but as she reached the threshold, heard footsteps on the veranda, and voices. Voices terribly close. Panicking, she turned around, faced the bedroom again, heard the creak of the first screen door, fell to her knees and felt along the underside of the bed.

It was too low.

She heard the latch.

They were in the house.

'I made some this year – it's so good.' A man's voice, a flood of chattering and the floorboards of the beach house springing beneath her knees. The light in the next room came on, casting its net over the floor of the bedroom. She crushed herself beneath the desk.

They were in the room. Two men.

'I have a CD here somewhere,' the first man said.

His bare legs stopped at the edge of the bed. His feet moved, pointing away from her.

'Somewhere . . .' the man repeated.

It was him. She heard the tick, tick, tick of the CD boxes, falling like dominoes as his fingers worked through them.

'Here,' Kemal Lekić said, 'is what I am . . .' Thoughts finished with the tick, tick, tick of the plastic cases.

Through the thin walls, Anya could hear the lounge filling with the excitement of a party.

She would act completely crazy, off-her-tits, fall through the crowd, roll her eyes, drunkenly apologise, run away, down the empty beach.

'Have you found it?' Another voice. Kiwi. The New Zealander from the boat house. Anya closed her eyes.

'I know I have it,' he said, 'I have volumes one and two. But then I'm sure I bought – ah!'

She thought the silence would kill her.

'Bullseye,' the Kiwi said. 'Awesome.'

'You see.'

She heard the bedroom door close.

Ljuba Crvenović's face had been held to the floor. Hand at the back of her head, pushing down as if it would never stop. As if the force didn't know her head could go no farther. Concrete. Not the floorboards against which Anya breathed in the bedroom of Kemal's beach house. The soldier held down the mother of two small children, and entered her from behind so he couldn't be seen. Her friends were close. Close enough for Ljuba to feel the spit of their breath, faces squashed against the floor like rotten fruit, all the goodness, all the life being squeezed out of them. At first Ljuba had closed her eyes with the will of a child who believes the world disappears when they can't see it. But her friend's screams opened them. The faces of her friends, the boots of the men. Who dared do this to them? The hand of the man appeared before her eyes, palm down, pressed to the floor, knuckles white, fingers grasping a cheap plastic bag, like the kind she would use to carry vegetables home from the supermarket. Before the bag was wrapped around Ljuba's head, the red sash fell to his wrist. The red sash of the commander.

The red sash of Kemal Lekić.

The red sash in the picture on the computer screen.

A bass rhythm broke out in the room next door. Anya listened to the music and voices, and tried to control her breathing. The quicker the better. She was on her knees. She was standing up. She was at the bedroom door with the wooden handle in her hand.

'That is not the toilet!' she announced, bursting into the room. But no one turned. No one appeared to even notice her entrance. A man wearing a baseball cap leant against the wall next to the bedroom door.

'Do you know where the toilet is?' she asked.

The man looked her up and down. A small group had gathered around him. She had interrupted a story.

'I've never been here,' the man said.

It seemed as if half the beach had emptied into the house. She pushed past the group next to the wall, and saw the German in the orange cycling mac, looking at her hopefully. Turning back, she wheeled into the middle of the room, where a gap had formed around a glass coffee table, and a man unloaded an armful of canned beers. Taking one, she opened it, drank from it and couldn't stop drinking. It was warm. Her hands were shaking. She drank again. She tried to hide her smile with the can. She had done it. She was safe.

She felt a hand on her shoulder.

'I rescued you,' he said when she turned around.

Anya tried to keep a fixed face. 'I'm sorry – you're . . . ?'

'From today,' he said. 'The boat.'

'Yes.'

'Chuck.' He offered her a wink instead of a handshake. In one pupil a silver fleck floated. Hypnotised by it, she wondered if something wasn't stuck in her own eye.

'Chuck,' she repeated.

'But I don't know *your* name.' He pointed with the can, knuckles white in his tan. The fist Ljuba Crvenović had seen.

'And your name?'

'Anya.'

'Anya. It's a good name. I knew a Dutch girl called Anya.'

'Chuck,' she said, 'Chuck. Is that a real name? I mean – I know it's real,' she chattered through her nerves, 'but I never heard of anyone called Chuck, and I guess it's American and you don't sound American.'

'I don't?'

'No, there's something—'

'Is not America the land of *all* nations?'

He was flirting with her.

'Yes, of course, I'm being – rude. But I would have to guess you weren't born in America, even if you lived there.'

'You would guess right.'

He looked around the party now, as if missing somebody. He was a big man. Broad. Hairs beneath his vest. His chest met the level of her eye. When she looked up, it was the muscles of his neck and shoulders that impressed her first. She felt sick.

'So where is it?' Anya asked. 'Where are you originally from?'

'Is your friend here?'

'Friend?'

'Your friend on the boat?'

He meant William. 'Oh yes. No. No, he's not. He had an early night tonight.'

'I never lived in America actually.' He smiled. 'I was born in Bosnia.'

In the suitcase in her apartment, Anya had a photograph taken at this man's funeral. Whatever she expected from a dead man, she did not expect the truth.

'Do you know Bosnia?' He saved her from her muteness. 'It is a small country next to Croatia and Serbia, which are next to Italy, on the beautiful Adriatic Sea.'

'So your name isn't really Chuck?'

He laughed, his fingers brushing her wrist. 'No,' he said. 'But it's what people call me. Like Chuck Norris. I used to be the big fan of Chuck Norris.' He made karate hands and a drop of beer jumped from the can onto her shoulder. He reached over and brushed it off. 'Although I would rather be Bruce Lee. I didn't like the name Bruce. Not so much.'

'You do – whatever it is Chuck Norris does?' she said hopelessly.

'Mixed martial arts? Yes. Jeet Kune Do, to be technical. It was very popular in Yugoslavia.'

Anya's mouth was dry.

'So. When you were born, the country was Yugoslavia, and then it became Bosnia. That was the war, wasn't it?'

'Please. Not the *war*.'

'Of course, of course,' she said. 'Sorry – ignore me, I'm always putting my foot in it.'

'I'm sure I don't need to tell you about the war.'

Anya pressed the can to her lips. It was empty. There was nowhere left to hide. 'Thank you so much for the fireworks and the party,' she said.

Kemal took a step back and opened his arms. 'You aren't leaving?'

'I really have to.' Anya bent over and tried to find a space for the empty can on the littered coffee table behind her. 'My boyfriend will start to worry.'

'Ah – of course. Not a friend then. A boyfriend. I understand. What a pity.'

He held her wrist and took the empty can. 'I'll dispose of this for you.'

They straightened up together. He let go of her wrist.

'You never found out my real name,' he said.

'Oh – your real name?'

'Marko.' Kemal Lekić offered his hand to be shook.

All her courage had suddenly left her. 'Well – goodbye, Marko.'

'It's a very popular name,' he shouted after her. 'In Bosnia!'

Anya almost tumbled down the steps of the house. She turned left and skipped at a pace across the beach. Each footfall in the loose sand seemed the effort of two. But the light and noise of the party dimmed. Safer in the dark she began to run, slowly at first, then faster.

Ljuba had run too. The next night. The women decided to run as darkness fell. Whatever lay in the forests beyond the factory would be better than what happened to them there. No one stopped them as they ran across the car park. No one stopped them as they climbed the low wire fence. No one expected anyone would want to leave. They ran along the road by which they arrived. Anya darted towards the shoreline, onto sand that was damp and compact, and easier beneath her feet. Ljuba had told her how it felt, when someone was at your back. To hear the sound of gunfire and not know whether it came from behind you, or in front. In the back of your head, or in your face. Ljuba had dived into the darkness of the trees. It was the last time she saw the other two women.

Anya slowed down, hand over her mouth, trying not to look back. But she did look back. She had to. The distant beach house resembled a ship sitting over the bay, a necklace of fairy lights strung along the veranda and figures floating in a pool of golden light.

Sunday 10 April 2005

Stovnik

Jujube berries float in water turned the pink of dental rinse. Marko is given a sponge from the plastic orange bucket. The imam turns out to be a stocky little man called Munib. He wipes his nose with a handkerchief and appears to have a heavy cold. To Marko's relief, Munib has washed the excretory organs already. Where the ghusl cannot be performed in full, Munib explains, *We must do our best.* Munib gives Marko a flannel cloth and tells him to dip it into the silver bowl of water. He must wash Kemal's hands and arms, three times, from the fingertips to the elbows. The water is tepid. They begin with the right side of Kemal's body, over the shoulders. Marko can't shake the idea he is not washing Kemal Lekić, but a *statue* of Kemal Lekić. Embalming and freezing have hardened his friend's body. The skin has the quality of wax, and the face, although certainly Kemal's, has the look of a beaten boxer. Is it something the brain haemorrhage has done? Kemal's eyes are closed and Marko wants to tell him to wake up, to look at him straight.

'In cleaning the body we clean the spirit,' Munib says.

Marko washes Kemal's feet, his toes. Parts of a body he has held before, parts he has gripped, trapped and pinned. This is all some elaborate joke. Any second now Kemal is going to leap from the table and grab Marko's wrist, wrench his arm behind his back and pin him to the floor.

To know oneself is to study oneself in action with another person. It is not the imam, it is Kemal speaking. Not the Koran but the *Tao*. Kemal circling Marko on the mats.

Look into the eyes of your opponent, the eyes will tell you not where the hand is, but where the hand will be. Learn the habits of your opponent's mind and you will learn the habits of his body.

The imam begins to mutter something, a prayer Marko doesn't understand. If Marko didn't know why Kemal had run away, who *would* know? Who could better anticipate Kemal than he could? Marko is not sorry Kemal survived the shelling. He is almost happy to see his friend lying here, reassembled. He is glad Kemal kept his body and walked around in it, lived another life, lived another future. He deserved a future. How could he blame Kemal for running away? To know oneself is to study oneself in action with another person. What hurts is to know this future didn't include him. What hurts Marko is to know Kemal could let him grieve for no reason. The years spent blaming himself for a death that never happened.

'We will wash with camphor,' the imam says. 'After the water.'

The mortuary hums. Its refrigeration units have a rhythm, and every minute or so there is a sound like a distant tide pulling over stones; a reminder the mortuary's body bags are still full of bones from the war. There is no mystery to the smell. The room is a freezer full of rotting things.

'Is this the first time you've met Kemal?' Marko asks.

The imam gives him the cloth soaked in camphor. 'Yes – but of course I knew him by reputation.'

Marko wipes the rag over his dead friend's shoulders. He only thinks of the tattoo, because the tattoo has gone. It is an absence. A missing piece of their past. There is a grey patch of scarred skin where the Bosnian lily of the brigade used to be. The patch left speaks of nothing, and everything; something from the life Kemal had after the war, after Marko. Samir had told him, you believe what you want to believe. He had told Marko he was there, at the camp, and that he knew Kemal did nothing. The ceremony is supposed to be about the forgiveness of Kemal's sins. But it is Marko who needs forgiving. He needs Kemal to open his eyes, sit up and forgive *him*. Forgive him for not believing. Forgive him for running away. Forgive him for Vesna.

Marko pulls the cloth over Kemal's face and it catches on the bristles still growing in his cheeks.

'It's a humane thing.' Marko is stopped by the sound of Kemal's voice in his head. 'To put them down, Marko. You are stopping the suffering.'

Bangkok

The field on the other side of the carriageway becomes a central reservation. Headlights sweep by, and out of the night, white lines shoot from the road. The scrub turns into a metal barrier, a fuchsia-coloured taxi overtakes, a late evening coach travels east, a limousine joins the airport road and distant downtown lights the clouds. Bangkok.

Leaving the border, Missy had attempted to start some kind of conversation. But William had held himself in. They had stopped to pick up some water (Dr Pepper for Missy), and afterwards she had wheeled her seat back and fallen asleep. Since then he has been alone at the wheel, dreaming the road.

The flyover carries them over suburb shacks.

Stratton, Stratton, Stratton. The joins in the concrete finally wake her.

'Good morning.' Missy wipes her mouth with the back of her arm. 'Or good evening.'

He hears her nails scratching at an armpit. He asks her where she would like to be dropped and she tells him any Skytrain station is fine.

The road rises past the glowing red neon of the Don Muaeng airport, where lights blink on the runways. William thinks about Anya's suitcase, about turning off and asking Missy to wait while he goes inside. At some point he will have to let her go. But not yet. They have passed the turning. The rear-view mirror is bright with headlights and billboards loom over them again; a pretty Thai girl in secretary's clothes riding a scooter right out of the picture, Samsung, INTOUCH mobile, a billboard with an extended, gold frame like a baroque mirror, containing a portrait of King Rama IX.

World Wide Girls Go! Go!
Wild West Boys. Boys. Boys.
The Sheba Club! The Sheba Club!

The toll road sets them down beneath the Skytrain tracks, the car washed red, blue and green in the din of the clubs. They squeeze into the traffic, among the pastel taxicabs and riots of tuk-tuks.

'Right back where we started,' Missy says.

A blinking red river of traffic carries them into the colder light of the business district where the signs mean even less;

Verstec, Zuellig, Translation, Bonnavure; past the steps to the station at Si Lom, the junction in all directions and a stone elephant, dwarfed by the concrete pillars of the tracks. The elephant stands in the central reservation, raising its trunk in a gesture utterly futile.

'I may as well drive you home,' William says.

'From here? Probably it's going to be quicker on the train.'

'Where are you going?'

'Sukhumvit. Down around soi forty-two.'

William takes the left, skirting Lumphini Park where the traffic is eased by the three lanes of Rama IV. After a few streets, Missy directs him left again. They cut over to Sukhumvit, down one of the narrow soi of walled houses, where night-hawkers line the pavement, their stalls beneath tired beach umbrellas.

'Angkor was just awesome,' Missy says, seeming to warm up with the relief of home, 'and this whole thing, however the school fucked up with the visa, I'm really grateful for how you've handled this. Hey. We turned a disaster into an adventure!'

Why does everything she says make him bristle? And why does he suddenly not want her to leave?

'Over here,' Missy says.

He pulls the car up by a tarpaulin-covered food court opposite one of the local hospitals. Strip lights hang from wires, over steaming mobile kitchens. There's a 7-Eleven and a soup stand. The covered court is full of nurses in their pink T-shirts and blue trousers.

'Here?' he asks.

'Well, I'm literally round the corner, but it's not good to stop at the next junction.' Missy opens the glove compartment and takes out her passport, complete with new visa. 'Don't want to forget this!'

He expects to hear the car door open, but she shifts in her seat. 'I'm sorry about what happened at the hotel, that's not really me.'

'Why does everyone keep apologising to me?'

'Sorry.' Her tone changes. 'I mean. No, I guess I'm *not* sorry.'

'If you want to fuck strangers, what business is that of mine?'

'Excuse me?'

'Maybe your boyfriend's business, but not mine.'

'My boyfriend?'

'The one all over your phone.'

If William takes his hands off the steering wheel, they will shake.

Missy looks at him, speechless, like a child slapped around the face. He wants to put back what he has just said but the anger he suddenly feels is boundless.

'Goodbye,' she says.

When she opens the door, it seems incredible to him she is actually going; offensive the chatter of the food court flooding in. She stands on the broken pavement with one hand on the open door, and lowers her head. 'I was *not* apologising for my actions!'

Then William is slammed back into the silence of the car, and Missy is walking around a party of motorbike couriers, into the night. He can't seem to let go of the steering wheel, can't lift his foot off the brake. His arms and legs feel weightless. As useless as he had been in the bedroom with Anya.

The car door opens. Missy is back. She sits down with a sigh, closes the door carefully and reaches into her back pocket to take out her mobile phone.

'This is my brother Ricky.' Her hands shake when she holds up the phone. She shows William the picture of the man on her menu screen, before returning it to her lap and flicking through to the gallery. 'He came to Thailand a couple of years ago. *We* came to Thailand, I mean. It was the first time I came, with Ricky. That's when I decided I wanted to come back and work here.'

At first, William thinks Missy is looking for a particular picture, but then he realises she is just thumbing through them, a tenderness in the gesture – adjusting here, stopping there. She shows William the picture of her brother on a river taxi floating past the Grand Palace.

'Angkor Wat was on Ricky's bucket list,' Missy says. 'The Far East. But we had to choose between Angkor Wat and Singapore in the end, and we went to Singapore.'

'I've never been to Singapore.'

'It sucks – I mean, it's prettier than Bangkok but compared to here? Dead.'

When he looks into her eyes, her face takes on a different shape. The point of focus has shifted. He sees a completely different painting.

'We did Bangkok, and went to Singapore, and Malaysia, and then we hopped the islands down to Australia. Our parents gave us some of the money, but we ended up so completely broke on our last days in Sydney, living off these cheap tins of hot dogs – I never want to eat another hot dog in my life!'

'I was never a hot dog man.'

'Oh, I used to eat hot dogs. Believe me I could eat hot dogs.'

'It's a New Jersey thing, isn't it?'

'Not so much, more Manhattan.'

'Yes, of course.'

Missy takes a breath. 'Never mind that you were looking through the pictures on my phone.'

William takes his hands off the steering wheel but doesn't know where to put them.

'Sorry. It was an accident.'

'The bucket list thing,' Missy says. 'What I mean is, at least I got to do that with Ricky. He was supposed to, like, *die* three times, but the treatments kept working so damn well it was almost a joke with us. You know? *So Ricky*, we'd say, *how many more months this time?*

William can't look at her. He looks out of his side window at a woman rooting through her clutch bag. She has walked out of the 7-Eleven, one of those miracles of Thai womanhood; clean black hair, perfectly fitted black dress and polished cream heels on a cracked pavement littered with food waste and plastic bags.

'With you. It must have been, almost the opposite,' she says. 'You didn't *know* like that. One minute your girlfriend is there and then—'

'She wasn't my girlfriend. I mean she *was*,' William begins. 'And she was more than – girlfriend just doesn't sound right.'

'I understand.'

'I don't know why she wasn't just in bed. In the bungalow. If she'd been there, we wouldn't even have been on the beach when the wave came. But she'd gone out that morning, back to the beach bar. I found her talking to this guy. We were all together when the wave came, at the beach bar. The same guy picked me up and drove me to the hospital. But I couldn't find him afterwards.'

The silence of the car is the reply he is used to. The silence in his head when he asks himself what happened. 'Not that any of it matters now.'

He watches the woman on the pavement clip her bag together and walk down the shattered street as if she were walking down a red carpet for the premiere of a film. He had never met another woman like Anya. He had never admired another woman as much. And he had thought when he called her in London that he wanted her. He did, he did want her. He just didn't know she was his best friend, not his lover.

'It does still matter,' Missy says, 'what happened matters. I think if that guy, the one who rescued you, if he might know what happened to her – Even if he just, shared that experience with you, you should try and find him at least.'

'I don't know where I'd start without a name,' William says. 'And I'm sorry about your brother. About the phone.'

Missy doesn't reply. They are both with their ghosts.

'You know, I would still like to start work on Thursday,' she eventually says. 'I hope that won't be a problem.'

In the hours before the Boxing Day Tsunami, people reported seeing flamingos, elephants and other wild animals, heading for high ground. Domestic dogs and zoo animals refused to leave their shelters. Approximately 283,000 people were killed, but very few animals were reported dead, or missing.

Boxing Day, 2004

Kao Lak

Anya eased herself up against the head of the bed and looked down on Will's long back, on the dimples of Venus. He coughed in his sleep. His right leg shifted, pulling the sheet down with it. A hand came out from beneath the pillow, bunching it under his head. She waited until the burr of his sleeping breath returned, and was about to step down from the bed, when something on the side table caught her eye. A drawing. The notebook was open. Not a proper sketchbook like the ones William would leave around their various homes, but something cheap and lined, with a picture of the Lion King on the cover. Not that it detracted from the skill of William's familiar hand. It was the skiff they had been on the day before, a few lines making the hull sit perfectly in the water, transforming the paper into the ocean. The boat balanced near the horizon, only two small smudges suggesting the figures occupying it. She put the notebook back, wishing now that she had woken him in the night.

Slipping off the bed, Anya showered quickly, and put on her bathing suit with the resort's robe. Before she left, she took one last look at him, soft, behind the mosquito curtain, like an aged painting.

Finding facts. It was in her job description. The presentation and analysis of facts. Fact: Kemal Lekić was alive. Fact: Kemal Lekić had been accused of rape, implicated in the disappearance of two women, the abuse of his military role and at least one breach of the Geneva Convention.

The *analysis* of facts in the advocacy of the victims of human rights abuses, this too was Anya's job. Ljuba Crvenović's human rights had been abused. She had related the circumstances of her case to Anya, and Anya had established facts in the case which were not known to the authorities in the country where those abuses took place. Wasn't this exactly Anya's purpose? Wasn't it her ability to do this job, and do it well, which had been the reason for the Stovnik policeman's call to her that afternoon in Sarajevo?

You were seen visiting Vesna Knežević.

Anya should have spoken to the regional office of the International Criminal Tribunal. She could at least have mentioned the rumours about Kemal. She could have asked the investigators there to scrutinise the findings of the Stovnik police. But she hadn't even reported Bogdan's behaviour. She had failed then, and if she did not report Kemal Lekić to the relevant authorities, she would be failing now.

In only a few weeks' time, those authorities would no longer be the International Criminal Tribunal but the War Crimes Chamber of Bosnia. This transfer of duties might play into Ljuba's hands. The country was being asked to clean up its own shit now, and by all accounts, there was a political willpower to do so. Cases like this, stalled by local authorities who had been reluctant to investigate, might be exactly the kind of case the new War Crimes Chamber would be eager to pick up. To not report what she had discovered would not only be a failure of Anya's function, but might be considered aiding and abetting a man wanted for questioning.

The mangroves leaned in on her hangover. On the treetop walkway, the day was so bright, and so hot, the events of the previous night seemed only more impossible.

'Have you seen my giraffe?'

It was a little girl suddenly at Anya's knee.

'Wow, that is a beautiful giraffe.' She smiled, and tapped the inflatable animal under the girl's arm.

'His name,' the girl announced, 'is Scarf. But Daddy said he will only get smaller and smaller.'

'Oh,' Anya said, casting around but seeing no parent. 'Smaller and smaller?'

'He *was* really big. But today he is really small.'

'I see.' Anya looked back past the cabin, down towards the beach. There was no one in that direction either.

'It's because of the hole,' the girl said.

'Are you on your own?' Anya asked.

The girl looked at her. Her mouth seemed so tiny and pink. 'I have a brother, a mummy and a daddy, and a baby sister. And lots of friends and cuddlies. And a Night Garden game. I can show you if you want to?'

'Are they all at the resort?'

The girl nodded. 'Daddy said the hole is very funny, isn't it, because it is in the giraffe's bottom.' She presented Anya with the giraffe's rear. It was patched over with rubber from a puncture repair kit. 'This stops the air coming out!' the girl declared proudly

'Oh – that's very good,' Anya said. 'Where *are* Mummy and Daddy?'

'We're on holiday,' the girl said. 'Are *you* on holiday?'

'Yes – just like you.' Anya felt breathless, it was so bloody hot. 'And you – you're staying in one of these cabins, do you know which one?'

The girl picked at the patch on the giraffe's bottom, but said nothing.

'I think we need to find Mummy and Daddy,' Anya said.

But all of a sudden, the girl turned and fled, giraffe bumping along behind her.

It was only when Anya reached the hotel's reception that she remembered she hadn't left a note for Will.

The presentation of facts in the advocacy of the victims of human rights abuses. Fact: Ljuba Crvenović had accused Kemal Lekić of rape. Fact: the parents of two other women wanted the Stovnik brigade questioned over the disappearance of their daughters. Fact: the Stovnik police had investigated the accusation and found no grounds for indictment, partly because Ljuba was the only named witness in the event. As for the missing women, the Stovnik brigade had logged their presence at the camp, and claimed not to have seen them after its disbandment.

Kemal Lekić could only be a wanted man if he was alive. But even then, Ljuba's case might go nowhere.

It all came back to the same thing. If Anya had any grounds to believe the case should be reinvestigated, the time to make use of them had been after her visit to Vesna, when the job should have been handed over to someone who knew how to build a case. Fact: Ljuba Crvenović had not explicitly asked Anya in her capacity as a researcher for Dignity Monitor to advocate on her behalf. For Anya, Ljuba Crvenović's story was only a fact in as much as it pertained to the report on problems for returnees. The rest was not her job.

But was it a duty?

Anya lay face down on the massage table. She closed her eyes. The affectionate patter of a bongo. Plucked strings, skipping with the rhythm of stones over water.

To remain impartial. To apply objectivity. To gather testimony and frame it for the record . . .

To take people at their word, and organise points of view for reports which made recommendations at a policy level . . .

This did not necessarily mean working with facts. It meant working with truth. Truths as people wanted to tell them. The truth of the world as they saw it. For Ljuba, in her apartment now, folding the ends of a toilet roll, getting her husband's dinner ready, the truth was this: Kemal Lekić was dead. The man who raped her was dead, and the fate of her friends would be forever unknown, and there was nothing more to be done about it. For the husband at work, looking forward to his dinner, his wife had survived the war unscathed, they had both survived, and now he had three children, and a good job, and an apartment in Belgrade. For those children, the truth was this: their parents survived the war. They lived in a happy family. Their mother was an angel who kept their bedrooms tidy, and folded the toilet paper, and read them stories every night. She was not a woman raped by Bosniak soldiers, who feared going home because of the men who treated her with less dignity than a goat.

So who was Anya to upset these truths with her facts? If she disturbed Ljuba's case, if she told Ljuba that Kemal Lekić was alive, would the new truth be better than the old?

The brace at the head of the massage table was tight. She heard the handle of the door, the door closing, the slippers of the masseuse over the tiled floor, a tap running, the sound of stones knocked together in a pail and the wheesh of steam.

For the briefest moment, Anya felt all the hairs on her body stand to attention. She had the sensation of her skin lifting, a premonition of touch, before the first brusque hand prepared her back with the oils.

Kemal Lekić had touched her. He had held her wrist, as he held the wrist of Ljuba Crvenović. He was alive now, but only for Anya. Anya who had only ever had the power to present truth, but now had the power make it.

'That's amazing,' Anya said more because she needed to make a noise than anything else. The hot stones seemed to open her, to make new acres out of the muscles in her back. A path of stones cut through grass silvery and thick, like a dog's fur.

It was springtime in the Brecon Beacons. With William she was walking over the hills. They broke over the tops, and one beacon looked on to another, like giant dogs watchful over the steep valleys. They stood on a summit, by a pile of slate stones marking the place where a Wellington bomber had crashed at some point during the Second World War, Will picking over the ribcage, rusted almost to nothing. It was a surprise to find the skeleton wreckage, left all these decades as a memorial. On a plaque, there was a story. It was something about a Canadian flight crew who had crashed in foul weather. Beneath them the shadows of clouds sailed over the valley. Will told her to face the blustering wind and open her mouth. And so she had. They had both opened their mouths and let the warm spring wind fill them like balloons. And when they were full, they had turned from the wind, and let it pour out of them like water.

'I'm pregnant,' Anya had gasped, bending over and holding her knees.

I'm pregnant. The words didn't feel real because they were words a woman rehearsed all her life.

The masseuse paused and positioned one hand on each of Anya's shoulder blades. Slowly but surely she pressed down, and Anya felt a sharp pain in her breasts as the air pushed out of her lungs. She sighed, but the pressure kept building. As her breath leaked out, Anya felt the world rushing in; the room first, then the buildings of the complex, then the mangroves, the island and the ocean surrounding the island, all sucked up into her empty chest.

Anya was an only child. She had never been good with children. Never had a chance to understand them. What use would she really have been at the age of twenty-four with a child? She still had her PhD to finish, a career to start. They said it would be fairer on the child this way. Those were the words they kept returning to. The mantra they repeated. Fairer on the child. The decision made together three weeks after that day on the hills. Fairer on the child.

The world rushed out again. The masseuse removed her hands and Anya felt as though she were being lifted; as though she were beginning to float above the massage table. She needed to know Will remembered. She needed to know he remembered the thing *neither* of them *wanted* to remember. How after the abortion they had never really been the same.

She couldn't bear it all herself any more.

The masseuse gripped her left ankle, and the other hand began to pull at each of her toes – click, click and click. She bent Anya's leg forward and forced her foot into an arch against the starched breast of her uniform, and when the hot stone was placed into the cracked sole of her foot, Anya almost cried in alarm.

'You would like to turn over?' The masseuse had finished with the second leg.

Sometimes she thought Will had wanted the child. Sometimes she thought the decision had been her own. That she had lacked the courage to make any other. But now a parent, not a child, seemed to be growing inside of her, and asking for more of her every day.

Anya pulled her sweating face out of the brace, peeled her body from the table and blinked into the silk ceiling-swag of the dim room. Somewhere a tap was running, the sound of steam again, the feet of a stool as it glanced the tiles and the presence of the masseuse, sitting down by her head, taking a hold of her wrist and in her lap opening Anya's palm. It was nice to be holding someone's hand. Anya wanted to turn over and hold the strange woman in her arms. To be held by her.

But the masseuse replaced Anya's hand on her chest, and picked up the chair. And as she did so, Anya felt something. Not the masseuse. Not anyone but some thing, bigger than them both. It was the bed. The bed trembled, bottles rattling on shelves, stones rattling in their pail.

The music stopped.

Monday 11 April 2005

Bangkok

What if he did try to find the man who had rescued him? Where would he begin? What would it change?

William wakes after a sleepless night. It is still dark. The lights are green as he joins the traffic on Nonthaburi, through the tuk-tuks bringing tourists back from the night market, through Nana junction where backpackers stream over the pedestrian crossing and a giant neon-green bottle of Chang pours LCD bubbles into a glass. The traffic crawls on this stretch; a golden shrine to Mitra at the steps of the Ocean Mall. Starbucks. Polo. Two lanes of taxis. A carpet laid out on the pavement. A waving wall of lucky Japanese cats.

He had felt the earthquake a good hour before the arrival of the wave. As if it were no more than the idling engine of a truck. Like the trucks which used to stop at the traffic lights outside the bedroom window of William's childhood. His eyes opened on Boxing Day in Kao Lak, not on to his bedroom in Stratton, but on to the beach bungalow; the shadows of a strange room, the mist of mosquito nets. The heat smothered him, pinned him to the bed.

When William woke again, the clock on the bedside table told him it was half past nine.

Half past nine. Anya not in her room. Anya's bed still made, not even slept in. The room still and empty. The distant sound of voices on the beach.

He pushes into the right-hand lane. Two blocks and right again. Up onto the Don Muaeng tollway, *Stratton, Stratton, Stratton.* The purple billboards of Air Phuket, the liquid green glass of the Eastwater building and the fleets of little Korean minivans, black windows, no drivers.

The traffic slows at the exits for Don Muaeng airport, robot vans piloting themselves off the road. At Short Stay Arrivals, pink taxis line up.

William turns into one of the car parks, and takes a ticket at the barrier. The low feeling of the car-park ceiling, of being crushed. He has no idea it is past eleven in the evening until he enters the airport and, looking up, sees the flickering arrivals board.

Sydney
Shanghai
Singapore
Auckland
London
Dubai
Moscow

At the check-in desks, rows of yellow-shirted agents are busy doing nothing. The floors of the hall have been buffed to a watery reflection. It is a softness – the air of expectation – which fills an empty hall built for thousands. There must be some odd pause in the stream of international air traffic, the world taking its breath. The wave moving silently, unseen beneath the sea.

Currency Exchange
Information

Sarajevo

Samir's house is perched over the old Sarajevsko beer factory, on the hills above Baščaršija, where the wooden shacks lean into each other as if they are trying to hide. But the house itself is a giant thing of unpainted concrete, three times the size of the old shacks. He shows Marko onto a balcony big enough for 'a dining table and a small jacuzzi'. While it is certainly big enough for those things, there is nothing here, just a plastic orange barrel containing dry concrete, and a yardstick set into it. The house is half finished, no carpets, wires sticking out of the electric sockets and a carpenter's bench with a circular saw covered in blue tarpaulin. He shows Marko the view over the tumbledown roofs of the neighbourhood, where minarets light up the beautiful early-evening mess of Sarajevo. The night smells of fried onions, meat, and all the things he really misses about Bosnia. Marko had forgotten what home felt like until he came back to it.

'You don't own a house until you've built it yourself,' Samir says. 'Five years I've been at this. How much would you pay for this space in a city like London?'

Marko tells Samir you couldn't get this much space in a city like London.

'One hundred and eighty thousand dinar,' he tells him. 'That's no more than twenty thousand euro.'

Jasmina walks out of the tarpaulin sheets that do for the windows of the empty lounge. She is barely out of college;

the square frames of her glasses and a roll-neck sweater. Her kisses glance Marko's cheeks, and when she puts her hands on his shoulders, he can smell the garlic of her cooking.

Samir digs his fingers into Marko's neck and guides him towards the kitchen. 'See, you do the important rooms first,' Samir says. 'The kitchen, the bathroom. The rest can wait.'

An electric generator hums behind their conversation. Jasmina serves lambs' necks, and they talk about the funeral. What a send-off Kemal had. Possibly the only man in Bosnia to have two graves. The council hadn't dug up the old one. They had placed Kemal in a small crypt of white marble, farther up the cemetery, next to Lovers' Hill. His reputation had *grown* with the years, not diminished.

'They have money for nothing,' Samir had whispered in Marko's ear. 'But when it comes to burying people, they throw it away.'

This time the coffin had the weight of a man. Bogdan on one corner, Elvis, Samir and Marko. Marko's feet sank into the fresh white gravel of the path.

The soldiers in new uniforms. Gun salute. Soil landing on the Bosnian flag.

Marko had looked over the grave and seen Sabina, the woman from Ladina.

'How many people would you say there were?' Samir is asking.

'Hundreds, maybe five hundred.'

'More than that,' Samir said. 'Nearer a thousand.'

It had been a strange carnival of faces. School friends wearing the masks of age. Another hand. Another arm around his shoulder. Another voice telling him what a great man Kemal was. Another story about Kemal's kindnesses. And *How is your mother?* And *When will we see your father again?*

'Are there really so many Negroes?'

Marko looks up from his plate. It is Jasmina who has asked the question. She points with a fork that has skewered a knuckle of meat.

'Negroes?'

'Africans. In Britain. I saw this programme about London, and it was just full of Africans.'

'Yes,' Marko says. 'Yes. There are.'

Samir pulls the meat off the bone, looking as much like Marko's own father as Marko's uncle. Jasmina asks if he wants any more lamb. He tells her he is full.

'Marko,' Samir says. 'I want to show you the rest of the house before you go.'

Marko has Samir alone now, but his cousin is too busy talking for him to raise the subject he wants to discuss. A spiral staircase leads off the empty lounge and upstairs Marko is surprised to find carpet. Here, the rooms are almost complete. The master bedroom looks over the balcony. The view of Sarajevo glittering in the dark. There are two more bedrooms, empty and half the size of the master, a large bathroom with a shower and whirlpool bath. Marko is finally about to ask what he has to ask when his cousin shows him a third bedroom, painted pink. There is a Moses basket in the corner.

'You didn't notice,' Samir says. 'You insult me! She has a bump already – what did you think, my wife was fat? We're having a girl.'

Bangkok

The entrance to the lost luggage desk is through a glass door below a tall escalator. The door closes behind him, shutting out the tannoy announcements. William presses a doorbell that is loosely taped to the counter and it chimes like the doorbells of his childhood. The man who emerges from the aisles of racks could be a car mechanic, blue overalls and black hair in oily curls. He takes the passport.

'I don't have the card posted to me,' William says.

'You need card.'

It had not occurred to him there would be any bureaucracy he couldn't circumvent with a British passport. 'I had the luggage shipped using my passport.'

The man opens the claret book, confused, flicking through its empty pages, until he discovers the picture where it isn't in any other passport – at the back.

'I urgently need my luggage,' William says. 'You can cross-check my details, can't you?'

The man looks at a computer screen. 'I can see the record,' he says. 'This arrived three month now?'

'Three months *ago*.' William still can't help himself.

'Sometimes we destroy,' the man says. 'But I can look for you.'

In Kao Lak, the woman at the reception desk of the resort listened to William trying to explain his girlfriend was missing. The woman had a number for a police officer who was assigned to the resorts to report crimes and emergencies. He could be with them in less than an hour. William told the receptionist to make the call, and headed back down to the beach. He wouldn't return to the reception until after the wave.

Perhaps the policeman had come to the resort, drawn down to the beaches on Boxing Day morning, called out on a holiday, dragged away from his family because another *Farang* had drunk too much and stayed out all night. William thinks about it every day. He thinks about whether the receptionist herself had been at her desk, or down by the beaches. He thinks about the family he passed on the gangway as he headed for the reception. It could only have been seconds, the moment he stepped to one side to let them pass. But when he thinks about that moment, he can picture every detail better than he can picture the face of his own mother. The boy walking stiffly with his inflatable armbands, the father trailing the girl who trailed the inflatable giraffe. It reminded William, in the middle of his panic, of those lines from Winnie the Pooh – *Here is Edward Bear, coming downstairs now, bump, bump, bump, on the back of his head, behind Christopher Robin.* His mother used to read those lines, voice in his ear, fingers tapping the crown of his head with each *bump*.

The man in the lost luggage department has returned with a suitcase. It is not Anya's suitcase, William is sure of it. It is something wrapped in layers of cellophane packaging. The porter pushes it into the rack at the side of the desk, and the label tied around the handle has William's name. When William pulls it out of the rack, the case is lighter and smaller than he remembers.

. . . it is, as far as he knows, the only way of coming down the stairs, but sometimes he feels that there really is another way, if only he could stop bumping for a moment and think of it . . .

William would suddenly like to hear his mother's voice more than anything in the world.

He signs the receipt, the suitcase in his left hand. He thinks about putting it down, and walking away, but holding the handle of the case, he feels like he did the one and only time he touched an electric fence. It was in a field of horses. The horses had turned and were running towards him.

William thought he was coming back for Anya. But it is Anya who has come back for him.

Sarajevo

The city has been pinched at the sides. On both flanks of the valley, the front-line remains almost where it was at the end of the siege, the capital of Bosnia poking into the thing they call Republika Srpska like a head in a noose.

Five streets up the hill from Samir's house they are not in Bosnia. Technically.

'Fucking ridiculous,' Samir says. He wants to drive Marko into Republika Srpska because the road around the valley to the airport isn't as busy as the more direct route at this time of night, and because: 'Look at it,' he says. 'This is fucking Sarajevo. How is this not Sarajevo?'

There are no signs marking the border. The street names are the same Sarajevo street names. The buses are the same Sarajevo buses.

'Look at this graveyard,' Samir says. White crosses and obelisks fill the slopes above them. 'Muslim, Christian, Muslim, Christian – half of those graves are our men. Even the dead aren't home.'

Marko decides not to remind Samir he had told him exactly the same thing on their way into Sarajevo.

'I'd thought about coming back,' Marko tells Samir.

'You did come back!'

'I mean staying. About staying. Going back into the business with Dad. Run the security company.'

They come off the hill, down to a crossroads where they wait for a tram to pass.

'What for?' Samir says. 'You don't want to live in England?'

They are in the suburbs of Butmir now, where the roofs of the houses are low, and the airport opens the sky over the flat valley floor. The familiar silhouette of Mount Igman, a sleeping giant in the blue night. On the other side of the airport, the apartment blocks of Dobrinja are lit up. The place where Vesna's father no longer lives.

Samir turns the car around one of the city's few traffic islands, before joining the airport road.

'We had to crawl under the airport last time,' Marko says. 'That fucking tunnel!'

Through the window he watches a plane touch ground. Cars zip by in the opposite direction, taxis bringing the new arrivals in. In the tunnel they had to bend down, folded in half beneath the runway, people pushing past in the opposite direction.

'When we came here with Vesna,' Samir says, 'Kemal couldn't have worried more if you really had been brothers. And not because he thought you were going to fuck her.'

'I talked to Sabina after the funeral,' Marko says. 'She was offended at the idea – of her and Kemal. She knew all about Vesna, about his plans to get married.'

'Oh yes.'

'I believed her.'

'Why?'

'If she'd been fucking Kemal, he wouldn't have told her about Vesna.'

'Who knows what people are like?'

'I talked to Bogdan too.'

'Did you see how nuts he is?'

'Not really.'

'Maybe he was having a good day.'

'He wouldn't absolutely rule it out. The allegations.'

'He takes his job too seriously.'

They drive through the gates in the barbed fences, and the signs saying, *Sarajevo Thanks You! Come Back Soon.*

'Here we are.' Samir pulls up the car, into a space. 'You can leave by plane. No tunnelling underneath the airport!' He opens the driver's door and starts to fix his leg. 'I'll help with the bags.'

Marko watches a couple in front of them climb out of their car, and begin to remove the luggage from the boot.

'It's not *what* you all say,' Marko begins.

Samir takes a breath, then forces it out in a long, bored groan. 'What will it be, Marko?' he says. 'Another ten years? Drop back in and see if we aren't all killing each other again?'

'It's what you *don't* say.'

'What?'

'I should know. Shouldn't I? He slept in our house. He was like a brother to me. If anyone should know it should be me. How could I not know what was going on with him?'

'I told you to believe in him. Stop picking at old scabs.'

'It changes everything.'

'Nothing has changed. Except you don't have to feel responsible for Kemal's death any more. Isn't that what you want?'

'I can't believe Kemal did it. But you all behave like he did.'

'How?'

'Because you all act like you don't care. Like there is nothing to even *think* about!'

Samir lets his head drop dramatically against the steering wheel. Then he sits up straight, and says, 'They raped his mother in front of him, Marko. Did you forget that? Did you think about what it might do to a man? No, you didn't. Because you didn't have to do the things we did. And that's not your fault. But you're not here now. And you're not dealing with the things we have to deal with.'

'You saw Kemal rape those women? I mean you actually saw him do that? You know he did it?'

Samir's eyes follow a girl out of the car park. The rumble of a plane fills the car, before retreating through the hills.

'Not *all* the women. There were some other men, not from Stovnik anyway, you don't know them. And Kemal talked about it. Afterwards. He felt bad about it. If it makes you feel any better. He wished it had never happened. I didn't – *watch* it. Why would I watch that?'

Marko knows he has to get out of the car but can't bring himself to move. He is suddenly aware of the process involved. His brain needs to send a message to the muscles in his legs. But if he is *thinking* about sending a message, the message can't be sent. Maybe it was how Samir felt when he tried to move his missing foot.

'I was going to tell you,' Samir says, 'but I thought – you could come here. You wouldn't have to know. You could be happy you hadn't sent him to his first death!'

Marko cannot move, because he knows he is not going to leave. Not yet.

'How do you think it feels?' Samir says. 'How do you think I feel? Knowing I should have stopped it?'

'A package of anti-biotics is worth two local phone calls. For a litre of cooking oil you can get a carton of cigarettes . . . for 2 litres of oil you can wear almost new Reeboks. A used, male, winter jacket costs 3 kilos of onions. A once standard package of 18 kilos of paint is being exchanged for any kind and amount of food. 10 litres of petrol, the amount which supplies energy for a two-hour shooting of a TV broadcast about the future of Bosnia Herzegovina, can be exchanged for 12 cans for your private survival. In handwritten ads on Tito Street: "I am looking for a woman to help me survive this winter."'

Bora Ćosić (*Sarajevo: Survival Guide*, 1994)

16 September 1994

Sarajevo

'You won.' Vesna leaned over from the back seat and punched Marko's shoulder. 'So stop moping.'

Marko looked out of the window of her father's Renault, at the twin towers, and the Holiday Inn, and the headquarters of *Oslobodenje*. On the television news, Marko always saw Sarajevo from the hills and the buildings looked small. But in real life, their size made the destruction even more unsettling – more undignified somehow. Seeing these tall buildings fallen to pieces, Marko had experienced the same sadness he felt when he saw his parents upset.

'*Sarajevo, ljubavi moja,*' Vesna's father began to sing.

THIS IS
SERBIA

someone had written over the shattered stucco of one building.

Another hand had written,

Fool this is
a Post Office

Marko felt until now he had been watching the war, watching the refugees running from it, watching Kemal fighting it. From the balcony of his home, he had seen smoke rising on the far side of Stovnik. In the summer months he had heard the whistle of shells, and counted the gap between the pop and the wheesh, as they stepped closer and closer. They buried young men in the cemetery. When sirens sounded they moved down into the basement. But the guns in the hills around Stovnik never had the range to reach beyond the university building and the blocks of Marko's estate had remained safe. On the 'safe' roads through Sarajevo, there wasn't a building untouched.

They slowed into a queue. Vesna's father stopped singing. The cause was a tram turned onto its side, a tangle of pipes and wheels stuck in the air. The tram was empty. Its frame had rusted and the windows were smashed out. Whatever happened had happened a long time ago. In front of the tram, the concrete blocks of the central reservation had been moved. The Renault humped over the rubble, before picking up speed on the wrong side of the dual carriageway. Between the city and Dobrinja, the road had become a frayed ribbon of potholed concrete, flanked by the burned-out wrecks of cars.

'Don't worry!' Vesna's father said. 'There's a ceasefire.' Then he laughed until he began to cough.

They passed a hill of bricks and twisted steel, a fire-gutted school, a bonfire of office desks. In the bruised evening light, the eyes of a couple advertising Nescafé on a roadside bill-board sparkled. The pupils had been skilfully removed by a sniper. When the car turned back across the central reservation, and into the estates of Dobrinja, the dark figures of the apartment blocks seemed to lean for support against the evening sky.

In the *Tao of Jeet Kune Do*, Bruce Lee claimed that by paying attention to the body, the mind can relieve it of pain. You just needed to concentrate, focus on accepting the pain. Pain was only a concept. In the *Tao of Jeet Kune Do*, the mind and the body are not divided, but the same organism, part of the same system, like people living in an apartment block, in the same country, on the same planet. Marko lay on a blanket on the parquet floor, beneath the dining-room table in the apartment of Vesna's father. He felt the poking fingers and burning hands of the boy from Foča, in every place pinched, and pulled, and pushed. The grips, the bruises of landing. Painful concepts.

The boy from Foča had coarse red hair and freckles, not just on his face, but all over his shoulders and chest. His breath smelled of rotten carrots. Marko had watched as he won his heats, and knew the boy from Foča was the one to beat. He was a better fighter than Marko, and when they met in the final, the boy's fingers had slipped like water through his hands, the cloth of his hems like grease.

Marko's face had been in the mat before he knew what happened. The boy's elbow dug into the back of his neck, the knot the boy made with his legs, unbreakable. A knee needled his back and pushed the air out of his lungs, and Marko felt not pain, or humiliation, but a deep admiration. He had been trapped by the perfect *Nippon*.

And he shouldn't have done what he did next. But the team cheered from the bleachers, their stamping feet ringing in his ears, and Marko became not just one boy, but the town itself. It was the first time he had ever experienced an overwhelming anger, and afterwards he had wanted to disown it.

Stovnik had dug its fingers into the boy's wound, not Marko Novak. Marko had spotted the stitches on the second pass, as they circled each other and the boy pulled his top together with his belt. The grey stitches and pink burn which could only mean a shrapnel wound.

On the parquet of the dining room, he turned over, but found no comfort. Vesna's uncle slept on the divan next to the dining-room table, and snored like a horse. They had offered the divan to Marko but he had turned it down in the hope Vesna might suggest her own room. She hadn't. They had finished dinner, the candles in the flat were snuffed and Marko thought her father might actually intend to drive him back to the barracks where the rest of the team were staying overnight. But Vesna had pleaded it was too late, and anyway too dangerous now, and her grandmother had agreed.

'Of course,' her father said. 'Marko stays with us tonight.'

He turned from the snoring uncle, and covered his ears. But in the seashell whistle, in the cheering stadium, the boy from Foča returned. After the match, Marko went to shake the boy's hand. Still clutching the wound with his right, the boy had offered his left. But the Foča coach stood with his hands on the boy's shoulders, and gave Marko a look which needed no explanation: the best man had *not* won.

He turned onto his back, and stared at the underside of the dining-room table, holding his idle dick for comfort, thoughts drifting to Vesna as she had been underneath the ping-pong table with Kemal.

Before she went to bed, they had been drawing on her wall. She had told him how her father tried to keep the room as she left it, but when the shooting came close that summer, they needed to take out the bed frame and legs. She had pointed to a line of bullet holes in the posters of Denis & Denis and Annie Lennox – a track as straight as any picture rail. The line showed the limit of the sniper's range. In two years, the family had worked out the sniper, whenever he decided to aim their way, could never get beneath this line.

'He's gone now, the sniper.'

'How do they know?'

'Because no one is dead.'

Marko turned on the dining-room floor and closed his eyes.

She was still there, at the bottom of it all, the girl in the kiosk at Vilnik. On his knees, Marko began to crawl through the grass. But it seemed a long time before he finally reached the dark hut, where the girl sat with her legs apart.

'I didn't mean to do it,' Marko told the girl.

The shadow of the door covered her face like a hood.

'What are you doing?' he asked.

Her lips didn't move but he heard the voice. 'I'm having a baby, can't you feel it?'

Marko looked down between the girl's legs, and found his hand inside her.

He woke with a start. The underside of the table hung over him. His body remembered the pain it was in, and rolling out from under the table, Marko stumbled out of the dining room, trying to recall the map of the apartment in his head.

They said if he walked around at night, it was still best not to turn any lights on, and to keep his head down.

He felt along the cold walls of the corridor, past Vesna's room and Vesna's father's room. He had managed to shut the bathroom door behind him and was fumbling for the lock, when Vesna spoke.

'Do you think she died giving birth?' She sat in the dark, on the tiles between the bath and the toilet. He could smell the vomit. 'Or do you think someone killed her?'

He knelt in front of Vesna, and reached out to feel her forehead.

'I threw up,' she said.

She was hot. By the toilet there was an empty bucket. He picked it up, scooped some of the emergency water out of the bath and started to pour it into the toilet bowl, flushing away her sick.

'I think it was an anxiety attack,' Vesna said. 'Did you ever have an anxiety attack?'

'Sure.'

'I thought I would be happier here – at home – I thought I would be happier. But I don't remember how to be. I should be back at my mother's.'

'You will be.' Marko put the bucket down and, shuffling knee to knee, he pulled Vesna's head to his chest, putting his nose to her hair.

'I'm eight years old in that room,' she said. She tried to kneel. But there seemed to be no bones in her legs, and she fell back into him – so much heavier than she was in his dreams.

Marko opened his mouth to tell Vesna not to worry. She knelt before him now. She clamped her hand over his lips. When she removed it, she pressed her mouth against his, missing at first, teeth knocking against his chin. Quickly she found her way in.

Then just as she had begun, she stopped. In the dark, her face soft like a bruised damson.

'What?' Marko whispered.

Vesna covered her mouth. She was laughing. 'When was the last time you kissed a girl?'

Marko didn't know how to answer. Instead, he took her arms, and pulling her into him, kissed her again. At first, Vesna's mouth remained closed. He pushed his tongue against her teeth. He felt her wrists in his hands. She tried to pull away. Then he felt a screaming pain and let go.

She had bitten his tongue.

'Are you a virgin?' Vesna giggled.

Marko slapped her. And Vesna's slap came back so quickly, Marko would often convince himself in the replayed memory of this moment, that she had struck the first blow.

When Vesna stood up, Marko expected her to leave. Instead, she locked the bathroom door, and turned around.

'Come here,' she said.

Monday 11 April 2005

Bangkok

It sits on the bed in William's apartment. Wrapped in plastic Anya's suitcase has the cold glow of an ice cube. Where the lids of the case meet, his scissors slip through the seam of cellophane, and after the initial resistance, the soft space inside. He picks away at the latch. It will open now. But he feels like someone is watching over his shoulder.

He is a thief. He lifts Anya's clothes out first. They are all a jumble, hastily crushed in by whoever collected the case from her room. He needs to order this mess, and begins to pull everything out – her dresses, her vests, her shirts and skirts. In the pocket of the suitcase, he finds white popsocks in a pack of three, a carton of tampons, all the blue socks rolled into balls, and gym shorts for sleeping in. There is a washbag splattered with dried toothpaste, essential oils sealed in a plastic zip-bag, a nest of hairgrips, a tube of something called Vagisil, a tub of Evening Primrose pills and the disgusting tarragon toothpaste she loved. He holds something in his hand. It won't let go of him. A disposable razor. Its blade still holds the short, sharp dashes of stubble from Anya's legs.

He had searched the hospital first, but Anya's name was not on the lists of those admitted. He needed to get back to the coast, but everyone said the roads from Phuket to Kao Lak were impassable, so he had registered Anya's details with the Red Cross people in the hospital grounds. He queued for an hour to use the mobile phone of a volunteer from the Red Crescent. But neither the resort nor Anya's mobile answered. He asked in the hospital about the man who had brought him in, but no one knew who he was talking about. He queued again for the mobile phone, and asked the school to book him a room somewhere, but all the rooms in the town were full, and the school couldn't even wire money because William had no identification to present to the bank. Somehow, he slept again, this time in the heat of the hospital steps. When he woke, the sky was milky, and the air seemed soft. It could have been late evening, or it could have been early morning. He signed for some cash from a Christian Aid worker, enough to hire a taxi driver who told him one of the roads to Kao Lak had been opened. They drove past a blue fishing boat, high in the palms of a tree, then aflame with the sun, a glinting bonfire of metal bikes and scooters.

Where the road ran along the coast, the front walls of shops and houses had all been pushed in, the innards of their rooms opened up.

The sign pointing down the road for the resort offered hope. The gates of the resort and its stone pillars were still standing. The wave had left only palms, turning brown and black, over the raised driveway. It was like this all along the coast, islands of normality amid the destruction, the caprice of geography. The tsunami was created by a concertina of energy, more powerful where it met precipitous land, dissipated by shallows. Spreading far where it met no resistance, snagging where it did.

The lost child is told to stay in one place, not to move. If Anya had made it to the resort, she might be in the cabin. This would be the place to wait if there were no other way of communicating. His hopes rose as he neared the hotel reception. She was probably sitting on her bed, reading magazines, more worried about him than he was about her.

On the reception veranda, a man in a grey pyjama suit swept leaves as if this were just a hotel out of season. The swamps beneath the walkways connecting the treetop cabins had risen, slick black water iridescent with oil. The wave which destroyed the beach and the shops along the front had rushed beneath the stilts of the beach huts, beneath the walkways, its energy absorbed by the knots of mangrove roots.

The cabin was how he had left it. Anya's clothes were still packed into the drawers and cupboards. In the bathroom her toothbrush and razor in a cup. On the bed, her laptop.

But Anya wasn't there. She had not come back. He sat on the bed of Anya's room, put one hand on the closed lid of the laptop as if resting his hand on a Bible, and tried to remember. They had been at the bar. When the first wave came, they had run from the bar. It had caught up with them on a small street of shops, the place he had been on Christmas morning to buy the things for breakfast. They had stood on the fire-escape steps of a wooden building as a second wave came. And then the steps had collapsed beneath them.

Anya's precious work. She would want that safe above all else. He put her laptop in its shoulder bag and took it with him. When he bumped into her later that day, as he inevitably would, she would thank him for taking it. He took some of the cash from her purse and left some in case they missed each other here, but he didn't think about Anya's passport. The one thing which might help him identify her.

He didn't think about it because he didn't want to believe he would need it.

The steps from the walkway to the beach had fallen into the sand, and William had to lower himself down. There was no beach as such, only this dark black mulch, like the ploughed earth of a field and, running from it in channels, the black bleed from the swamp. The sand was littered with broken timber and glass, the door of a refrigerator, the frame of a window, the cistern of a toilet; the smell of sewage and seaweed baking in the sun. Down by the headland, a paper chain of students worked to pass debris onto the back of a dump truck. They were singing in Thai, one of those see-saw melodies, as if the job were just some away-day, bonding exercise. He walked around the smashed hulls of fishing boats, over the heads of beach umbrellas poking from the black sand, the towels of Disney princesses, bottles of suntan lotion, a picnic basket, the refrigerator of an ice-cream seller and sandals. Blue sandals, pink sandals, leather sandals, a swimming costume, the plastic of an inflatable swimming ring, broken sunglasses, a child's colouring-in book.

Where the beach bar had stood, he walked over matchwood; broken glass, smashed bottles, half-buried nets, plastic anchors, plastic boats, the black skeleton of a Christmas tree. Only the toilet block of the bar remained – two cubicles and the wall dividing them. Standing over all this, the elephant, its trunk fishing in one of the unbroken toilet bowls. Its unblinking eye.

As if commanded, William sat down before it, on a step leading nowhere, the laptop on his knees.

He begins to fold the clothes; the slacks, the shorts, the vests, the skirts. He folds Anya's arms into her chest, and her legs at the knee. When she is back inside the suitcase, he takes the laptop, and slides it under the first layer of clothes. The teeth of the zip won't meet, and he has to push down on the lid. Which is when he notices there is another compartment, a pocket to the case, still wrapped tightly beneath the cellophane. Anya's passport. The thing he should have taken from the room because she was missing. Not the stupid laptop he was trying to protect. The passport in which she wears the shorter hairstyle which had marked their last years together, in which the stamps for Bosnia and Serbia and Croatia fill almost every page. The pocket gives up an opened packet of chewing gum, a printout of the flight tickets and the resort reservation. Tickets for the Heathrow Express. Things she must have thrown in at the last minute in London. Things to keep to hand. Something wrapped in Christmas paper, just bigger than an envelope.

'Happy Christmas William!' Her handwriting stops him. It is her voice. He turns the card over. 'Good times!'

He sits on the floor, his back to the bed, fingers fumbling with the Sellotape.

It is a Snappy Snaps packet. His hands shake as he pulls the first photograph out. Girls in school uniform, claret shirts and blue blazers; faces William doesn't recognise beneath savagely permed hair. Friends bunched up against a wall, flicking V's to the camera, sleeves rolled, legs straight, making stiff A's of their skirts. Anya is at the end, her curled hair dyed black and shoulder length, tips threaded with beads. The child she was when he first met her.

The photographs come in different sizes, different aspect ratios, some Polaroid, some stuck together with the sticky rings of tea cups. There is a picture of her mother's car, the old red junk-bucket parked up in a brown field. That car which had changed their world. It is next to a small orange tent. In another picture, a circle of faces looking up into the camera, surrounded by the ashes of a fire, packets of Rizla in a girl's lap. Another girl, whose face he knows, but whose name he can't remember, is Anya's chubby school friend. Anya is wearing the old jumper which hung to her knees, the one with holes in the cuffs where her thumbs poked through. In the next picture she is standing on the bend of a tight Mediterranean road, next to a saint's shrine, a wash of hot white light behind her and barely a trace of the snow-capped Alps William remembers seeing when he took it. In the next picture he recognises the boy standing with his arm around Anya. It is William, it is him, barely nineteen, his face so young, his flesh so doughy, he can hardly believe he was any more than fifteen. And yet there they are, in the holiday pictures, heads resting together as they stand in front of Lake George at sunset, pine trees and a jetty, and at the end of the jetty, a small steam-riverboat, red propeller wheel on the side, and the words *Captain Allegheny* written in gold. This is the year they left school, before they started university, in those days when everything was new and life was a very, very simple promise they would stay together for ever.

William is crying.

This is why he had called her at the end of the monsoon season. This is what he supposed they might have for a few days. She had packed it in a suitcase, and brought it with her. Anya and William grinning, their thumbs up before the Golden Gate bridge; Anya standing on a downtown pavement, her finger positioned so it makes a miniature out of a distant Empire State building; Anya and William in a picture he took with his arm extended, their faces close to the camera lens and their mouths mocking WOW as a whale jumps over a bar at Sea World; Anya and William, older now, sitting anxiously at a Bosnian wedding table groaning with food. But somehow, different in this picture; her hair has been straight-ened. Her face is pinched. But it isn't really something the picture tells him. It is something he knows.

It is Anya after the abortion. It is Anya and William falling apart.

Hands still shaking, he puts the photographs back in the pocket of the suitcase like something he needs to hide. And pulling his hand out, he finds something else. It is a leaf of A4 paper folded in half. At first he doesn't know what it is he recognises about the picture. It is a photocopy of a newspaper article from some Balkan paper. Something to do with Anya's work. *Stovnik.* A town in Bosnia, wasn't it? There is no reason why a newspaper from a Bosnian town should mean anything to him.

It is the man. Younger when this picture was taken, his head shaved. But still him. The face he had looked up at as the man reached down and pulled him out of the mud. He had held on to this man's shoulders, locked his arms around his chest, the burn of the exhaust pipe against his calf. It is the man who rescued him, the man who had been sitting with Anya at the bar and the man she introduced him to before they turned to see the tide retreating. The man who has a name now because it is beneath the picture. Kemal Lekić.

Tuesday 12 April 2005

Sarajevo

Someone is practising piano scales. Someone operates a drill. Someone hammers a metal beam in the tight streets of Baščaršija. Marko has not left Bosnia. It is almost midday, but he wants to lie on the bed and watch the brick dust turning in the open window. In Cambridge, Marko sleeps fitfully in the days, waking to the sound of his upstairs neighbour watching horror movies; the long periods of quiet suspense followed by sudden stabs of music, shouts and screams. Sometimes he falls asleep to the vibration of a washing machine. But England is a quiet place.

He feels underneath the covers. They had come back drunk and he is still wearing his jeans. He thinks about calling Millie, but texts her instead. He tells her he is going to miss his philosophy class. He doesn't suppose the tutor needs to know, but it would be good if she could call in. He has decided to stay just a few more days.

What he cannot tell her is why. Because he is not entirely sure why. And the part he *is* sure about – making his apologies to Vesna – would involve telling Millie what he has to apologise for.

He buries his hungover head back into the pillow, and listens to the muffled noises of the market. In Stovnik, the families were always in and out of each other's apartments. No one locked their doors. During the war, they shared the basement. But even before then, Marko had always been a light sleeper. He would wake in the night to the sound of Kemal's breathing; the small, sudden snaps of blocked airways, and dreams that sounded unwanted. The candle painted an uncertain picture of the soldier boy sitting on the chair by Marko's homework desk, his white shorts turned grey, combat gear at his feet, tan line where the sleeves of his fatigues were rolled and the fleur-de-lis tattoo on his bicep. The brigade were strict about keeping the hair of soldiers short, but over time the rules had slipped. Like the rest of the brigade, Kemal had a fringe which hung in a square black handkerchief at the front of his shaven skull.

Marko turns in the bed and thinks of the shaven head in the morgue. The patch on his bicep unnaturally smooth. Had Kemal sat in some Thai tattooing parlour as they blasted it off? It was hard enough to imagine Kemal as a man in his late twenties, growing out of the boy, a man turning thirty; but to imagine him in the heat and light of a Far Eastern country? Had he turned Buddhist? Had he kept his head shaved to a shadow of stubble, and recited mantras in an orange robe? Had he remembered the *Tao of Jeet Kune Do?*

Had Kemal been following Lao-tzu?

'It's a mercy, isn't it?' Kemal asked in the candlelit bedroom.

'What is?'

'Shooting them. Did you shoot any today?'

He was talking about the dogs. But he wasn't looking at Marko. He was looking down at his hands, fingers spread on the homework desk, as if contemplating which ones to keep.

'Did you sleep the sleep of the just?' Samir says.

The old shop window is bright with afternoon light. At the open door, Samir sits in shorts and a straw hat, holding a guitar and picking out notes which are hopelessly lost to the shriek of a stonecutter in the building site across the road.

'It's the first spring day we've had!' Putting down the guitar, Samir crosses to the back of the small room and over to the reception desk, where he starts the complicated business of making a coffee in the plastic kettle. There is no plug on the lead, so he carefully inserts the bare wires into the socket on the wall.

Marko can't imagine how this tiny room was ever his uncle's copperware store. Cavernous in his memory, the store had dripped with copper coffee pots, copper skillets, copper bathtubs, copper vases, copper scenes of Sarajevo, copper portraits of Bosnian heroes. Marko picks up a model tank on one of Samir's shelves. It is fashioned from copper-tipped bullets, and sells for $50. It is impressive, Samir's business, the bed and breakfast, the house he built himself, the child he is going to have. How hard it must have been to put it all together.

'Those model tanks?' Samir says. 'I saved a bunch when we sold everything off.'

A television above Samir's head shows an Italian football match. Scattered over the table of checked oilcloth are tourist leaflets: rafting on the Drina, mountain climbing, coach trips to Dubrovnik, fishing trips on the Sava. In Marko's room there had been dried flowers in frames, and the theme is continued here.

The picture of the judo team is above the table, on a shelf of its own. They are standing together before the coach which will take them to Sarajevo. Four soldiers flanking them: Elvis, Samir, Bogdan and Kemal. There was always a risk in leaving Stovnik that goodbyes could be final. It stops him when he thinks of how they ever lived like that.

'What's the plan?' Samir pours the coffee, holding back the grains with a spoon. 'How long are you going to stay?'

'I think he was guilty about something in the end.'

His cousin walks outside, puts the coffee on the table and gestures for Marko to follow. The sun is breaking over the hills, and in his eyes when he sits. Samir begins to pick out notes on the guitar, and for a moment they are both stopped by the sight of girls tripping along the pavement. Unbearably young in their summer vests and bouncing skirts.

'*Zumbul, lale, jorgovani . . .*' Samir sings quietly, but he struggles to find the right chord.

'There was a lot he never told me,' Marko says. 'The more I think about it. The more I think of how much I didn't know. Who were the women? The ones who went missing?'

'I don't know their *names . . .*' Samir shakes his head. He has found the chord he is looking for, '*Jorgov-a-a-a-ni . . .*'

'Was it just Kemal?'

Samir stops again. 'There were other times, you know. Other soldiers who did it. Some of these soldiers we were with, they had the brains of Albanians.' He pulls the cigarette pack over the table. 'You know why this kind of thing happened? Because when everyone says you're drunk, you better start rolling around on the floor and acting like you're drunk. Kemal got lost in it. That's all. It happened. So he wasn't perfect. Don't over think it. *You* lose your temper too, Marko. Lose yourself. No one's perfect.'

Across the street, tarpaulin blows into the empty windows of an Austro-Hungarian building, and a welding torch flashes in its dark heart. Samir puts the guitar down, taps a cigarette on the table, smells it and rolls it over to his cousin. Marko doesn't pick it up.

'What's that book you've been reading?' Samir asks. 'Philosophy?'

'Just something. My girlfriend's,' he lies. 'I picked it up for the plane.'

'When I say I can't *remember*, Marko, I mean – *maybe*. If I tried. But I don't want to. You understand that?'

Marko nods.

'Kemal was a good man. Most of the time a good man. And I don't want to remember him like he was this one time, just this one time.'

Marko picks up the cigarette and lights it. He can't believe he has stayed. He should have gone home. He should be preparing for his class. They could rebuild the market all they wanted. They could park their Audis and Mercedes on the kerbs. They could set up new businesses and make their money, and spend it in the cafés, but this place – his home – would never be right.

'Let me give you the best piece of advice I have to offer,' Samir says. 'And then you can do as you want. You have to *choose* what to remember.' Samir taps each word on the table with a coffee spoon. 'It doesn't-do-you-any-good-to-remember-everything. Remember it all and you just go crazy.' He puts the spoon down and raps his knuckles against his own forehead. 'That, my little cousin, is a medical fact.'

He wants to tell her more. He wants to tell her there was an elephant on the beach, nosing among the toilets left standing in the wreck of the bar, and how this elephant had looked at him with its unblinking eye, and he had looked at it with all the joy and wonder of a child looking at an elephant in a zoo. It wasn't just an elephant. William had seen the creature as if he had never before seen or heard of an elephant. As if he were reborn. Anya was gone and he felt relief. In that moment, he had thought about leaving her laptop among the debris of the wave. But then the feeling of relief had passed and he had kept it.

One of the food-court girls brings Missy's smoothie.

'I saw a documentary,' Missy says. 'About how the seabed opened up. That's how it starts. With the earthquake, a canyon opens up in the seabed, and at first the water is sucked down.'

'I felt the earthquake in my sleep.'

'And no one connected the earthquake to a tsunami?'

'It felt like a very mild, very short quake. When I found Anya at the bar, it was about an hour later, no one was thinking about the tremor. When we saw the sea, it was going out, not coming in.'

Missy shakes her head. The girl returns with their food. A moment is filled with the business of steam and opening chopsticks. When he had dropped off Missy and returned to his apartment, Anya had started speaking again. She told him he was being a dick. She told him to man up and apologise.

It was simple enough to suggest lunch over in the mall. He told Missy he would give her the lowdown on the school before her starting on Thursday. But he wanted to repair the bridges after their argument. She had suggested he meet her at a skatepark. But he didn't skate. *I owe you at least a lunch,* he confidently told her.

Where is that confidence now? He chases a slippery mushroom in his noodle soup. Despite his road trip with Missy, he feels like he is starting over. Not just with Missy, but with the business of seeing people, of being out. Gripping the fishy mushroom in the chopsticks, he brings it to his mouth, but it drops back into the soup and burning drops splash the back of his hand. His stomach is unsettled. After packing Anya's suitcase he had thrown up.

'I can't imagine the sea just retreating like that,' Missy says.

'I suppose it was like an estuary tide. I thought it must be some local phenomenon.'

Missy shakes her head. More disbelief.

He wonders what is supposed to be happening here. He needs to tell her things, but why does she have a desire to know? 'You could see the fish. In places on the seabed. Where the sea moved so quickly, they were left behind.'

'And you ran?'

'Running would have been a good idea.'

They hadn't run. Not at first. At first they stood like everyone else, looking out at the retreating sea and shading their eyes from the sun. They followed their feet to the edge of the veranda where the corner of the building pointed out at the coast.

'I was still trying to make polite conversation,' he tells Missy. 'I'd woken up with this idea in my head. She had been murdered or kidnapped or raped at the party. I ran to the resort reception and made a flap about it. But then I came down to the beach, and there she was, having coffee with this guy. I didn't know who he was.'

'No one was running?'

'I don't think so, not until the last minute.'

As they watched the tide retreat, William had seen the family who were staying in the bungalow next to their own. The girls stood in the water left behind. Later he had seen the father running, carrying a child in each arm, another on his back. Absolutely hopeless. They had all run eventually. Up the beach, where it sloped to a road of small shops and where they thought they would be safe, on the higher ground.

William looks down, through the glass walls of the mall, to where the lights on Pattapaya hold the traffic, cars stacking up, then shooting out like bearings in a pinball machine. When the cars stop, a lone man pushes an ice-cream vending-fridge over the pedestrian crossing.

'I'm sorry you couldn't find the guy from the resort,' Missy says.

William shrugs. At least he knew. Kemal Lekić had died of a brain haemorrhage in a Bangkok hospital on the 3rd of January. Until then, William's rescuer had been in a coma. For the final two weeks of his life, Kemal Lekić had been completely unknown, an unidentified man. There was no Bosnian Embassy in Thailand. Kemal didn't come to the attention of the Bosnian Embassy in Indonesia until staff and friends at the resort identified him. Over the phone, the man at the Embassy in Indonesia had told William the body had been repatriated. There was a brother in Bosnia.

At least Will *thinks* this is what the man was trying to tell him. The embassy man gave Will a number. If he wanted to share his story about Kemal, he could call the brother.

But none of this told Will what he wanted to know. He would never find out if Kemal saw Anya's body, or if he knew what had happened to her.

'Anya was a workaholic,' Will says absent-mindedly.

Missy looks up from her soup and Will realises he is not talking to someone who knows anything about him or his life with Anya.

'She loved her job,' he adds. 'One of those people who lives for their job.'

'What did she do?'

'She was a researcher. A human rights researcher.'

'Cool job.'

'She helped people,' he says. And understands for the first time: now Anya is dead, he is more responsible for her than ever.

He looks at Missy, her neck cocked, raised eyebrows and wide eyes. Now he knows what is going on. People are like those tipping cups in Japanese gardens, filled with a constant stream of water, compelled to tip. She will take what he has told her, and at some point or another, it will be tipped into someone else. And like this, drop by drop, the water will recede from him, taking Anya with it.

Sarajevo

Marko squats against the fence, and watches a street cat on the opposite wall. The cat's eyelids grow heavy, closing for only a second before startling awake. He watches as if the cat might impart some wisdom, but it just licks a paw and returns to its somnambulant routine.

From the cobbled streets of Bjelave the city is a distant roar. The air above the town is filled with the smell of spring cherry blossom. It is heaped so deep against the walls of gardens you can stand in it. He is here now. There is no going back. But what he sees through the chain fence of Vesna's garden has stopped him.

Marko had thought she might reject him over the phone. But he hadn't wanted to walk into her workplace again. In truth, he hadn't known what he was going to do. But wandering around the old town that afternoon, he had found himself drifting down the street of the travel company, walking past the windows once, twice, three times, before persuading himself the café with the Tito ashtrays, across the road from her office, was as good a place as any to stop and have a coffee. It was nearly six o'clock, and he could see the office was shutting down. His next plan was to 'bump' into her as she left, but all of a sudden, Vesna had walked out of the office door, and Marko had scrambled to put money on the table.

He almost caught up with her at the corner of Maršala Tita, but when she crossed the road, a tram cut between them. He was about to shout after her as they climbed the steep steps of the alley between the banks and Veliki Park, but she reached the top, and disappeared from sight. Then he was following her. Following her, not trying to make contact. They climbed the cobbled streets that shot straight up the hillside above the city centre. She was a block of houses ahead when Marko began to slow with questions. What was Vesna going home to? Had her mother moved to Sarajevo? Had there been a ring on her finger when they met in the café? This woman shared her childhood with him, but what did that really mean? What did their childhood mean when her lover and his best friend was a rapist and a murderer? When the war had finally taken everything?

He followed Vesna past the fenced platforms of a school playground and through the thundering feet of children. A car passed between them, rolling down the street, red brake-lights pumping in a yellow cloud of dust that climbed in a slow explosion over the garden walls. When he next saw her, she was unlocking a crooked, rusting door in a crooked chain-link fence, and walking into a small, overgrown garden at the corner of a narrow alley. The little girl came tearing around the side of the cottage and across the garden, throwing herself into Vesna's legs. She picked her up, and brushed the hair from her face, and with the girl's chicken-bone legs wrapped around her hips, they walked up the stone steps of the house.

Bangkok

In the mall, William holds his fingers to his nose. When he thinks about the temples, he can smell the air of that day on his hands. He has grown to need it. It is like the hawthorn smell which rises from English hedgerows in the spring. Sweet and sickly and as full of life as it is of death.

After he had combed the beaches by the resort, he took the waiting taxi to the nearest temple. A red marquee stood next to the temple gates. Beneath the marquee, people had gathered to study Polaroid photographs. Red-robed monks pinned the photographs on noticeboards. The monks ferried in and out of the temple gates with shoeboxes full of them. Behind the walls of the temple, students of forensics had arrived from universities in Bangkok, Singapore, even as far away as Mumbai, and stood in their blue sanitation suits over white body bags, one shooting, one compiling the photographs in the shoebox. The bodies themselves were unloaded from the back of a dumper truck by teenagers in student clothes, with scarfs and ripped T-shirts tied around their mouths and noses. The dump trucks had come from the beaches where the chain gangs were singing, where William had been.

At the third temple, William stood next to a middle-aged woman whose pale skin, and drawn features, told him she had just stepped off a plane from some wintering European country. As she looked at the photographs, the fingers of one hand dithered at her neck, and the other hand gripped a baton of rolled papers.

He called his parents from the mobile phone of an aid worker. They had been trying to reach him in Bangkok, and had no idea he was on the coast. He told them to find a number for Anya's mother, and to let her know he was looking for her daughter.

But he hoped he wouldn't find her. He hoped he wouldn't find her at the temples where the bodies in the photographs had spent forty-eight hours bloating in stagnant water, burned black by the sun, infested with insects. When he didn't find Anya's picture, he was invited into the temple grounds to inspect the bodies which hadn't yet been photographed. They were laid out in neat rows. An open cemetery. William felt as if he were floating over the burned and bloated limbs of these oddly inflated people. Their faces had swollen into oversized party masks, and although he looked at them, they were somehow incapable of looking at him. Limbs arranged like abandoned puppets, their small white eyeballs stared out from behind the flesh and bone, or their heads were empty with black sockets, no eyes at all. The mouths of the tsunami dead were left in silent screams and permanent grins, their lips pulled back, their teeth protruding, their open mouths stuffed with a black seabed mud, like something left halfway through the process of taxidermy. Dead children stared at him as though in disbelief, others smiled as if they knew him. But once William started looking he couldn't stop. It seemed almost rude to turn away.

The charred little babies were the strangest of all. Not at all like flesh and bone, more like plastic or china; castaway firings slated for return, eyes and mouths shut tight, in a moment that could have been fear or joy.

When William couldn't find Anya in the grounds of the third temple, he moved to the next, eight kilometres up the coast. The next, eight kilometres down. At each temple it was the same. He hoped he would find nothing. He hoped he would bump into her, walking among the photographs, walking among the bodies like him.

Anya's mother called him three days later. He was in Bangkok by then. She wanted to get a flight out. She wanted to know how to find her. William told her what he had done. He told her he had been to all the temples. He told her it was no use. And so she wanted a story from him. She wanted to know what had happened in the final moments. But what could he tell her?

He told her not to come.

A week later, Anya's mother called to tell him she had been contacted by the forensics team to whom William had given Anya's details. The team had asked for anything which might provide Anya's DNA; an old tooth kept from childhood; hair if she had been living at home. She had driven down to London, and collected her toothbrush, some underwear and a hairbrush from the house in Walthamstow. She told him she wished she had come to Kao Lak, and asked whether she should still come.

He told her not to come.

What use would it be? He had asked for Anya's belongings to be forwarded from the hotel and promised he would arrange to have them sent on.

They have finished eating, and Missy is in the bathroom. The busyness of the tables at the food court spreads to the counters and cashiers, the frantic kitchens behind them, the shops across the mezzanine, the escalators delivering shoppers and taking them away, lifts taking people up, taking people down. It feels as though the entire mall is moving around him, the people and the reflections of people in the windows of storefronts, the ripple over the glass walls as another Skytrain slows into Nana Station. He watches as the doors of the train slide open, pouring people into the atrium. Such a thin line between the living and the dead. A thin, watery line. They should be running, all of them, running for their lives.

'Until Thursday then,' Missy says.

'Yes,' William says. Though it is clear that neither of them is convinced.

'I'll be at the skatepark tomorrow night. If you want to check it out.'

On the day of the wave, before they began to collect and catalogue the bodies, before they realised how many bodies there were, the Buddhists had burned the first to come to the temple. To the Christians it felt like the priests were murdering the dead. With no body, no identification, no funeral. But the Buddhists saw it differently. Burning released the human spirit from the degradation of the flesh. Some of the Buddhists even whispered that the wave was karma. Some kind of awesome reckoning. William envied the religious their belief in anything. Not because he could ever believe in the truth of any particular religious story, but because the Christians shared their belief with other Christians, and the Buddhists shared their belief with other Buddhists. Because the Muslims shared their belief with other Muslims, and William would have to make up his own story.

Missy has gone.

He wanted to tell her Anya had nothing to reckon for. No sins to atone. He wanted to tell her she had been his closest friend. He wanted to tell her it was his fault. He had asked his former girlfriend to come to Thailand, his first lover, the lover he thought he would have again. But the woman he greeted at Kao Lak airport, had turned out to be more than his lover, she had turned out to be his greatest friend.

He wanted to tell Missy that he hoped they burned Anya's body. Whatever the fucking Buddhists and Christians and Muslims thought, he hoped she had been burned, not left to rot, and that as he stood there in the temple grounds, looking at what the ocean had left behind, Anya had been falling in the white ash.

Sarajevo

'Look at that blossom, all over the clean clothes!' Vesna says.

Ivory-pink petals drift across the scrappy lawn, catching in the white sheets, and the blue-white vests, and the pink-white blouses. They sit on a hollowed log beneath a small damson tree. Vesna smokes her Dunhill, and Marko smokes with her. He had come to apologise. Apologise for what they did to Kemal. And somehow apologise to her for what Kemal had become. But now Vesna is the one doing all the talking.

'We went to visit his grave when Amelia was five. I'd always talked about him. She used to say, *Daddy went away with the men who look after us.* Like he was still out there, being a soldier.'

Her daughter sits in the long grass, on the other side of the washing line, playing cat's cradle with the little girl from next door.

'She's very nurturing,' Vesna says. 'She likes younger children.'

The more Marko looks at Amelia, the more he can see. Her hair is Vesna's natural colour, a mousy blonde. She has her mother's feline eyes, and her mother's heart-shaped face. But the strong nose and the long chin belong to Kemal.

'So I was mad when he called me, Marko. If you think you were angry to find out, can you imagine how *I* felt when he called me from Thailand? Amelia was seven years old by then. Seven!'

'I guess Kemal didn't know he had a daughter,' Marko says. 'When he called you.'

'Jesus, I thought it was some kind of joke. Of course he didn't know he had a daughter – we all thought he was dead!'

Marko thinks of the body in the morgue. The shaved head. He thought he had come to tell Vesna about the camp, but now he wants to tell her about Kemal's dead body.

But he doesn't. Instead, he asks, 'What was he like? In Thailand?'

Something about the memory of it makes Vesna smile. 'I went to see him twice. I didn't tell him about Amelia the first time. I just wanted to see him. To see what he was like. He was – *calm*. You know, like he'd been getting into Buddhism or something.' She is resting her elbows on crossed legs, and brings her fingers together in mockery of meditation. 'Gone all *Zen*. Which made me even madder at first. I wanted him to feel my anger, but it all seemed to bounce off.' She stops and barks, 'Hey! Amelia! Be kind to Daša!'

Tall and thin, Amelia is standing with one foot on the smaller girl's chest, but at her mother's instruction, she lifts it, before demonstratively offering the younger girl her hand.

'You see, I tell you how good she is, and she does something to prove me wrong. She's getting to an age when she knows she can stop listening to me.'

Vesna can't seem to take her eyes off the children. He envies her that.

'So when I finally told him about Amelia,' Vesna says, 'it was on the second trip. I was nervous. You know, going back a second time, it meant I was *interested*, right? At least he thought so. We had some argument, and by the time I told him about Amelia, it came out like it was spite. Like I was trying to shock him. I wasn't nice. I told him about the English woman too, the one who was on to them.'

'So you knew?'

Vesna nods but says nothing else. After her second trip to Thailand, she tells him, Kemal had wanted to meet his daughter. 'But I kept putting off the visit. Money wasn't a problem, Kemal was prepared to pay for the flight, but he said he couldn't come back to Bosnia. It was too complicated.

'And how was I supposed to tell Amelia? Amelia was seven at the time. The days of thinking Daddy had just "gone away" were long gone.'

Vesna says she would try to imagine the conversation she should be having. But she couldn't just tell her daughter Daddy had come back. How could she explain why Kemal made himself disappear? How could she explain he had never *known* about her? *Next month*, she would keep telling herself — *when Amelia was through this year at school, when Amelia had finished her exams, when she was over this flu, when things weren't quite so difficult at work.*

'I was thinking about it last Christmas. To do it just *after* because I didn't want to spoil things!' Vesna screws her cigarette into the bark of the hollowed log. It joins others rotting in the crook of the branch. Her stash of stolen moments. 'And now, he really is dead.'

She had started to worry when she saw the news about the tsunami. Kemal had owned a bar right on the beach. 'I knew that if he had been there when the tsunami came—'

It is a strange thing. Every time the tsunami is mentioned, conversation stops. As if the idea of it needs the space in their minds, the room to pass. They watch Amelia, her hand, the hub of a wheel on the little girl's head, turning a circle, and reciting the rhyme, *Ide, maca, oko, tebe* . . .

'What English woman?' Marko asks.

'Oh, there was someone from a human rights organisation interested in Ladina, and what happened at the camp.'

'She came to see you?'

'Only briefly. I told her to get out.'

Vesna bends over her knees, and lifts her toes from her flip-flops. The chipped varnish of her toenails, the small hairs on the joints.

So she knows about Kemal already. And she lives with it. Marko is relieved the news is not his to tell.

'Do you ever think about the woman in Vilnik?' Marko says.

'Of course,' she says. 'I said I *try* to forget things. Not that I can.'

'I never told anyone about it.'

Vesna looks at him, something like warmth in her eyes. A reflection of how they were.

'I used to blame you,' she says. 'After Kemal died on the Kapija. After we *thought* Kemal had died. I know I shouldn't have done it. It was because I didn't want to blame myself.'

Out of nowhere, Amelia appears in front of them. 'Are we eating tonight or can we go over to Daša's?'

Vesna touches her daughter's hair in a way that makes Marko feel strangely jealous. 'Of course we're eating tonight, honey – since when don't I feed you?'

'It's eight o'clock.' The girl is talking to her mother but is looking at Marko. She is assessing him.

'This is Marko, Amelia. Marko and I were friends when we were children.'

Amelia pulls her face into a polite smile, and it is like she has pulled his memories of Vesna and Kemal together. They are in the garden again, at Kemal's parents' house. Before the war. Before Vesna was a girl who kissed his best friend. Before Kemal's father died of a heart attack in front of the television. Before the soldiers came into that garden, and made Kemal watch as they raped his mother. Before Kemal turned into a rapist himself.

'He knew your father.' Vesna surprises Marko.

'Your father was like a brother to me,' Marko tells Amelia. 'I slept in a bunk bed with him. Your father slept in the top bunk. Above me. We used to play games at night.'

'What kind of games?'

'Oh. We had a game – I would be Chuck Norris and he would be Bruce Lee.' But Marko can't explain it. 'We would tell each other stories – it was in the war, you know. When your father came home. Our home was his home.' But he is telling her a story he doesn't believe any more.

'What else?' Amelia says.

'Your father had a terrible snore.'

Amelia smiles, and the more she smiles, the more she looks like her dad.

'He was a good man,' Marko says.

'Will Marko come to tea?' Amelia asks her mother.

'You can go to Daša's, Amelia, maybe we'll see Marko later.'

And with that, Kemal's daughter runs headlong into the drying sheets.

'Thanks,' Vesna says.

'I had to tell her that. That he was a good man.'

'He really was.'

'I suppose good people can do bad things.'

'What do you mean?'

Marko has to look at her. But her face expresses the confusion in her voice. She really doesn't know what he means.

'Ladina,' Marko says. 'The camp.' But even as he says this, he realises they are not talking about the same thing.

'Is that you, Mladić?'

'Yes, it is you old devil, what do you want?'

'Three of my boys went missing near . . . and I want to find out what happened to them.'

'I think they're all dead.'

'I've got one of their parents on to me about it. So I can tell them for certain they are gone?'

'Yep. Certain. You have my word. By the way, how's the family?'

'Oh, not so bad thanks. How's yours?'

'They're doing just fine, we're managing pretty well.'

'By the way, now I've got you on the line, we've got about twenty bodies of yours near the front and they've been stripped bare. We slung them into a mass grave, and now they're stinking to high heaven. Any chance of you coming to pick them up? Because they really are becoming unbearable.'

Bosnian Serb General Ratko Mladić talks by phone to the head of the Croat Interior Ministry, 1992, in a recording played to journalist Misha Glenny, in *The Fall of Yugoslavia*

5 May 1995

Stovnik

A spring breeze hurries the clouds, and the light plays over Slatina's apartment blocks; over stucco the colour of dirty skin, concrete balconies of mustard-yellow, rust-red and sticking-plaster pink. When a cloud darkens the estate, the blocks across the courtyard seem to lean over the playgrounds below. Then the sun returns, and the day stretches out again, keeping its promise of a long evening on the Kapija and the 'Youth Day' party. It will be the first time in five years the day has been celebrated on the square. The latest ceasefire has held for a month. Convoys of food and clothing have made it through and, watching the estate from the window over the sink, Marko peels potatoes delivered from Croatia, challenging himself with each stroke of the peeler to produce a thinner skin.

'The war turned you into a housewife.' Kemal passes through the kitchen in nothing but a towel.

'And you an arsehole.'

Insults don't feel as easy in Marko's mouth as they did before he fucked Kemal's girlfriend.

Kemal shuts the bathroom door. Marko is only cooking because his parents are visiting the black market at Babunovići, or *Arizona*, as everyone is calling the market now the Americans hold the road. Fish have started to arrive. They have bought four rainbow trout. There is enough gas to heat the water for Kemal's bath. A little luck and the war might be over. Shouldn't everyone be feeling happy? Maybe it is because they have been here before, but the end of war seems almost as frightening as the beginning.

The phone rings. He dries his hands and dashes into the lounge with the wet towel, tucking the receiver between his shoulder and chin.

'Yes?'

'Marko?' It is Vesna. 'Is this thing actually working?'

'Yes,' Marko says. 'It's working.'

'Well?' Vesna says.

'Well what?'

'Is he in?'

Marko peers down the hall to the bathroom door. It is closed. Water is running. Jon Bon Jovi sings 'Living on A Prayer'.

'He's out.'

'Oh,' Vesna sounds disappointed. 'I told him I'd call at three.'

'I can take a message.'

'Where is he?'

Marko sits down on the sofa and picks up a leaflet on the coffee table: *Citizen Information: UNPROFOR in Stovnik and Surrounding Areas*. A picture of a tank and an African-American soldier at a crossroads.

'He's gone to the market with my mother. In Babunovići.'

'Babunovići?'

'*Arizona*. The road is open.'

'The Babunovići road is open?'

'For the last three days.'

'We haven't got radio reception,' Vesna says. 'I didn't know.'

'Well, it's open.'

'Then maybe Kemal could collect me? From my mother's?'

'What for?'

'The Kapija. The party tonight. Tell him – *ask* him to come around seven thirty or something, will you?'

Ask him yourself, Marko thinks. Since Sarajevo, Marko and Vesna seem to speak even *less*. She hasn't mentioned what happened in the bathroom of her father's apartment. This phone call should be for *him*, about *them*.

'Seven thirty,' Marko says meekly.

He is about to put down the phone, when he hears Vesna's small voice in the receiver and snatches it back to his ear.

'Yes?'

'How is he?' Vesna says. 'Is he still acting weird?'

'He's fine,' Marko cuts her off. 'I don't know what everyone is worrying about.'

Boxing Day, 2004

Kao Lak

Kemal tells Anya to order anything she likes. *On the house.* Anya orders a filter coffee. Kemal asks the boy for Turkish. She watches the boy walk into the bar. A European family sit at a table on the veranda, an Asian couple at the next. It seems extraordinary that normal life goes on as she sits in front of a dead man.

'Did you try coffee in Bosnia?' Kemal asks her.

'Of course.' Beneath the table she can't stop jogging her leg. Though the beach is warming up, she feels cold, and pulls the resort's robe around her chest, tightening the belt, shifting uncomfortably in the seat of her swimming costume. He approached her on the walkway as she returned from the massage, and somehow she knew she hadn't got away with it. But how does he know who she is?

Kemal pushes the cigarette packet across the table. 'We have a saying – *a coffee without a cigarette is like a mosque without a minaret.*'

'I don't smoke.'

He nods and replaces the cigarette packet on the flickering cover of a magazine. It is something to do with motorbikes. This is the bar-owner's table. His magazines. His cigarettes. A Russian thriller he has been reading. His hunting knife (or is it fish-gutting?).

Kemal briefly shakes his arms, like a dog throwing off water, then sets his elbows on the table and steeples his fingers. 'My friends came to see me. Vesna. Bogdan. You met them in Stovnik.'

Anya nods.

'They told me an English woman called Anya came from an organisation called Dignity Monitor. And Dignity Monitor publishes photographs of its employees online.'

'I see.'

The boy brings the filter coffee with Kemal's Turkish coffee, laying out a proper brass pot with a separate sugar bowl, a small cup, a saucer and a glass of water.

Kemal indicates Anya. 'Another water?'

'Thank you.' Anya surprises herself by managing to smile at the waiter like a normal person in a normal situation.

'But I wondered when I saw you hiding under the table in my room. Is this what they do at Dignity Monitor? Not very dignified.' He tries to disguise his smile by drinking from the glass, but in the water his teeth are as big as a horse's.

Anya picks up the milk jug, steadying it with both hands, and pours some into her coffee. 'I'm sorry,' she begins, but doesn't know where she is going with it. The coffee is steaming hot, and the low morning sun is on the back of her neck.

Kemal waves her apology away, eyes scanning the beach before turning back to her. 'How did you like Stovnik? I can't tell you how much I miss it.'

Stovnik

The water has reached Marko's feet. He steps back from the kitchen sink, and the heel of his sock makes a small plash in the warm puddle. At first, he thinks he has spilled something. He grabs a towel and starts to mop. But the puddle stretches beneath the kitchen table and the towel immediately soaks through. Walking around the table, he follows the water where it spreads on the tiles, over the threshold of the kitchen door, flowing in a thick and constant stream over the hallway parquet. The floors must slope gently towards the kitchen because, thank fuck, the water has streamed away from the lounge and its carpet.

He hammers on the bathroom door. 'Kemal? What are you doing!?'

It gushes over his feet. His socks are heavy. He tries the handle and the door opens.

The water falls in curtains over the lip of the bath. Kemal floats like something brought to the head of a spring; his legs and chest a hairy moss, his penis a giant, blind worm. He holds himself still with the sides, eyes closed, the taps of the bath still running. Marko turns them off, and hits the stop button on the tape player.

Kemal opens his eyes, a man waking from a deep sleep. 'I was listening to that!'

'You've flooded the fucking kitchen!'

'What?'

Kemal shifts, sending another curtain of water over the sides of the bath. He smiles. 'Four years of water shortages, then you get too much.'

'Fucking maniac.' Marko leaves the bathroom to find the towels, and clean up the mess. The flood uses every towel in the airing cupboard. The parquet will be stained for days. He strains the mop, empties the bucket, strains the mop, empties the bucket. What would Kemal say? What would he do if he knew? What would he do if Marko told him every last detail? How she had wanted him to fuck her on her knees?

He is down to the last corners of the kitchen when he stops to rest on the handle, and sees his friend, across the lounge and through the open door of the bedroom, naked and sawing his crotch with a towel.

Everyone had been treading on eggshells around Kemal, too afraid to say anything. *Fatigue*, his mother called it – a little shell-shock. His father said it was all completely normal. They just had to give Kemal space, time and their understanding.

Kemal took his space and time at the house in Kletovo. He said he was doing the garden there. He would return covered in soil and earth, using all the hot water for his baths.

In the bedroom Marko finds Kemal putting on the jacket of the new tracksuit his parents bought from the *Arizona* market; a Kappa, pearl with a lime-green stripe down the arms and legs.

'It looks good,' Marko says. But Kemal has lost so much weight the tracksuit is about a size too big.

Kemal looks into the mirror and adjusts the sleeves. 'Top 5 Bundesliga goal scorers, 1993?'

'Kuntz,' Marko says. 'Chapuisat, Heesen, Bäron and Kirsten.' He sits down on the bottom bunk. The back of his head rests against the frame of Kemal's bed. He is too tall now to easily fit beneath it. With his back to Marko, Kemal puts his left foot on the window ledge and begins to tie the laces of a white trainer. Another gift from Marko's parents.

'You're going to the Kapija tonight?' Marko asks.

'What for?'

'The big Youth Day thing. Everyone's going.'

Kemal swaps legs, and ties the second trainer. 'I'll probably go to Kletovo, work on the garden.'

'But the curfew's lifted,' Marko reminds him. 'Everyone's going.'

Kemal straightens up and appears to be staring out of the window at something Marko cannot see.

'What happened with the bath?' Marko says.

'I fell asleep.' He crosses into the kitchen, opens the tool drawer and starts to rifle through it.

'You feel tired?' Marko asks.

'Tired?'

'In general. Do you think you're exhausted?'

'Why would I be exhausted?'

'I don't know. You know. That's what Dad thinks.'

'In the pocket of my jeans!' Kemal shuts the tool drawer and heads back into the bedroom where he throws clothes across the room. 'Come on.' Kemal opens the front door. 'I've got something for you.'

The lift is still out of order. He follows Kemal down the stairs of the block, from the warm late afternoon light, to the cold of the stairs, back to the warm light again. At the turn of each staircase, the glass has been smashed. Kemal doesn't stop for Marko, but jogs down at a methodical pace. By the time they reach the bottom, Marko's knees are trembling, and it feels as if the playground between the blocks is facing the wrong direction.

'Where are we going?' Marko pants.

'You'll need to be fitter than that.' Kemal claps Marko on the shoulder.

'What for?'

'When they call you up. It isn't long, you know. But hopefully you'll be sitting in the barracks all day anyway.'

Marko pulls a cigarette packet out of his pocket. He can't seem to walk outside without wanting to light up. They take a cigarette each, sit on the pavement banked above the football pitch and say hello to Mrs Lilic as she passes with her shopping trolley.

'I think she sells organs,' Kemal says. 'On the black market. She's *always* shopping. But where does she shop?'

'What did you want to show me?'

Kemal shakes the arm of his new tracksuit, and looks at his watch. 'Maybe nothing. Maybe something.'

This could be it, Marko thinks. If Kemal knows, this could be it. They are waiting for the friends who are going to take him away, and beat him up. He watches the boys playing football on the concrete pitch. It couldn't be them, could it? Marko knows every one of them by name. Burim raises a hand and waves them over but Marko shakes his head and dismisses him.

'He'll go with you, will he? Burim?' Kemal says.

'What?' Marko tries to hide the panic in his voice. 'Go where?'

'The call-up?' Kemal says. 'Conscription. You're both eighteen this year, aren't you?'

'Oh yes. Yes, there'll be a few of us.'

The game is quick and ruthless. Elvis threads the ball through Samir, through Zurab, through Alexander. An orange Volkswagen Vanagon pulls up on the road right in front of them, roof blocking their view of the goal. It is Bogdan. An older boy and one of Kemal's closest friends. He has brought a van, and they are going to take him away in it.

Bogdan climbs out of the driver's door. Wearing the fatigues of the brigade, he walks around the bonnet to the pavement. Kemal stands up to meet him, and Marko thinks about running. But where would that get him? He couldn't hide forever.

When Kemal and Bogdan shake hands, Bogdan leaves a set of keys in Kemal's palm and Kemal slips him a note.

'Enjoy.' Bogdan looks at Marko. Then crosses the playground, heading for the main road.

When Kemal turns around, he throws something at Marko.

The keys.

'Happy birthday,' Kemal says. 'An early present. I feel bad I didn't get you anything last time.'

Marko jumps down the bank and onto the road. He doesn't know where to begin. He paces around the van.

'We liberated it,' Kemal says.

Marko looks at his friend.

'Not like that – it's all good. Ex-army. We registered a new owner.'

He runs his fingers along the paintwork. Beneath the hot orange, a faint trace of camouflage paint. Kemal opens the driver's side door. The cab smells of warm leatherette.

'Diesel,' Kemal says.

'How did you get it?'

'Someone owed us a favour.'

'You can't afford this.'

They climb inside. Kemal punches the buttons on the radio and the news comes on.

'I didn't need to afford it,' he says. 'So don't worry about it – I told you, the army owe me.'

Kemal opens the passenger door. 'Drive it. Drive it all the way to Croatia if you need to. Get out of this shithole.' He bangs the roof. 'I have to go and meet someone.'

He steps out of the car, closes the door and climbs the bank to the pavement.

He is not going to be beaten up. Kemal does not know. Marko puts the key in the ignition, and turns the engine over. The van starts first time, engine shaking his seat. Kemal has stopped on the pavement, detained by Elvis.

He leans over the seat, and winds down the passenger window.

'Vesna called!' he shouts.

Kemal looks back at the van.

'She said to meet her at the Kapija. The New York – seven thirty! By the theatre wall.'

Kemal walks back to the van and hangs over the window. 'Vesna wants to meet *tonight*?'

'Sorry, I forgot. She wants to go down to the square, for the Youth Day thing.'

It is half the truth. He needs the other half himself.

'I'll call her and tell her I can't make it.'

'No,' Marko says.

'Why not?'

'She's not in,' he improvises. 'Not by a phone any more. At a friend's. You know. She said she was going round a friend's to get ready.'

'Jesus. Seven thirty?'

'On the Kapija. By the theatre wall.'

Kemal shakes his head. 'All right.' Then he leans through the window of the van, and pinches Marko's cheek harder than he needs to. Pinches his cheek so it will leave a blue bruise which Marko feels half the way out of town. 'Drive safely.'

He is passing the cooling towers of the electricity plant when he remembers he is supposed to be cooking dinner. But the Stovnik sign feels like a point of no return.

Shithole, he thinks. He has never heard Kemal say anything bad about his home.

Kao Lak

In the past ten years of her profession, Anya had listened to countless victims of human rights abuses. Usually they were voices over the phone. Most often, she heard them through a translator, but sometimes, when a case began to build, she sat and listened to victims of inhumanity, in the cafés and homes of villages in Bosnia, Serbia, Croatia and Kosovo. Until now, she had no reason to wonder how it might be different to listen to the story of the perpetrator. Only at The Hague had she breathed the same air as war criminals. And the court was different. The men on trial didn't begin with the trickle of places and people, of times and dates. They didn't slowly unwind themselves. The men at The Hague answered only what they were advised to answer, giving up the facts in shockingly dull itineraries of horror. Most of these men had at some point been assessed as psychopaths. She didn't really believe these assessments, but it was easier to *want* them to be psychopaths than to believe them to be normal.

This wasn't a courtroom. Kemal didn't talk like the men at The Hague. For a start, he *was* talking; like a man who'd been rehearsing this conversation for years. And as he did, Anya was reminded of something a military police investigator once told her: silence is the best means of interrogation.

It started with how he missed Stovnik, but now Kemal was telling her about a place called Kletovo. He had grown up in Kletovo, in his father's farmhouse, but his father had died before the war, and then his mother had been taken by Chetniks. Kemal had been made to watch while the Chetniks raped his mother. He tells her this without emotion, with his eyes on the beach, as if he were waiting for someone to appear.

She looks down at her hands.

'Maybe you think this is what turns a man into a rapist.' A breeze picks up the smoke of his cigarette and throws it in her eyes.

'I'm sorry about your mother.'

Of course, he really had been rehearsing these lines. But to what purpose? So when the time came he had a good story? So he could absolve himself with the right excuses? She heard this too in the mouths of lawyers at The Hague, as they tried to build the mitigating circumstances for their clients; as they tried to construct the story of how a man comes to do the unspeakable.

Now she was the lawyer.

'I was told by a witness you raped a woman. At least one. At an aluminium factory called PK Musapa, sometime in August 1994. Two other women at that factory went missing.'

Anya hears the words come out of her mouth and feels they do not belong to her. They belong to the ideal Anya. The woman she is supposed to be. And while she knows that her accusation is dangerous, she experiences the thrill of becoming this person.

' "At least one"?' Kemal doesn't take his eyes off the beach. He leans forward and crushes his cigarette into the ashtray, tap, tap, tapping it down.

'Ljuba Crvenović,' Kemal finally says. 'That was her name, wasn't it? You spoke to her, did you?'

Jasenica

Marko hasn't been to Vesna's house in Jasenica since the beginning of the war. Thirteen years old! They had played in the front garden. He parks the van on the gravel slope, but it begins to roll back. He has to pull harder on the handbrake, frantically forcing the gearstick into first. The van creaks, and holds, just. The terraced lawn he remembers has turned into mire, relieved only by a few rows of vegetables, bamboo tents for beans and tomatoes, stunted peppers under sheets of plastic. The house has only half a roof. Across the white plaster wall, beneath the blue sheets of UNHCR tarpaulin, someone has sprayed:

WELCOME TO ZAGREB

'Hello?' He hears music playing; Bijelo Dugme singing *'Da te bogdo ne volim'*. The porch smells of the stagnant rain water collected in plastic barrels by the front door.

'Who is it?'

'It's Marko!'

The door unbolts. Edita's face appears in the crack.

'Mrs Knežević!' Marko smiles.

'You!' she says. 'My God, look at you.'

She is shorter than he remembers. Or he is taller. Her face is thinner. Her black hair threaded with white.

'Who did this, Mrs Knežević?'

Vesna's mother shakes her head at the graffiti. 'Oh, some kids – local – years ago.'

He follows her into a hallway of bare concrete floors. The walls have been recently set and have a clayey smell.

'My parents were Croatian of course,' she says. 'So apparently this graffiti is hilarious.'

The kitchen is bare; walls half-skimmed, pale shadows where the kitchen units used to stand. The only furniture is a table in the middle of the room, where a camping cooker is hooked up to a gas cylinder.

'Vesna told me Kemal was coming to collect her at seven thirty.' She picks up two coffee cups and puts them in a washing bowl.

'He couldn't,' Marko lies. 'So I've come to get her while I can.'

'Well. She's upstairs getting ready. Which means you may be here for weeks.'

'You should have told us about this graffiti,' Marko says.

'Us? Told *you*?'

'I know people,' Marko says. 'We could find those guys.'

Vesna's mother laughs, and wipes the coffee cups with a dishcloth. 'And that's how it all starts, isn't it?'

Marko offers her a cigarette.

'Now let me see.' She takes the packet. 'What is this?'

'Real Marlboros, from Denmark – I get them from Lorens.'

'Lorens? The man you work for, is it?' She takes one of the cigarettes and smells it, knuckles like cracked acorns. Leaning over the table, Marko lights the cigarette, and Edita's lips print a plum ring around the filter. She blows the smoke at the ceiling in one long plume, like a whale shoots water for the joy of it.

'It was just some kid's joke,' she says. '*Welcome to Zagreb.* But we can't get it off, and we'll have to paint over it, and no one seems to have any yellow paint. I want yellow this time. I want a change.'

'Have the packet.' Marko offers her the cigarettes.

'Marko!' Vesna stands in the empty frame where the kitchen door used to be, barefooted, in a sleeveless white dress, which describes her figure so perfectly Marko is speechless.

Kao Lak

Kemal remembers Ljuba. She arrived on the second day. Her party walked out of the woods. With a team of four soldiers, Kemal manned a roadblock of overturned cars. The refugees were directed to the factory. They came in small groups at first. Each one of them approached the block, in the sights of the soldiers' guns, arms and hands raised above their heads. Refugees had been used as Trojan horses before. At Gruvo Brdo, six of the 3rd brigade were killed, along with twelve refugees who approached a roadblock. The Chetniks were sitting in the trees behind the refugees, forcing them out. Kemal didn't want anything like this to happen to the 2nd brigade. He hated forests. More than anything he hated forests.

The men with him at the factory were not in good humour. The brigade had been split by Chetnik troops attacking the valley from two sides. On the west flank Kemal and his men seemed to have pushed them back. But his troops in the east had not been so successful.

During the night, shots echoed over the eastern hills, where his men tried to hold off the attack, fighting their slow retreat to the factory. These men were supposed to regroup with the troops commanded by Kemal, but had been cut off.

There was no shelling in the area, but if the Chetniks brought shells in, the factory in which they were taking refuge would make a clear target.

What to do? It was Kemal's decision. He didn't trust a flight to the west. Perhaps they really had managed to push back the Chetniks there. But only two roads were passable, and he knew they were manned with roadblocks. The more difficult routes might prove too slow, giving the Chetniks time to outflank them. The south wasn't an option either because eventually, they would meet the river, and if they couldn't cross it, they would be trapped. Besides, the 2nd brigade had been chased into the valley from the south, and he had no intelligence on whether this threat was still present.

Kemal thought they should wait until they could gauge the Serbs' next move. Until headquarters could give them better information on the radio. When the radio worked.

They were thinking about pushing on north, when the refugees started arriving from that direction too, bringing with them news of what sounded like a large Serbian presence.

'That is one place I would not go back to.' He looks over the beach. The clatter of cutlery surrounds them, the laughter of a child, the soft voices of lovers and the tinny noise of a radio drifting out of the bar.

'I remember Ljuba arriving,' Kemal says. 'Because she came with the other women and they were pretty. Eight of them including Ljuba, you are right. Younger than most of the others. They kept close. Slept together on the floor.'

Kemal paws at his face. He rocks back on the legs of his chair. Rocks forward, and brings his big hands down onto the table, palms flat.

'You know what I thought when I saw those women? I thought, here's trouble.'

Stovnik

It is nearly seven by the time Vesna is ready to go. Kemal will be waiting in the square at 7.30. They have half an hour. Marko has so much to say, but when Vesna climbs into the van, he is paralysed by the sight of the gold zip that runs all the way from the dark pit of her arm to the nut-brown skin above her left knee.

'I thought you said you had a new *car*?'

Marko doesn't understand. His head fills with hairspray. Vesna pulls down the passenger visor, but there is no mirror. She opens the gold handbag on her lap and takes out a compact. 'Whatever this thing is. Are you going to drive it?'

The van jumps. Vesna's hair falls about her face. He takes the engine out of gear and tries again, letting down the awkward handbrake as smoothly as possible. They descend the hairpins over the valley at Jasenica. The only road barrier is the flickering yellow tape indicating a mined area. The van clatters over the potholes. Vesna says nothing. When they turn onto the Zagreb road, the indicator doesn't cancel itself, and when he tries to turn it off, it switches in the other direction, then back again, before mysteriously stopping.

On the way to Vesna's, Marko had sailed along, the windows open, the invigorating smell of fertiliser in the air; the sedimentary layers of the mountains on either side of the valley were speed stripes. He had been full of confidence. He would get to Vesna first. They would finally talk about what happened. He would let her know he wanted her, and that what had happened in Sarajevo couldn't just be ignored.

Now the van climbs through its five gears at an excruciating pace, and every change seems to mark the distance between Marko and the girl sitting next to him. Trapped in the cab, this is the closest they have been since Vesna's bathroom floor, since Marko so painfully found his way inside her. But they couldn't be further apart.

He winds down the window, and rests his elbow in the cool running air, free hand feeling in his pocket. Then he remembers he gave the cigarettes to Vesna's mother.

'Do you have cigarettes?'

'I'm giving up.'

'Giving up?'

But she doesn't answer. Out of the passenger window, she watches the blackened frames of Tinje's houses sail by. An army transporter is suddenly in front of them, and Marko has to slow behind the open tailgate. Inside the men sit on benches holding their rifles. The wheels of the truck ping small stones against the van's paintwork and windscreen. Marko tries to drop back.

'When are you drafted?' she asks.

'June,' Marko says. 'Probably. I don't know yet.'

'What do you think about Kemal?'

'I don't want to talk about Kemal.'

Marko feels he has taken a real step with these words, but she seems to ignore him.

'Do you think it's a kind of shell shock? His mood?'

'I don't know.'

'He isn't himself. Seems to want to spend all of his time in that garden.'

'Yes.' Marko realises he is going to have to placate her. 'He took a bath today.'

'So?'

But he doesn't get to finish the story. The army truck in front suddenly stops. They brake sharply. Vesna bounces forward. She has her hands on the dashboard. When the dust clears, the boys in the truck appear to have taken notice. One of them comes to the back and stands with his arms hanging from the metal frame of the tarpaulin roof. The soldier sways forward, and says something Marko can't quite hear. Another soldier appears at the shoulder of the first, shapes a cock out of thin air and mimes his masturbation.

Vesna gives them the finger. Marko opens the door of the van and steps out.

'Marko!' He hears her shout. 'Don't!'

'What's the fucking problem?' Marko yells at the soldiers.

But they don't even look at him. Marko is left in a faint cloud of exhaust fumes and sand which clear to reveal an American soldier, and a tank at the side of the road.

Kao Lak

Ljuba's testimony to Anya matched what Kemal told her. The first time she saw the brigade commander with his red sash was at the roadblock. Over the next two days, she found the presence of the man with the red sash reassuring. He always seemed calm. He was always in control. He didn't go with the soldiers who manned the roadblocks any more, but stayed behind as part of the team defending the factory. He spent a lot of time with the radio, communicating with the brigade headquarters. When an argument broke out between two women accusing each other of stealing the food rations, it was Kemal who stepped in and sorted out the matter.

Ljuba confessed she had felt safer for the presence of someone like Kemal.

'We decided to investigate a route to the south-east,' he is telling her, 'there were two villages we might be able to use – as staging posts. I had information they were still defended. The idea was we could reinforce those defences and protect the refugees in the houses. But we needed to see first. If we would meet any Chetniks on the way. Send a "probe".' He uses the technical word proudly, as if holding up a gem to the light. It is the English he has learned from his expat customers in Thailand. 'I was away two nights. And when I came back – it was at night.' He stops. Somewhere else in his mind. 'Fuck it,' he mutters, 'she should have kept still.'

He stops to sip from his coffee but when he puts the cup down he doesn't start again. Something is in his way. Something in the forest which Anya can't see. He paws at his face, pulling down on his nose and sniffing.

'Vesna told me she threw you out.' He shakes his head. 'She's got fire – yes?'

Anya colours. The way she had bumbled around, asking stupid questions. 'Yes.'

'Did you meet my daughter?'

'Your daughter?'

'Amelia. Did you see a girl called Amelia?'

'I didn't meet a girl.'

She looks at Kemal's hands, as if they will tell her what they have done. 'When you came back it was at night? What do you mean, she should have kept still?'

He is watching the beach, absent-mindedly scratching at a patch of what looked like scalded skin on his left bicep.

'I was on the Kapija, you know.'

'Where?'

'You can't hear anything. When a shell hits so close. It's like an explosion of silence in your head. You can't hear people screaming. I could see them. But I couldn't hear them.'

Kemal holds out his hands and arms. 'How do you explain? Not a scratch. Nothing touched me. Afterwards, my ears were bleeding. Perforated drums. The sound of the shell perforated my eardrums, but the shell itself – the shrapnel. All around me, everyone in pieces. But me? Nothing. How did that happen?'

'Do you want to talk about what happened at Ladina?'

'I thought – *I should be dead*! What if I *was* dead?'

'But in Ladina?'

'I want to go to Bosnia and be in my daughter's life.'

She is losing him. She needs to take him back. She needs him in that factory. She doesn't want Kemal the father. She wants Kemal the soldier. Kemal the brigade commander.

'How did it happen?'

'Hmm?'

'Ljuba?'

'I don't know,' he says. 'I wasn't there.'

This is what he has been trying to pull out of himself. When he picks his coffee up, his hand is shaking.

Just his hand. And then Anya realises. She sees what Ljuba saw. The red sash of the commander on the concrete floor. Just his hand. His wrist. The red sash.

'When you left the camp,' she starts, 'For the probe. You left someone else in charge?'

'If I was a dead man,' Kemal says, 'how could I betray anyone?'

She opens her mouth to speak. Kemal breaks her gaze. He is looking beyond her. He is smiling. He is standing up to greet someone, and when Anya looks around, it is William. He is red-faced. Out of breath.

'Here you are!' he says.

And despite all the questions Anya still has, she has never been so happy to see anyone in all her life.

By the time they have passed the roadblock, it is almost a quarter past seven. Barely fifteen minutes before Vesna is supposed to be in the square with Kemal, and still they have talked about nothing. Marko pulls away as fast as the van will manage. The engine complains as he racks through the gears.

All Vesna can do is moan. Moan about the van. Complain they'll be late. The road steepens, and the van likes it even less. He pulls up on a Ford Transit packed with people, and gears down to overtake. When he does, it is a mistake. As they crawl on the wrong side of the road, an old man his grandfather's age is looking down on them through the window of the minibus, shaking his head.

'What are you doing?' Vesna asks.

The grocer's van is heading towards them. The gap between this and the bus is only just big enough. He twitches at the steering wheel. The grocer's van takes their wing mirror. Marko applies the brake, and the minibus they are trying to overtake shoots forward.

'Jesus, Marko!'

'You wanted to get there on time,' he snaps.

'And alive!'

The minibus is slowing now. They are at the junction above town, next to the water-cooling towers of the electricity plant. The bus turns left. Marko turns right. They pass the Stovnik sign, and the abandoned petrol station. Around the bend are the blocks of Marko's estate; beyond this, the red roofs of the old town, and the Kapija where Kemal is waiting. Where Marko has told Kemal to be.

Marko decides this will be the last time he will see Vesna. And if this is the last time he will see Vesna, perhaps it will be the last time he will see Kemal. He will be eighteen next month. He will move out. Come summer he'll be barracked with the army anyway.

He pulls onto the gravel verge of the last bend into town.

'What are you *doing*?' Vesna asks.

'Nice view.'

'Marko,' she says. 'Let's go. He's waiting.'

Marko grasps Vesna's wrist and pulls her into him. Hadn't it been like this on the bathroom floor? The hard kiss, hard teeth and biting? Wasn't this what she liked? Wasn't this what *they* had shared, wasn't this the thing only they shared? Or did she share this with Kemal?

Vesna pulls away. When she slaps him it is harder than he has ever been slapped. She has slammed the car door, and is walking over the dirt and scrub of the lay-by towards the edge of the hill.

'Vesna!' He climbs out and shouts after her, 'Vesna!' Marching now, easy to catch up as she stumbles in her heels.

'What if I told him,' he yells, 'about us!'

She stops and turns around. 'Tell Kemal?'

'Who do *you* think?'

'Kemal knows, you dickhead. No one has to tell him. He just knows.'

Marko looks at her face. She is crying. He has made her cry, and he feels wonderful and terrible at the same time.

'Are you going to drive us down?' Vesna asks. 'Or are you going to hit me?'

He watches as Vesna wobbles in her shoes, out over the gravel verge, towards the clump of flickering linden trees looking down over the roofs of the town. He thinks she is going to disappear on the path, but then she stops and bends over and a clear vomit pours out of her mouth. When he reaches her, Vesna raises her hand, and shakes her head. She sits down at one of the picnic benches. After a moment, he sits down beside her.

'Sorry,' he says.

'It's my fault too.'

When it comes, it doesn't make any sense, to hear the whistling sound up here. Marko has only ever heard it in the town. He spins around because he thinks a truck is passing by, but the road behind them is empty. A small 'pop'. Like a tyre exploding. Turning back to the town, a white cloud is already unfolding silently over the Kapija. For a second it might be something else: then its terrible beauty blooms, and it cannot be anything but what it is. From up here, it all happens slowly, silently, as if underwater. With the noise of sirens and screams, the first black smoke unfolds from the white. This is how it must look, to the men who fire the shells from the hills.

Tuesday 12 April 2005

Sarajevo

Samir's mobile phone does not answer. He is not at the B&B. The reception desk is watched by an elderly woman who turns out to be the shopkeeper from next door. She tells Marko that Samir has gone up to the park. 'Off Jekovac, you know? Above the Širokača cemetery? He had some idea about getting flowers for Jasmina, I said why don't you buy flowers from the market? You won't find flowers up there, unless you plan to take them from somebody's grave!' The woman screws a finger into her temple to indicate that Samir is mentally unsound. 'All the flowers on the market are from North Africa, he says. Spring flowers, he says. They have to be *real* spring flowers! He's crazy about them.' She gestures at the walls and their framed blossoms.

Jekovac is the street winding up above the market, above the noise of street sellers and vans in the tight market lanes, above the hammering of metal beams in the old Austro-Hungarian buildings that seem to require endless renovation. Marko has walked down one side of the valley today, and now he is climbing up the other. Jekovac rises on a cliff, above a hook in the Miljacka, and when the road turns, he can see over a crumbling wall, down to the green river. He stops to catch his breath. He has been smoking for the first time in years and hasn't eaten.

He is above the Širokača cemetery now, where the white obelisks of graves pour down onto the terracotta carpet of the city's roofs. The sun is beginning to set at the western end of the valley, drawing the eastern end beneath a curtain of cool shade. The black glass monstrosities of the Unis towers strike twin silhouettes. *Momo* and *Uzeir*. These were the names they gave them. One tower Bosnian, one tower Serb; a local legend of which the liberal politicians liked to remind the population during the war. *As long as Momo and Uzeir are still standing . . .*

And nationality hadn't mattered to them, it really hadn't mattered. Marko's father was born in Serbia, his mother in Croatia. So what did that make him? A boy born in Bosnia of Serbian and Croatian parents. They had *lived* in Bosnia, that was the point. Kemal's parents were born in Kletovo, and were Muslims both, but none of the family went to mosque. Samir's parents had Slovenian, Serbian and Hungarian blood. But no one in Stovnik really talked about where they came from, or who went to mosque and who went to church. They were better than all that. They were proper socialists. They were better than the idiots of the villages who did what they were told. They were better than the politicians in Serbia who destroyed Tito's communism and grabbed the army for themselves. In Stovnik they were better. In Sarajevo they were better.

How could you believe that about Kemal? In the garden Vesna's eyes had accused him.

Them, she had said. When Kemal told her about Ladina, she had told him about the English woman who was on to *them*.

Marko follows the steep road around the back of the cemetery until it splits at the tall walls of the yellow stone bastion, an octagon tower that rises two storeys. He is confused. He is not sure where this 'park' is supposed to be. There is a small patch of land planted with plane trees on the bastion, but up the cool stone steps of the tower, he only finds a few teenagers, and schoolchildren sharing cigarettes; aimless boys throwing stones at the trees; lovers sitting with their knees up, toe to toe on the wall, so their raised legs strike the shape of half a heart. The city spreads to the west, and climbs the hills to the north and east. But on the south side of the bastion, the hill drops precipitously from the road, and there is a single sandy pathway through the woods.

How is he supposed to find Samir here? He should have waited at the B&B, or gone back to his cousin's house. Jasmina would be cooking. Above the city, the early evening air is filling with the smell of frying peppers. The sinking sun sharpens the lines of the cliffs and hills. Why did this country have to be so fucking beautiful?

He sits down on the old wall of the bastion, and closes his eyes to the sun; the kids' voices swim around him, punctuated only by the hollow bell of stones striking the tree trunks. In England, he had once been taken to a cricket match, where the man who took him talked about the sound of leather on willow – the English sound. When he opens his eyes he is not in England. Two men in caps are laying prayer mats on the balding grass. Like a siren the call to prayer begins.

'It was *Samir* he didn't want to see!' Vesna told Marko of her conversations with Kemal. 'Samir and the others. That's why he didn't want to come back. He couldn't stand to look at them. Neither can I. Not even for Kemal's funeral. He came around here once, your cousin, wanting to know where Kemal was. I couldn't let him in the house.'

Marko faces Mecca and closes his eyes. He listens to the call to prayer. He is not observant, never has been. It is not his religion, but the sound is something like a childhood lullaby. When it is over, he drops down from the wall, and at that same moment, his phone rings.

'I had a missed call,' Samir says.

'Where are you?'

'Most people don't even know these are orchids,' Samir tells him.

They are standing beneath the cool canopy of the wood, beneath the bastion. Trees cling to the sides of a steep hill, roots like long fingers scrabbling in the rock and earth. In places, the land here falls away to a sheer cliff. Marko found his cousin on an outcrop, before a small tumble of moss-covered boulders, over a drop thick with tangled bushes and stunted trees. Samir holds the flower out, stem in one hand, head laid over his palm like a market seller presenting a fine cloth.

'*Cephalanthera longifolia*, a common white orchid in Bosnia, usually flowers in late May or June, but this year? I blame climate change.'

He lays the flower with a small pile by his feet, and kneels down with his prosthetic leg to clip another with a penknife. A breeze brushes the heads of the trees, the forest whispering.

'Cut it right, and they grow again.' He clips another, and places it with the bunch before using his good leg to push up, dragging the prosthetic until he can flip it straight. This is done in one seamless action that still elicits Marko's admiration. The descent into the woods had been hard enough on *two* legs.

'We spent so much time in forests,' Samir says. 'As soldiers. You wouldn't think I would want to spend another minute in them. But it's funny. There's something I like about being here. I think it's where I started looking at things differently. You know – "nature". And human nature.' He reaches over to one of the lichen-skinned boulders, touching a flower Marko hadn't even noticed. It grows in a green cup between the stones.

'This one is *Neottia nidus-avis*,' he says. 'Because of the bell-shaped heads and the lighter colour. Usually I find these, and they have quite brown petals. But this one seems very yellow.' He cups the flower like a lover's neck, but doesn't cut it. 'Maybe because of where it grows.'

'The Bosnian lily. Kemal had burned the tattoo off his arm.' Samir doesn't seem to have heard him. 'I saw Vesna again. She had Kemal's daughter. But you knew that.'

'I'm going to leave this one.' Samir removes his hand from the orchid.

'You knew Vesna had been to see him in Thailand.'

Samir has his back to Marko, looking up over the boulders and into the canopy of the woods. 'It's good to know, that there is no one hiding behind these trees. I'm not sure you can understand that.'

'Kemal contacted her three years ago.'

Marko is aware of taking a step towards his cousin, but not aware of the decision to place a hand on his shoulder.

'It's a victory for me. To come back into the woods,' Samir says.

Marko tightens his grip, but Samir slips it off. 'You were quite a naive kid, Marko. What made you think we were so fucking virtuous? We weren't. We were stupid fucking kids like everyone else. And you didn't have to face up to that, did you? You could just run away, and leave us to face up to it like you owed nothing. Maybe you did owe nothing.'

When his cousin finally turns around, Marko punches Samir square on the nose.

Samir steps back, holding his face. The blood comes quick between his fingers.

The trees dance around them.

'Done?' Samir says.

Marko waits until his cousin looks up again. Samir wipes his face so the blood paints his cheek, puts his hands on his hips and presents the other side like a target. 'There's more than that. Isn't there?'

Marko has taken his shot before Samir even finishes. This time his cousin goes down, falling back, over his good leg. Marko isn't sure whether he hears, or sees Samir's head hit the boulder. He grabs the collar of his shirt, picks him up and punches his face like a pillow. He doesn't know how many times he does this before he stops.

Up the path and over the outcrop, the trees marching with him now. He knows if he stays there will be more. He can feel it in his fists, it is what the beat of his heart is telling him. He knows he will not stop.

The path meets the road, and offers him a choice he is not ready for. Down to the town, or up into the hills. He follows his feet up, because it is harder this way, because this way there is more energy to spend. Samir helped carry Kemal's coffin up the hill of Lovers' Park, when he knew Kemal was not dead, but on his way to Croatia. Kemal was out of the country, out to wherever he would no longer have to look at the faces of the men who let him down. Marko tries to remember now if Samir had wept. If he had ever seen Samir weep.

But he can't remember having ever wept himself.

He reaches a broken stone wall, separating a field of meadow grass from the road, and sits down, breathless, the city falling away.

When people in England asked about the war, Marko used to say to them: 'War is war. What can I tell you?' He has never known what this meant. Only it stopped a conversation he didn't want to have. When people asked about the war, he did not see the war at first. He did not see the things people wanted to hear about. He did not see orange tracers unzipping the night over Stovnik. He did not see the mouth of the tunnel beneath the airport in Sarajevo at just the moment before he took a deep breath, and bent down to hurry through. He did not smell the sewage, and the sweat in damp clothes. When people asked about the war, at parties, on the doorstep of a club, around a dinner table, it was Kemal he saw first. Kemal in his bedroom, putting his uniform on. The boy his cousin Samir met on a beach in Bečići, the boy who turned out to be from the next village. The boy who encouraged them to chase the girl who was down by the breakwater. The boy who discovered Vesna. He'd loved Kemal more than any of them. Those friendships were his war. When people asked Marko about the war, he saw Kemal, because Kemal was the one victim of the war whom Marko believed he'd killed.

A song is playing somewhere. Playing through a cheap radio among the clatter of pots and pans. He hears a mother shouting at her children. A dog barking. The chime of his mobile phone playing along in all this; it is a sound he doesn't recognise until he feels the phone buzzing insistently against his thigh. He doesn't make the decision to answer but finds himself pressing the right button, and holding the phone to his ear.

'Hello?' It is an English voice.

'Speaking.'

'Sorry – who am I speaking to? Is that Marko?'

Perhaps William has the wrong number. He almost wishes he has. He has spent the afternoon preparing himself to make this phone call, and now he feels like it needs a rehearsal, a false start. If this is the wrong number, he can try again, get himself into a better frame of mind. Or if this is the wrong number, perhaps fate is relieving him of the responsibility to make the call. Because if this is the *right* number (and yes, the voice on the other end of the line has just confirmed his name is Marko), he has no business visiting his grief on the unsuspecting.

'I was given your number by the Bosnian embassy in Bangkok,' William says. 'As next of kin for Kemal Lekić. I understand you were his – *brother*?'

William looks down from his apartment, on to the familiar lights of Sukhumvit at night. It is reassuring to place his hand on the cool glass and remind himself of where he is.

Marko listens to the English voice telling him Kemal Lekić was his brother, and like a suggestible believer listening to the words of an imam thinks, yes, he *was*. There is also something reassuring about the English voice. Something of his real life, with Millie, with his business, with his rent and his bills, with all the wonderful dullness of his normal life, far away from the hillsides where he has just assaulted his cousin.

'Who is this?' Marko asks.

'Sorry. My name's William Howell. I met your brother in Kao Lak.'

'Kemal?'

'As a tourist. I was a tourist. In Kao Lak. We happened to be together when the wave came.' There is a pause. Every time William mentions the wave, it's as if he has to wait again, to stand on the veranda with Anya and Kemal, to watch the tide retreat.

'We were together when the wave came,' he begins over. 'And I suppose, I believe, I may have been one of the last people to see him alive. Before the coma.' William should have begun the entire conversation with his condolences, but it seems too late now. There is no sound on the other end of the line, and when he tries to imagine the Bosnian man who has answered the phone, he realises he is picturing Kemal himself. The voice comes out of nothing, but is close, like a man standing next to him in a dark room.

'You were with Kemal when the wave hit?' Marko asks.

'We were together, at his bar. We'd just met. But afterwards – '

William cannot think why he had imagined this was a story he could tell over the phone to a stranger.

'Afterwards?' the Bosnian man says.

'Sorry. I'm calling because I wanted to tell you, your brother saved my life. He picked me up, and put me on the back of a bike, and got me to the hospital. I was almost unconscious.'

'Yes.'

'There were other people too,' the English man says, 'in the sea. We found a place, a fire escape which we were standing on. And Kemal stepped down into the water. He was pulling people out. I thought – I thought it's something someone should know about.'

'Yes,' Marko says, 'yes, it is.'

The first wave turned out to be nothing more than a rehearsal. The ocean had given up, tipping over the car park, water from a spilled glass. As the spill retreated and sucked at their toes, they watched where Kemal's bar had become a wooden boat, sea turning at the skirts of its veranda. The car park was as far as the first wave came. Where the beach had been, a black lake of umbrellas rocking like buoys, a vending freezer capsized, the seller, standing among his floating stock. People stood waist deep, the panic on their faces slowly turning to relief. Parents held their children above the waterline, chattering voices full of a nervous joy. Some people had even begun to play. He remembers a group of brown-skinned teenaged boys, wrestling in the water, seal slick in the sunlight. Others waded to the road, women holding excited children above their heads. It all happened in the silence left behind after a great noise. The silence created when you take something away. Below the lip of the car park, bobbing on the surface of the black water, floated a sign with the English words *No Dog Walking*, on a piece of green sheet-metal, and a picture of a small black terrier crossed out with a red line. William has often wondered if Kemal or Anya had said something as they stood on the warm, damp tarmac of the car park. If they had said their final words to each other. But *No Dog Walking* is all that ever returns to him, the sign turning on the surface before it slips away – slowly at first, gathering pace. Not floating, but pulled. They were standing in a moment where everything that mattered was what *couldn't* be seen, what *couldn't* be heard. The yawn of the ocean pulling the water back, as the horizon slipped silently towards them. The value of their life reduced to scale; how small they were.

William has said goodbye to Marko, and with his thoughts, Bosnia retreats to the other side of the world. He lies back on his bed and the ceiling of the apartment tips over him, glowing red and then black, red and then black, the conversation of altitude lights on the needles of Bangkok's skyscrapers, the cars picked up and gently turned over, a shoal of refrigerators, a washing machine pushing through the window of a shop, the air cracking in their ears. It was not the first wave they had to fear. It was their ignorance. They couldn't see the first wave for what it was. The kindness of the world. A warning. William read somewhere, in the days when he followed news with the hope Anya's name might appear, how very few domestic or wild animals were killed in the event. National Park keepers in Burma reported how the earthquake sent their elephants trekking to higher ground. Forest wardens in Sri Lanka reported monkeys which took to the taller trees of the deeper jungle, hours before the wave arrived.

On Kao Lak beach, even after the first wave made land, children played, and their parents watched. Only humans, with their human arrogance, possess the instinct to stand and stare at what they have never seen before. Because what had happened was not a wave. It had no height, like the hands of water that form from troughs and end in the fingers of crests. It did not reach up, and break in a fist. It was not a wind wave which, however big it may appear to a surfer, is only a brief tantrum of energy, the wind picking up the sea, and throwing it at the shore. The ocean had rolled up like a carpet. The energy of the earthquake had travelled, silently beneath the deep sea, gathering the shallow water from the coast, and pushing it onto land. Land which had only ever been a temporary home for humans, land which had for much longer been the seabed itself. The wooden boat of Kemal's bar simply disappeared inside the second wave. And then they ran.

It is Anya who finds the fire escape. William follows her up the wooden steps. Kemal behind. They climb to the top where a man in Sponge Bob boxer shorts and a Lakers vest films the swollen river of debris filling the street below. No longer just the force of water, but the weight of what is *in* the water. A man holds on to the branch of a tree. A woman uses a television as a float. A child hangs on to the saddle of a bicycle. The wave does not drown people. It crushes them first. They are buried beneath brick walls, pinned by cars, torn open by glass. William watches as, on the first flight of the fire escape, Kemal steps into the water and stretches across the torrent with a metal pole. It is one of those poles with a hook, the kind used to close the shutters of shops. The fire escape they stand on is screwed to the side of a two-storey building, but the roof above the last step is more than the height of two men. There is no way to reach it.

At first, William can't see what Kemal is doing. A hand emerges from the water, and a boy's naked body flickers in the river, like a dream, a white ribbon, caught on the rear fender of a car which is nosing up against the side of the store. The boy's free hand catches the pole, and draws it back. Kemal pulls him, grasping the crook of the boy's arm, and throwing him onto the steps. The boy crawls up. Holding on to the railings and extending the pole again, Kemal jabs at a round, pale thing bobbing against the trunk of the car.

What did you do?

The question repeats across the blinking altitude lights of Bangkok. The neon-white skeleton of the Shangri-la Hotel, the green veins of Lumphini Park. The temples of the Grand City piled up, like towers of gold coins, spilling into the bend of the river.

What did you do to deserve to be here?

The pale thing in the black water is a baby. The shine of its arched spine and tiny bottom in the air. Kemal uses the pole to poke the baby but it doesn't respond. It bobs like an apple.

Things knock together in William's dreams. In the wave he can swim. When he touches a refrigerator, it spins away. And always, last of all, before he wakes, William is holding Anya's hand. Her hair fans like seagrass and they float above the reef, the fish showering beneath them, and Anya pointing up at the shimmering light. They surface and pull off their masks, and Anya says, 'Happy Christmas.'

Another car crashes hard into the first, as though, accelerator down, someone inside were really driving it. The baby disappears between the teeth of the cars. When the steps fall in the water, William holds on to Anya's hand. He holds on with both hands, one around her forearm and one around her wrist. His fingertips feel the cheap plastic of her Chairman Mao watch, but she won't come with him. She won't come the way the water wants. He holds on to her, but she is stuck and the water is tearing him. Pulling at his legs, the wanting water. He holds on to Anya, but she will drown him. The water will take him up, and Anya will pull him down.

Sarajevo

Empty your cup so that it may be filled; become devoid to gain totality. At the time, Marko and Kemal had thought the mantras belonged to Bruce Lee. They were written in the pages of his martial arts manual, the *Tao of Jeet Kune Do*, the book which for years was the only one they read; the pages whose drawings they interpreted and followed in the fights on their bedroom floor. Jeet Kune Do was a martial art without form, only an attitude. It combined karate, kickboxing and t'ai chi. Some of its moves improved upon the positions Marko learned in his judo classes. But really, it was the words that mattered most; the philosophy in which they were trying to train themselves. Bruce Lee stole it all from Lao-tzu. *In the world there is nothing more submissive and weak than water, yet for attacking that which is hard and strong, nothing can surpass it.*

Chuck Norris's yang to Bruce Lee's yin. In some ways, Chuck Norris was a more powerful fighter, but his characters fought out of revenge and violent emotion. Chuck Norris sweated. Bruce Lee was style. An *expression* of emotion, not a slave to it. To watch Bruce Lee was to fall into a trance, into a kind of forgetting. And without knowing it, this is what the boys wanted. The war was asking them not to think, but to become. *Into a soul absolutely free from thoughts and emotion, even the tiger finds no room to insert its claws.* Marko was a godless socialist, and even though he was born to Muslim parents, Kemal was a godless socialist too.

I have heard that one who knows how to nourish life,
On land meets no tigers or wild buffaloes,
In battle needs to wear no armours or weapons,
A wild buffalo has nowhere to butt its horns,
A tiger has nowhere to sink its claws,
A weapon has nowhere to enter its blade.
Why?
Because such a one has no place of death.

Kemal was a man who had to make use of violence, not a violent man.

Marko is relieved to find his cousin, not lying face down, but sitting up against one of the boulders, head in his hands. Kneeling, he reaches out and feels the back of Samir's head. His cousin flinches. There is no blood, but the swelling is the size of an egg.

'It's good you have a lump,' Marko says. 'I'd be more worried if you didn't have a lump.'

'I'm fine.'

But when Marko looks at his cousin's face, he sees his nose is out of joint, and there is a pink glow all around it, as if he has left the impression of his fist.

'We'll have to tell Jasmina you fell and broke your nose.' Marko hooks his hands under Samir's arms. When he pulls him up, the artificial leg is left behind.

'I never fall,' Samir leans up against the boulder. Marko hands him the leg.

'There's a first time for everything.'

'I'm sorry,' Samir says. 'He was ashamed of us. He blamed himself. Me. Bogdan. I felt sorry for Bogdan.'

Samir fixes his leg, and tries to pick up the flowers, bending down, one hand reaching for the back of his head. 'Jasmina had her second scan today,' he says. 'All clear. These flowers were supposed to be for her.'

Marko places a hand on Samir's chest, and stops him. He picks up the flowers and shoves them into his cousin's arms.

'You fell,' he tells him. 'You say that you fell. That's all.'

Boxing Day, 2004

Kao Lak

The water has made a river of the street. The river lifts the cars and they come to life, drunk on their freedom. One noses into the wooden struts of the fire escape and the platform beneath Anya's feet creaks. William is on the step below her, and Kemal is on the bottom step, at the end of their human rope. Letting go of William, Kemal grabs some kind of metal pole and extends it into the rushing water. The boy catches on it like a wet rag. Kemal pulls him in, this naked thing. This naked thing slips out of the wave like a birth, crawling up the steps with the instinct of an animal, until he reaches the top, until he reaches Anya.

Face in Anya's belly, the boy breathes, back heaving, the knots in his spine tightening. He coughs. He begins to choke. Anya hooks her arms beneath the boy's and pulls him up. With her fists she pounds on his back. She pounds on the boy's back and the water pours out of him. He is on his hands and knees and still the water pours. So much water it will drown them all. Then the fall, the fire escape collapsing, and the water full of salt. The sea cannons in her ears. The flapping of a bird's wings. The pigeons scrapping on the scaffolded tower of Our Most Holy Redeemer. The peeling bitumen beneath her feet. She couldn't hold William's hand. It lay there between them, a lost glove. The masseuse opening Anya's palm; and slowly but surely pressing down on her back, a sharp pain in her breasts, the air pushed out of her lungs; then music like stones skipping over water and the moon laying a carpet of light over the rolling sea, and the voices of the choir filling like a sail and – *three* years.

'Hello, what have you been up to?'

The fire escape leads to the school roof. The steel boxes of air-conditioning units. Little white mushroom caps with spinning fans. White plastic domes glowing in the ceilings of classrooms, and down there, on the other side of the earth's curve, patterned with rotten leaves stuck fast where in Algebra classes she stares, and out of the leaves worlds appear.

She lies on her back. The bright sky blinding them. The boy from school resting his head in her lap, the weight slightly uncomfortable, pressing on her – what had they called it in class? – her *pudendum*. The gloved hand inside her. Not taking the thing away. Only checking. It will be a pill. It will be a word she cannot say. Mifepristone.

Mifepristone. Above them, the clouds break into creatures. The creatures unfold into animals. A burning pig. The blue sky giving birth to an elephant. The cramps, like giving birth to a death. She closes her eyes and waits for the elephant to cover the sun. For the world to darken. And when she opens her eyes, the boy from school has gone.

Gone. The absence a sound like a bell. Anya gets to her feet. The ocean is deep and meets the roof of the school, surface a mirror, black in the dying day. Like hands, treetops reach out of the water. William. The Bosnian man. He is kneeling before one of the metal boxes housing the air conditioning. Scrape. Scrape.

Scrape, with a penknife. Not William. Not the Bosnian man. The boy from the river, crouched in a puddle, wet spine of knots. Slipping out of the sea. Slipping into the sea, chain of a boat's anchor released. Scratching his name into the tin panel with a knife.

A knife in her hand. Anya has never done anything like this before. She has never trespassed the school grounds. Never left her mark on the world. Kneeling, she scratches her name in the metal: A N Y A.

'Anya!' Her mother is calling from the porch, 'Come in now – you're late!'

'Losing too is still ours; and even forgetting
still has a shape in the kingdom of transformation.

When something's let go of, it circles;
and though we are rarely the center

of the circle, it draws around us its unbroken,
marvelous curve.'

Rainer Maria Rilke, 'For Hans Carossa',
translated by Stephen Mitchell

Wednesday 13 April 2005

Bangkok

At the Emporium Skatepark, Missy sits on the lip of the vertical ramp hatching a plan. The Emporium has a metal 'vert' and two concrete bowls, one deep, one shallow, back to back, broken by a soft, rolling spine. Out on the concrete beach, a box, a jump and a rail.

She watches the schoolkids pump round the park. Most of them fly into the bowl, and straight out the other side, but Angel pops out of the vertical, slips all the way to the edge and drops down the spine without taking a beat. It is beautiful. Angel has a great low-down style. He pulls his hand around the steeps of the bowls, hair trailing like a black banner, so much *speed*. With some skaters you see the sweat; bodies bobbing up and down like springs, as they pump. The build-up to a trick is just ugly grunt work, something to get them there. But Angel never seems to be working. When the trick comes, it is just part of the line he is taking, part of his way around things, part of the way he plays with the wave. He comes straight at Missy. Wheels whistling, loose shirt like the flapping of a bird, board almost glancing her and the metal lip of the rail, a knife sharpening. When he comes at her like that, she knows she can trust him, sure as a girl in hot pants trusts a magician throwing a sword. He drops left off the spine, cutting out the bowls altogether, jumping the box.

Before the Emporium, skating in Bangkok sucked. The streets were begging for it, all those plazas around the malls, clean steps and wide pavements. But there were *No Skating* signs everywhere, the police were harsh and the locals were shy. Missy's longing for Queen's Park, and the street corners of Brick, had been physical. Just to spend a summer's night in the cool breeze off Mantaloking Beach! She dreamed of grinding the rail outside the QuikTrip; of the line she used to take around Queen's, dropping in from the vert, pumping off the edge of the bowl, low to the ground, air off the short hump, land on two wheels. It was Angel, a Spanish Embassy brat, a fifteen-year-old private tuition student no less, who had shown Missy the Emporium. Even with the floodlights and towers leaning over them, Missy knew she was home.

Spotting a gap in the flow of skaters, she stands up, and drops in, off the vert, pumping again over the concrete nipple, straight into the shallow bowl, leaning back hard to gather the line around it. She wants to switch over the crest and into the deepest bowl, just at the right spot, giving her the highest possible line, at the fastest possible speed. The run is good but she can feel it might be faster.

Popping out of the deep, Missy gets a little air, but not enough to land on two wheels or jump over the box. She hits the flat on four wheels, dives around the box and cruises back over to the vert with just enough speed to carry her to the lip, where she sits on her perch next to William.

'Incredible,' William says.

Missy feels the jelly in her legs. She is out of touch, sketchy after these past few days, still sweating out the alcohol from the hotel in Cambodia. And then there are her knees: Missy has never minded the cuts and bruises of skating, but the carpet burns she picked up in the hotel with Henry are scabbing over, and something inside her, a new voice she doesn't really want to hear, is telling her not to break them, to let them heal sensibly. In other words, at the age of twenty-four, she is getting lame.

'Could be better,' Missy says, and stands up, drops in, lower this time, higher off the spine, harder over the nipple, quicker into the shallow pool. Too quick. She can't switch back. She can't find a line around the bowl, and is forced instead, to cut directly across, right up and out of the other side, running off the board as it flies from beneath her feet.

Missy is good enough at bailing to stumble onto the spine between the two pools, but the board is high in the air, and she watches as it crashes, nose down into the deep bowl, missing the head of a Thai kid by about an inch. A little self-conscious now, she turns to look up at William on the vert. He is on his feet. She waves to signal there is no problem; then Angel – Angel! – cruises around, not stopping for a beat, and leaves the board in her hands.

Chastened, Missy pushes off again, negotiating the kids, back over to the top of the vert. The deck has taken a chip to the nose. But nothing crucial. As she crashes on her back, she has that wonderful feeling of the blood pumping in her head.

'You OK?' William asks.

Missy shades her eyes from the floodlights hanging high above William and making a silhouette of his face. Those floodlights with the big heavy heads on their long thin necks, bowing down and emitting this pale light. So much *pain* there. Is that how it had to be? Getting older and sadder. More loss. More losing. Pale light.

'I know how to bail,' Missy says.

It had felt strange to talk to her boss about Ricky. Not just strange talking to the boss she hardly knew, but to be talking to *anyone* about Ricky. She thought about Ricky all the time. She visited him in that place somewhere between imagination and memory. But to think of him, then to feel his name in her mouth, on her lips – *leaving* her lips. After the whole headfuck in William's car, she had visited the corner store to buy some cranberry juice for the morning. Turning from the counter, she had seen a dead man. Ricky in his baseball cap and ripped jeans, ferreting through a basket of old DVDs. She thought: *Why has he decided to wear his jeans halfway down his ass like that?*

'You don't wear a helmet,' William says.

'Yeah?' She sits up and holds her ankles. 'I never have.'

'I had a friend who used to work in a hospital. He said skateboards were responsible for maybe sixty per cent of the worst accidents he saw.'

'You want to try it?' Missy asks.

William sits down next to her. 'Here?'

Talking to William about Ricky hadn't brought her brother back to life. It had not helped her find new memories. In some ways, it had even felt wrong, almost like talking about him behind his back. But Missy had fallen asleep last night, and found herself weeping as she hadn't since the week after the funeral. Weeping for so long, in the end she had been laughing. Laughter welling up in the space emptied out by the tears. And that was when she realised, she needed to talk to William again.

'Not here, that *would* put you in hospital. Down there on the flat.'

'I'm too old,' William says.

She watches Angel. Angel is busy killing it. Just fucking crushing it.

Missy stands, flips her board up, back foot holding the tail down, front foot feeling the tension of the vertical drop beneath her.

'Climb down, and I'll see you round there. I'm a good teacher.'

Not concrete but water. Not something to hit but something to dive into. Not something to master but something to ride. Not something still but something moving, changing, feeling – smooth down the vert, high off the spine, pumping over the nipple, gliding into the shallow, coasting over the crest and into the deep; a high, high line – the unbroken, marvellous curve; not riding now, but being ridden, letting the concrete wave carry her up and into the air where the landing is too awkward for the back wheels she wants, but better; tips her onto the front wheels and – Hey! She holds the trick all the way to the box, where she flips the deck around and jumps clean.

Halle-fuckin-lujah!

When Missy lands it is not on concrete but on a cloud.

And when Angel glides by, he slaps the palm of her hand and says, 'Yeah. All right – *Fucking* "A", girl – *Fucking* "A".'

Thursday 14 April 2005

Bangkok

White morning light cleans his office. He switches off the air-conditioning unit. In the silence it leaves behind, he opens the old sash window, letting in the honk and zip of mopeds navigating the tight soi of the neighbourhood. At the back of the school is a patch of scrubbed lawn leading up to a yellow rain tree which decorates a wall of breeze blocks beneath a tangle of telephone wires. The tree belongs to the era of the clapboard colonial lodge. The new breeze blocks screen the old compound from tall wire fences built for a storm drain created when the downtown skyscrapers went up.

It is the kind of morning that makes him want to smoke again. He sits with his back to the window. Instead of smoking, he takes a packet of ginger biscuits out of his desk drawer. While the kettle boils, he lays three of them, one on top of the other, next to the computer keyboard.

Sitting is painful. The burn stretches from the small of his back, over the lower vertebrae of his spine, catching when he moves. But there is something pleasurable about being reminded of the moment the board left his feet, leaving him to slide down the concrete bowl.

When the computer asks for his password, William thinks of Anya's words. Anya's laptop has been packed away in her suitcase. Her case is sealed and standing by the door of his apartment, ready to go.

It does not take him long to find the address of Anya's mother on the new 'maps' thing Missy showed him. Into the computer he types *Stratton*. From a distance he recognises nothing, but zooming in, sees the names of the roads he would walk to school. The road names return the memory of friends who lived on Middlefield Lane and Station Road, Monument Drive and Chapel Street. Lanes running into fields and farms, or into the bigger estates, which belonged to the edges of towns, growing out of the great sponge of the city.

The greenbelt, on the edge. Where they lived. Anya's family home on one of the newer estates. She went to the Catholic school, and William went to the state, which meant as children, their paths never crossed. It was only when William left school that he got to know Anya properly. A summer job at a restaurant called the Four Winds, on the dual carriageway between the suburbs.

He drags the little orange man over the screen, and drops him down at the place where the white loop of Lodge Crescent begins, a lace tied to Park Road. When the 'Street View' appears, he thinks for a moment he is in the wrong place. This is some other, Hobbit world. It is so *green*. Perfectly doctored trees line the pavements, the edges of lawns nail-scissor straight, manicured bushes screening one life from another. Theme-park hedges. He scrolls down the freshly painted white lines of the road, and the picture jumps, lost in a blur before puzzling back into place. It is like having the eyes of God.

There is so much space between the houses, each with its own driveway, the white doors of garages, and white window frames, red-brick pairs of seventies-built semi-detached houses interrupted by Victorian mansions. Is this how he grew up? As a teenager William was horrified by the suburban uniformity of his existence; but now, turning the image so he is facing the front of the house owned by Anya's mother, England feels like the extreme ideal of an extreme culture. An *extraordinary* place to live.

Anya's old house is partially hidden by a row of fern trees. But it is there: the golden mahogany of the front door, a porch window next to a carport where Anya would park her mother's car. There is no car in the picture, the curtain of the porch window is drawn back on the hallway. When he tries to zoom in and see through the windows of the house, he gets as close as the pixelated folds of a russet curtain. This was the place Anya had grown up with her divorced mother, the place where he stood on a ladder and trimmed the fern trees for Diane, a nineteen-year-old boy, eager to impress his girl-friend's mother.

Number 56, Lodge Crescent.

He cross-references the address with a postcode, and writes it down for the suitcase and letter he is sending to Anya's mother. He will let her go. It is what he has always been afraid of. It is why he felt so relieved that day on the beach. Why he split up with Anya in the first place. He was never strong enough for the things he loved. Better not to love than to lose love. He is still staring at the closed door of Anya's house in Stratton, when someone knocks on his door in Bangkok.

'William, good.' It is Karin. 'William, I wanted to intro-duce you to Melissa Ammanucci, she starts today.'

Missy steps into William's office. Everything about her is different. Her bob is clipped back, opening up her face. No shorts or vest or skatepark clothes but a pair of modest cargo-pants, and a black V-neck T-shirt, with black pumps. Missy in her role as a teacher.

'Great to meet you.' She extends her hand over the desk and William finds himself standing up, playing along.

Karin says, 'I thought I would show Ms Ammanucci the staffroom and facilities. She is scheduled to be teaching in the B corridor today.'

'It's great to be starting.' Missy smiles.

'It's great to see you again,' William says. 'We were very impressed with your interview.'

'Thank you.'

'Will there be anything else?' Karin asks.

'I don't think so,' William says.

When he sits down, the burn reminds him it is there.

He looks at the disorganised desktop of his computer. *A little mental housekeeping and organisation can save you a lot of time*, Anya says.

From the drawer in his desk, he takes the new sketch pad and unwraps its cellophane, turning his desk chair to face the open window. Holding his pencil straight, he lines it up with the yellow rain tree.

Sarajevo

Marko has the seat over the wing. The thunder of the plane fills his ears, and beneath the spinning black holes of the turbines, his country falls away. Beyond the city's suburbs, there appears no order to the place, no straight lines between towns, no cul-de-sacs or planned streets at the heart of ancient villages, only a shatter of terracotta roofs, caught in the green folds of the mountains, and silver rivers which can't make up their minds about where they are going. What idiot would try and draw borders in a place like this? Borders where each valley is already a world away from the next? A land where mountains rise between Asia and Europe, as if a direct consequence of all human efforts to crush east and west together. The perfect place to divide and conquer, divide and conquer, divide and conquer. He reads the landscape like he reads the pages of Millie's history books. From a distance.

Marko didn't want to hear Samir's story, but Samir wanted to tell him. And so he had listened. It seemed like a better reason to come to Bosnia than the ghusl.

Kemal left the camp with a party to recce a potential route of escape in the south-east and left Samir in charge. When he returned he discovered what the men had been doing. He had intended to visit the women, to reassure them, to let them know his soldiers would be punished. But the women had run. It was in the early evening. Ljuba and the others had simply sprinted across the car park towards the fences. The soldiers were dumbstruck. It was their job to keep people out, not in, and the women were over the fences before anyone made a move. Kemal gave the order. Samir and Bogdan followed. The three women ran along the road, not even keeping to the treeline. They were running in the failing light, no telling what they might be running into. Kemal signalled for the men to keep their guns down. They were going to catch up, that was all, bring them back. Then the firing started from the trees; bursts from a bend in the road, only a hundred metres or so ahead. Ljuba dived into the treeline. Everyone else hit the ground. Samir, Bogdan, Kemal. They scrabbled in the dust of the road to get their stupid Russian rifles into firing position. Samir fired into the trees. He was trying to save the life of the woman he had just raped. Funny thing, he told Marko, life.

One of the women stood up, and as soon as she did, fell down. The second woman knelt up to reach the first, and went down at her side. The soldiers held their position. Sometimes, Samir felt like he was still holding that position. But reinforcement came, and when someone pointed a grenade launcher into the trees, the firing stopped.

They had crawled to the bodies, uncertain of being clear. The women were still alive when they reached them. Samir remembers they were breathing. The woman he knelt beside – her breath sounded like it was being pushed through a hole the size of a needle puncture. She stared at him, unblinking. Lips powdered with the yellow dust of the road.

The first woman had taken a Chetnik bullet in her chest. The second, a bullet in her back. Kemal believed he had shot her. And he never forgave himself. Not as far as Samir knows. They took the bodies when they left the camp, and buried them the next day. A full funeral, deep in Kemal's back garden. Kemal had spent the following spring terracing the slopes, building up plant boxes. He said he was tending the garden. But really he was tending their graves.

The plane's shadow slips over patches of green forest, snow on the higher ground, sudden lakes.

Had Samir forgiven himself?

'That's not my job,' Samir said.

Marko picks up another shadow; a train of black clouds which form into a single trail of smoke and narrows to a point before stopping abruptly over a concrete tower in the middle of nowhere.

Filter down, smoking end up.

Marko, Samir, Bogdan and Vesna were just kids when they planted cigarettes in the soil of Kemal's first grave. To Marko, it would always be the real grave. The grave among martyrs. The town's martyrs were the children who wanted to celebrate Youth Day with a drink on the square; boys who wanted to see girls in their patched-up dresses, and girls who wanted to see the boys looking. In the months after the shelling, it became a tradition among the kids left behind in Stovnik to visit the graves together. The survivors would sit among their friends, drinking homemade plum šljivovica from emptied Pepsi bottles, transistor radios playing whatever they could catch in the air. Cigarettes were still expensive, and Marko would pass one between them. Between himself, Vesna, Bogdan, Samir, before planting it in the soil for Kemal. Filter down, smoking end up.

Marko undoes his seat belt. He takes a magazine from the seat pocket, feeling the tight skin of his knuckles, still swollen from Samir's face. The magazine is called *Heart of Bosnia*. The editorial page tells him this first edition is generously funded by USAID, and BHTourism. The magazine's mission is to promote the beauty of the people, and the nature of 'the heart-shaped land'. He recognises some of the photographs from the leaflets in Samir's reception. White water rafting on the Drina. Mountain walking in the north-east. A golden statue of Bruce Lee. His heart can still quicken at the sight of the man. The article tells him the statue has been erected in the town of Mostar. In the picture, Bruce Lee stands in first position, right arm outstretched, tensing his famous fist. Bruce Lee in Mostar. The subject of the statue had been chosen by the youth of the town, Bosnian Muslims and Croats alike. They were asked to agree on a suitable figure to symbolise the struggles of the recent past. 'Martial arts is a shared passion,' the spokesman of something called the

Mostar Urban Movement said, 'We will always be Muslims, Serbs or Croats. But Bruce Lee is one thing we can agree on.' A sudden brightness fills the window of the plane. Marko puts down the magazine and cups his hands against the cold, toughened plastic. The clouds have broken. The plane banks over a blinding sea; the Adriatic, between Italy and Croatia. A cloud whips beneath the wing and the metal tube in which he sits buoys up. For a moment, Marko doesn't know whether he is flying or falling.

AUTHOR'S NOTE

THE BOSNIAN TOWN OF Tuzla suffered a terrible shelling and massacre on 'Youth Day' in May 1995, and this served as an inspiration for the shelling of my fictional town of Stovnik. The account of Svinjare's burning is based upon Human Rights Watch reports, and testimony given at The Hague contributed to the facts surrounding historical incidences of rape in Foča and Miljevina. At the time of writing, the Association of Women Victims Against War is still fighting to have 'Karaman's House' memorialised. The young citizens of Mostar erected a statue of Bruce Lee in November 2005. Other events, and all characters in the Bosnian narrative of this novel are an invention. The realities of the war and its aftermath were researched through documented history in order to create a plausible fiction. The British Council does not run a Cultural Action Project Fund, or charge $85 for filling out forms.

To distance the story from the lives of real Bosnians, I have changed place names, and confused the geography of the country; some of the place names are fictional. Only Sarajevo appears as itself.

The novel grew from a desire to capture the humanity, solidarity and kindness of my Bosnian friends, and I am deeply indebted to them.

I am also in debt to those who helped me report events in the aftermath of the Boxing Day tsunami.

A wealth of books on the Balkans informed my research but I am particularly indebted to Misha Glenny's *The Fall of Yugoslavia*; Dubravka Ugrešić's *The Ministry of Pain*, her essays in *The Culture of Lies* and *The Museum of Unconditional Surrender*; Zlatko Dizdarević's, *Sarajevo, A War Journal*; Wojciech Tochman's *Like Eating a Stone*; Emir Suljagić's *Postcards from the Grave*; and Elvira Simić's moving diary, *The Cry of Bosnia*.

ACKNOWLEDGEMENTS

I HEAR SOME WRITERS write books all by themselves. Not me. If it takes a village to raise a child, it has taken a small town to make this book.

It required inspirational and sympathetic friendships. Thanks to Ryan Davis, Oliver Williams, Simon Muttitt, Brett Humble and Joanne Bevan for putting up with me in the days of music, French literature and big mistakes. Thanks to Nicola Tyler, who shared so much, and taught me to be an adult. And to Carrie Rossiter for the letters.

I was never a brilliant journalist, and required the patience and tutorship of better journalists. Thanks to Steve Grandison and Esther McWatters. Thanks to Susie Mesure for giving me something to do in Georgia, Nadia and Lika Lubinets for living next door, Angie Calton for living *with* me, Dimitri Bit-Suleiman for taking the punches, John Shields for the headlines, Olly Bootle for being a dude, Jo Grace for the organisational skills, Natalia Antelava and Shahida Tulganova for being inspirational, Karen O'Connor for running the show, and sending me to Bangkok.

For allowing me to share a corridor at St Mary's University, thanks to Russell Schechter, Peter Howell (who allowed me to borrow his fine surname), Mike Foster, Pauline Foster, Richard Mills, Cian Duffy, Brian Ridgers, Kathy Grant and Allan Simmons. Moreover, thanks to the students of St Mary's

University for allowing me to teach them, and to take so much inspiration from doing so. Thanks to Helena Blakemore and Tim Atkins for giving me a break.

I know the value of teaching because I had the privilege of being taught by some of the best. Thanks to the legendary Mr Brush, Julia Bell, Jeremy Sheldon, Toby Litt, Russell Celyn-Jones, Paul Magrs, Jean McNeil and to Richard Skinner for all his kind support.

No one ever had a writing circle as brilliant. Thanks to Thea Bennett for the wisdom, Martha Close for her understanding, Pippa Griffin for her passion, Anna Hope for her sensitivity, Keith Jarrett for the poetry, Josh Raymond for the red pen, Philip Makatrewicz for the knowledge, Matthew Weait for his mind, Ginevra White for her integrity and Cynthia Medford-Wilson for her acuity. You are all wonders. A special thanks must go to Olja Knežević, my Balkaniser and the best novelist Montenegro ever produced. Also to the early readers who dragged themselves through the bad drafts – Tanya Datta, LaDonna Dee, Nicola Mann, Zoltan Moll, Teresa Pearce and Sue Tyley.

In Bosnia, thanks to Dragan Išrilija who told me the story of his judo adventures. I am much indebted to Dragan's family and friends, including Zlatko Isabegovic and Amel Išrilija. Although the story took a turn to fictional war crimes, my relationship with Bosnia is defined by the generosity, bravery and humanity of Dragan and the teenage boys who in the summer of 1996 taught me so much about life.

My experience reporting on the aftermath of the 2004 tsunami was shaped by my encounter with the brothers Fergus and Guy Miller. In the heart of a tragedy, they had the courage to tell the world their story.

None of the stories in this book would have been told without the patience and kindness of agents and publishers who thought they were worth telling. Thanks to Kevin Conroy-Scott for taking a shine to my writing, to Marika Lysandrou for encouraging me and to the obscenely talented Sophie Lambert for sticking it out over nearly five years. You are a marvel, Sophie.

Thanks to Helen Garnons-Williams for understanding what I was trying to do, and for working so hard. Thanks to Alexa von Hirschberg for picking up the baton, and to Lindeth Vasey for spotting things I could never have spotted. Thanks to Imogen Denny, Ros Ellis, Myfanwy Nolan and all the team at Bloomsbury.

Much of this book was completed at the residence of Nicolette and Bryan Neville-Lee, and I owe them a lifetime of hot dinners.

It simply shouldn't be possible to have such an understanding, wise and caring family. Anna, Ben, Aggie, Pearl, Thora. Thank you. And thank you, Mum and Dad, Maureen and Christopher Savill, for making my own story such a happy one.

Finally, I would be nothing without Penny, Oren and Robin, who are continuing that story every day.

CREDITS

The author and publishers acknowledge the following permissions to reprint copyright material:

Extract appearing on page 11 from 'The Right to Know' by Amnesty International. Text copyright © Amnesty International, 2012.

Extract appearing on page 67 from *Sarajevo: A biography* by Robert J. Donia. Reprinted by permission of Hurst Publishers.

Extract appearing on page 241 from *Winnie-the-Pooh* by A.A. Milne. Text copyright © The Trustees of the Pooh Properties 1926. Published by Egmont UK Ltd and used with permission.

Extract appearing on page 285 from *The Fall of Yugoslavia: The Third Balkan War* by Misha Glenny (Penguin Books, 1996) Copyright © Misha Glenny, 1992, 1993, 1996. Reproduced by permission of Penguin Books Ltd.

Extract appearing on pages vii and 333, 'For Hans Carossa' from *Ahead of All Parting: The Selected Poetry and Prose of Ranier Maria Rilke* by Ranier Maria Rilke, translation copyright © 1995 by Stephen Mitchell. Used by permission of Modern Library, an imprint of Random House, a division of Penguin Random House LLC. All rights reserved.

A NOTE ON THE AUTHOR

IN 1996, DAVID LIVED as a teacher and a student among the refugees of Srebrenica, helping to organise a summer university for students in the safe haven of Tuzla. Over the past twenty years he has returned to Bosnia several times. Tuzla, and the real story of its 'Youth Day' massacre, became the inspiration for the fictional town of Stovnik. In an eight-year career as a BBC Current Affairs journalist, David worked on *Panorama*, *This World*, *Real Story*, *World at One* and *PM*. In 2004, he arrived on the beaches of Phuket two days after the Indian Ocean tsunami. He spent the next six months in Thailand and Sri Lanka, where he made two documentaries about the aftermath of the disaster. David has two children and teaches Creative Writing at St Mary's University, London.

A NOTE ON THE TYPE

The text of this book is set Adobe Garamond. It is one of several versions of Garamond based on the designs of Claude Garamond. It is thought that Garamond based his font on Bembo, cut in 1495 by Francesco Griffo in collaboration with the Italian printer Aldus Manutius. Garamond types were first used in books printed in Paris around 1532. Many of the present-day versions of this type are based on the *Typi Academiae* of Jean Jannon cut in Sedan in 1615.

Claude Garamond was born in Paris in 1480. He learned how to cut type from his father and by the age of fifteen he was able to fashion steel punches the size of a pica with great precision. At the age of sixty he was commissioned by King Francis I to design a Greek alphabet, and for this he was given the honourable title of royal type founder. He died in 1561.